THE SHOWDOWN

Neither man lifted his gaze from the other. Each knew that the test had come.

Both had killed. Both searched now for an advantage in that steady duel of the eyes. Neither had any fear.

The emotions that dominated were cold rage and caution. In just a split second, two guns would roar and one man would go down.

GUNSIGHT PASS
WILLIAM MacLEOD RAINE

POPULAR LIBRARY • NEW YORK

CHAPTER I

"CROOKED AS A DOG'S HIND LAIG"

It was a land of splintered peaks, of deep, dry gorges, of barren mesas burnt by the suns of a million torrid summers. The normal condition of it was warfare. Life here had to protect itself with a tough, callous rind, to attack with a swift, deadly sting. Only the fit survived.

But moonlight had magically touched the hot, wrinkled earth with a fairy godmother's wand. It was bathed in a weird, mysterious beauty. Into the crotches of the hills lakes of wondrous color had been poured at sunset. The crests had flamed with crowns of glory, the cañons become deep pools of blue and purple shadow. Blurred by kindly darkness, the gaunt ridges had softened to pastels of violet and bony mountains to splendid sentinels keeping watch over a gulf of starlit space.

Around the camp-fire the drivers of the trail herd squatted on their heels or lay sprawled at indolent ease. The glow of the leaping flames from the twisted mesquite lit their lean faces, tanned to bronzed health by the beat of an untempered sun and the sweep of parched winds. Most of them were still young, scarcely out of their boyhood; a few had reached maturity. But all were products of the desert. The high-heeled boots, the leather chaps, the kerchiefs knotted round the neck, were worn at its insistence. Upon every line of their features, every shade of their thought, it had stamped its brand indelibly.

The talk was frank and elemental. It had the crisp crackle that goes with free, unfettered youth. In a parlor some of it would have been offensive, but under the stars of the open desert it was as natural as the life itself. They spoke of the spring rains, of the Crawford-Steelman feud, of how they meant to turn Malapi upside down in their frolic when they reached town. They "rode" each other with jokes that were familiar old friends. Their horse play was rough but good-natured.

Out of the soft shadows of the summer night a boy moved from the remuda toward the camp-fire. He was a lean, sandy-haired young fellow, his figure still lank and unfilled. In another year his shoulders would be broader, his frame would take on twenty pounds. As he sat down on the wagon tongue at the edge of the firelit circle the stringiness of his appearance became more noticeable.

A young man waved a hand toward him by way of introduction. "Gents of the D Bar Lazy R outfit, we now have with us roostin' on the wagon tongue Mr. David Sanders, formerly of Arizona, just returned from makin' love to his paint hoss. Mr. Sanders will make oration on the why, wherefore, and how-come-it of Chiquito's superiority to all other equines whatever."

The youth on the wagon tongue smiled. His blue eyes were gentle and friendly. From his pocket he had taken a knife and was sharpening it on one of his down-at-the-heel-boots.

"I'd like right well to make love to that pinto my own se'f, Bob," commented a weather-beaten puncher. "Any old time Dave wants to saw him off onto me at sixty dollars I'm here to do business."

"You're sure an easy mark, Buck," grunted a large fat man leaning against a wheel. His white, expressionless face and soft hands differentiated him from the tough range-riders. He did not belong with the outfit, but had joined it the day before with George Doble, a half-brother of the trail foreman, to travel with it as far as Malapi. In the Southwest he was known as Ad Miller. The two men had brought with them in addition to their own mounts a led pack-horse.

Doble backed up his partner. "Sure are, Buck. I can get cowponies for ten and fifteen dollars—all I want of 'em," he said, and contrived by the lift of his lip to make the remark offensive.

"Not ponies like Chiquito," ventured Sanders amiably.

"That so?" jeered Doble.

He looked at David out of a sly and shifty eye. He had only one. The other had been gouged out years ago in a drunken fracas.

"You couldn't get Chiquito for a hundred dollars. Not for sale," the owner of the horse said, a little stiffly.

Miller's fat paunch shook with laughter. "I reckon not—at that price. I'd give all of fohty for him."

"Different here," replied Doble. "What has this pinto got that makes him worth over thirty?"

"He's some bronc," explained Bob Hart. "Got a bagful of tricks, a nice disposition, and sure can burn the wind."

"Yore friend must be valuin' them parlor tricks at ten dollars apiece," murmured Miller. "He'd ought to put him in a show and not keep him to chase cow tails with."

"At that, I've seen circus hosses that weren't one two three with Chiquito. He'll shake hands and play dead and dance to a mouth-organ and come a-runnin' when Dave whistles."

"You don't say." The voice of the fat man was heavy with sarcasm. "And on top of all that edjucation he can run too."

The temper of Sanders began to take an edge. He saw no reason why these strangers should run on him, to use the phrase of the country. "I don't claim my pinto's a racer, but he can travel."

"Hmp!" grunted Miller skeptically.

"I'm here to say he can," boasted the owner, stung by the manner of the other.

"Don't look to me like no racer," Doble dissented. "Why, I'd be 'most willin' to bet that pack-horse of ours, Whiskey Bill, can beat him."

Buck Byington snorted. "Pack-horse, eh?" The old puncher's brain was alive with suspicions. On account of the lameness of his horse he had returned to camp in the middle of the day and had discovered the two newcomers trying out the speed of the pinto. He wondered now if this precious pair of crooks had been getting a line on the pony for future use. It occurred to him that Dave was being engineered into a bet.

The chill, hard eyes of Miller met his. "That's what he said, Buck—our pack-horse."

For just an instant the old range-rider hesitated, then shrugged his shoulders. It was none of his business. He was a cautious man, not looking for trouble. Moreover, the law of the range is that every man must play his own hand. So he dropped the matter with a grunt that expressed complete understanding and derision.

Bob Hart helped things along. "Jokin' aside, what's the matter with a race? We'll be on the Salt Flats tomorrow. I've got ten bucks says the pinto can beat yore Whiskey Bill."

"Go you once," answered Doble after a moment's apparent consideration. "Bein' as I'm drug into this I'll be a dead-game sport. I got fifty dollars more to back the pack-horse. How about it, Sanders? You got the sand to cover that? Or are you plumb scared of my broomtail?"

"Betcha a month's pay—thirty-five dollars. Give you an order on the boss if I lose," retorted Dave. He had not meant to bet, but he could not stand this fellow's insolent manner.

"That order good, Dug?" asked Doble of his half-brother.

The foreman nodded. He was a large leather-faced man in the late thirties. His reputation in the cattle country was that of a man ill to cross. Dug Doble was a good cowman—none better. Outside of that his known virtues were negligible, except for the primal one of gameness.

"Might as well lose a few bucks myself, seeing as Whiskey Bill belongs to me," said Miller with his wheezy laugh. "Who wants to take a whirl, boys?"

Inside of three minutes he had placed a hundred dollars. The terms of the race were arranged and the money put in the hands of the foreman.

"Each man to ride his own caballo," suggested Hart slyly.

This brought a laugh. The idea of Ad Miller's two hundred and fifty pounds in the seat of a jockey made for hilarity.

"I reckon George will have to ride the broomtail. We don't aim to break its back," replied Miller genially.

His partner was a short man with a spare, wiry body. Few men trusted him after a glance at the mutilated face. The thin, hard lips gave warning that he had sold himself to evil. The low forehead, above which the hair was plastered flat in an arc, advertised low mentality.

An hour later Buck Byington drew Sanders aside.

"Dave, you're a chuckle-haided rabbit. If ever I seen tin-horn sports them two is such. They're collectin' a livin' off'n suckers. Didn't you sabe that come-on stuff? Their pack-horse is a ringer. They tried him out this evenin', but I noticed they ran under a blanket. Both of 'em are crooked as a dog's hind laig."

"Maybeso," admitted the young man. "But Chiquito never went back on me yet. These fellows may be overplayin' their hand, don't you reckon?"

"Not a chanct. That tumblebug Miller is one fishy proposition, and his sidekick Doble—say, he's the kind of bird that shoots you in the stomach while he's shakin' hands with you. They're about as warm-hearted as a loan shark when he's

10

turnin' on the screws—and about as impulsive. Me, I aim to button up my pocket when them guys are around."

Dave returned to the fire. The two visitors were sitting side by side, and the leaping flames set fantastic shadows of them moving. One of these, rooted where Miller sat, was like a bloated spider watching its victim. The other, dwarfed and prehensile, might in its uncanny silhouette have been an imp of darkness from the nether regions.

Most of the riders had already rolled up in their blankets and fallen asleep. To a reduced circle Miller was telling the story of how his pack-horse won its name.

". . . so I noticed he was actin' kinda funny and I seen four pin-pricks in his nose. O' course I hunted for Mr. Rattler and killed him, then give Bill a pint of whiskey. It ce'tainly paralyzed him proper. He got salivated as a mule whacker on a spree. His nose swelled up till it was big as a barrel—never did get down to normal again. Since which the ol' plug has been Whiskey Bill."

This reminiscence did not greatly entertain Dave. He found his blankets, rolled up in them, and promptly fell asleep. For once he dreamed, and his dreams were not pleasant. He thought that he was caught in a net woven by a horribly fat spider which watched him try in vain to break the web that tightened on his arms and legs. Desperately he struggled to escape while the monster grinned at him maliciously, and the harder he fought the more securely was he enmeshed.

CHAPTER II

THE RACE

The coyotes were barking when the cook's triangle brought Dave from his blankets. The objects about him were still mysterious in the pre-dawn darkness. The shouting of the wranglers and the bells of the remuda came musically as from a great distance. Hart joined his friend and the two young men walked out to the remuda together. Each rider had on the previous night belled the mount he wanted, for he knew that in the morning it would be too dark to distinguish one bronco from another. The animals were rim-milling, going round and round in a circle to escape the lariat.

Dave rode in close and waited, rope ready, his ears attuned to the sound of his own bell. A horse rushed jingling past. The rope snaked out, fell true, tightened over the neck of the cow-pony, brought up the animal short. Instantly it surrendered, making no further attempt to escape. The roper made a half-hitch round the nose of the bronco, swung to its back, and cantered back to camp.

In the gray dawn near details were becoming visible. The mountains began to hover on the edge of the young world. The wind was blowing across half a continent.

Sanders saddled, then rode out upon the mesa. He whistled sharply. There came an answering nicker, and presently out of the darkness a pony trotted. The pinto was a sleek and glossy little fellow, beautiful in action and gentle as a kitten.

The young fellow took the well-shaped head in his arms, fondled the soft, dainty nose that nuzzled in his pocket for sugar, fed Chiquito a half-handful of the delicacy in his open palm, and put the pony through the repertoire of tricks he had taught his pet.

"You wanta shake a leg to-day, old fellow, and throw dust in that tinhorn's face," he murmured to his four-footed friend, gentling it with little pats of love and admiration. "Adios, Chiquito. I know you won't throw off on yore old pal. So long, old pie-eater."

Across the mesa Dave galloped back, swung from the saddle, and made a bee-line for breakfast. The other men were already busy at this important business. From the tail of the chuck wagon he took a tin cup and a tin plate. He helped himself to coffee, soda biscuits, and a strip of steak just forked from a large kettle of boiling lard. Presently more coffee, more biscuits, and more steak went the way of the first helping. The hard-riding life of the desert stimulates a healthy appetite.

The punchers of the D Bar Lazy R were moving a large herd to a new range. It was made up of several lots bought from smaller outfits that had gone out of business under the pressure of falling prices, short grass, and the activity of rustlers. The cattle had been loose-bedded in a gulch close at hand, the upper end of which was sealed by an impassable cliff. Many such cañons in the wilder part of the mountains, fenced across the face to serve as a corral, had been used by rustlers as caches into which to drift their stolen stock. This one had no doubt more than once played such a part in days past.

Expertly the riders threw the cattle back to the mesa and moved them forward. Among the bunch one could find the T Anchor brand, the Circle Cross, the Diamond Tail, and the X-Z, scattered among the cows burned with the D Bar Lazy R, which was the original brand of the owner, Emerson Crawford.

The sun rose and filled the sky. In a heavy cloud of dust the cattle trailed steadily toward the distant hills.

Near noon Buck, passing Dave where he rode as drag driver in the wake of the herd, shouted a greeting at the young man. "Tur'ble hot. I'm spittin' cotton."

Dave nodded. His eyes were red and sore from the alkali dust, his throat dry as a lime kiln. "You done said it, Buck. Hotter 'n hell or Yuma."

"Dug says for us to throw off at Seven-Mile Hole."

"I won't make no holler at that."

The herd leaders, reading the signs of a spring close at hand, quickened the pace. With necks outstretched, bawling loudly, they hurried forward. Forty-eight hours ago they had last satisfied their thirst. Usually Doble watered each noon, but the desert yesterday had been dry as Sahara. Only such moisture was available as could be found in black grama and needle grass.

The point of the herd swung in toward the cottonwoods that straggled down from the draw. For hours the riders were kept busy moving forward the cattle that had been watered and holding back the pressure of thirsty animals.

Again the outfit took the desert trail. Heat waves played on the sand. Vegetation grew scant except for patches of cholla and mesquite, a sand-cherry bush here and there, occasionally a clump of shining poison ivy.

Sunset brought them to the Salt Flats. The foreman gave orders to throw off and make camp.

A course was chosen for the race. From a selected point the horses were to run to a clump of mesquite, round it, and return to the starting-place. Dug Doble was chosen both starter and judge.

13

Dave watched Whiskey Bill with the trained eyes of a horseman. The animal was an ugly brute as to the head. Its eyes were set too close, and the shape of the nose was deformed from the effects of the rattlesnake's sting. But in legs and body it had the fine lines of a racer. The horse was built for speed. The cowpuncher's heart sank. His bronco was fast, willing, and very intelligent, but the little range pony had not been designed to show its heels to a near-thoroughbred.

"Are you ready?" Doble asked of the two men in the saddles.

His brother said, "Let 'er go!" Sanders nodded. The revolver barked.

Chiquito was off like a flash of light, found its stride instantly. The training of a cowpony makes for alertness, for immediate response. Before it had covered seventy-five yards the pinto was three lengths to the good. Dave, flying toward the halfway post, heard his friend Hart's triumphant "Yip yip yippy yip!" coming to him on the wind.

He leaned forward, patting his horse on the shoulder, murmuring words of encouragement into its ear. But he knew, without turning round, that the racer galloping at his heels was drawing closer. Its long shadow, thrown in front of it by the westering sun, reached to Dave's stirrups, crept to Chiquito's head, moved farther toward the other shadow plunging wildly eastward. Foot by foot the distance between the horses lessened to two lengths, to one, to half a length. The ugly head of the racer came abreast of the cowpuncher. With sickening certainty the range-rider knew that his Chiquito was doing the best that was in it. Whiskey Bill was a faster horse.

Simultaneously he became aware of two things. The bay was no longer gaining. The halfway mark was just ahead. The cowpuncher knew exactly how to make the turn with the least possible loss of speed and ground. Too often, in headlong pursuit of a wild hill steer, he had whirled as on a dollar, to leave him any doubt now. Scarce slackening speed, he swept the pinto round the clump of mesquite and was off for home.

Dave was halfway back before he was sure that the thud of Whiskey Bill's hoofs was almost at his heels. He called on the cowpony for a last spurt. The plucky little horse answered the call, gathered itself for the home stretch, for a moment held its advantage. Again Bob Hart's yell drifted to Sanders.

Then he knew that the bay was running side by side with Chiquito, was slowly creeping to the front. The two horses raced down the stretch together, Whiskey Bill half a length in

14

the lead and gaining at every stride. Daylight showed between them when they crossed the line. Chiquito had been outrun by a speedier horse.

CHAPTER III

DAVE RIDES ON HIS SPURS

Hart came up to his friend grinning. "Well, you old horn-toad, we got no kick comin'. Chiquito run a mighty pretty race. Only trouble was his laigs wasn't long enough."

The owner of the pony nodded, a lump in his throat. He was not thinking about his thirty-five dollars, but about the futile race into which he had allowed his little beauty to be trapped. Dave would not be twenty-one till coming grass, and it still hurt his boyish pride to think that his favorite had been beaten.

Another lank range-rider drifted up. "Same here, Dave. I'll kiss my twenty bucks good-bye cheerful. You 'n' the li'l' hoss run the best race, at that. Chiquito started like a bullet out of a gun, and say, boys! how he did swing round on the turn."

"Much obliged, Steve. I reckon he sure done his best," said Sanders gratefully.

The voice of George Doble cut in, openly and offensively jubilant. "Me, I'd ruther show the way at the finish than at the start. You're more liable to collect the mazuma. I'll tell you now that broomtail never had a chance to beat Whiskey Bill."

"Yore hoss can run, seh," admitted Dave.

"I *know* it, but you don't. He didn't have to take the kinks out of his legs to beat that plug."

"You get our money," said Hart quietly. "Ain't that enough without rubbin' it in?"

"Sure I get yore money—easy money, at that," boasted
15

Doble. "Got any more you want to put up on the circus bronc?"

Steve Russell voiced his sentiments curtly. "You make me good and tired, Doble. There's only one thing I hate more'n a poor loser—and that's a poor winner. As for putting my money on the pinto, I'll just say this: I'll bet my li'l' pile he can beat yore bay twenty miles, a hundred miles, or five hundred."

"Not any, thanks. Whiskey Bill is a racer, not a mule team," Miller said, laughing.

Steve loosened the center-fire cinch of his pony's saddle. He noted that there was no real geniality in the fat man's mirth. It was a surface thing designed to convey an effect of good-fellowship. Back of it lay the chill implacability of the professional gambler.

The usual give-and-take of gay repartee was missing at supper that night. Since they were of the happy-go-lucky, outdoor West it did not greatly distress the D Bar Lazy R riders to lose part of their pay checks. Even if it had, their spirits would have been unimpaired, for it is written in their code that a man must take his punishment without whining. What hurt was that they had been tricked, led like lambs to the killing. None of them doubted now that the pack-horse of the gamblers was a "ringer." These men had deliberately crossed the path of the trail outfit in order to take from the vaqueros their money.

The punchers were sulky. Instead of a fair race they had been up against an open-and-shut proposition, as Russell phrased it. The jeers of Doble did not improve their tempers. The man was temperamentally mean-hearted. He could not let his victims alone.

"They say one's born every minute, Ad. Dawged if I don't believe it," he sneered.

Miller was not saying much himself, but his fat stomach shook at this sally. If his partner could goad the boys into more betting he was quite willing to divide the profits.

Audibly Hart yawned and murmured his sentiments aloud. "I'm liable to tell these birds what I think of 'em, Steve, if they don't spend quite some time layin' off'n us."

"Don't tell us out loud. We might hear you," advised Doble insolently.

"In regards to that, I'd sure worry if you did."

Dave was at that moment returning to his place with a cup of hot coffee. By some perverse trick of fate his glance fell on

16

Doble's sinister face of malignant triumph. His self-control snapped, and in an instant the whole course of his life was deflected from the path it would otherwise have taken. With a flip he tossed up the tin cup so that the hot coffee soused the crook.

"Goddlemighty!" screamed Doble, leaping to his feet. He reached for his forty-five, just as Sanders closed with him. The range-rider's revolver, like that of most of his fellows, was in a blanket roll in the wagon.

Miller, with surprising agility for a fat man, got to his feet and launched himself at the puncher. Dave flung the smaller of his opponents back against Steve, who was sitting tailor fashion beside him. The gunman tottered and fell over Russell, who lost no time in pinning his hands to the ground while Hart deftly removed the revolver from his pocket.

Swinging round to face Miller, Dave saw at once that the big man had chosen not to draw his gun. In spite of his fat the gambler was a rough-and-tumble fighter of parts. The extra weight had come in recent years, but underneath it lay roped muscles and heavy bones. Men often remarked that they had never seen a fat man who could handle himself like Ad Miller. The two clinched. Dave had the under hold and tried to trip his bulkier foe. The other side-stepped, circling round. He got one hand under the boy's chin and drove it up and back, flinging the range-rider a dozen yards.

Instantly Dave plunged at him. He had to get at close quarters, for he could not tell when Miller would change his mind and elect to fight with a gun. The man had chosen a hand-to-hand tussle, Dave knew, because he was sure he could beat so stringy an opponent as himself. Once he got the grip on him that he wanted the big gambler would crush him by sheer strength. So, though the youngster had to get close, he dared not clinch. His judgment was that his best bet was his fists.

He jabbed at the big white face, ducked, and jabbed again. Now he was in the shine of the moon; now he was in darkness. A red streak came out on the white face opposite, and he knew he had drawn blood. Miller roared like a bull and flailed away at him. More than one heavy blow jarred him, sent a bolt of pain shooting through him. The only thing he saw was that shining face. He pecked away at it with swift jabs, taking what punishment he must and dodging the rest.

Miller was furious. He had intended to clean up this bantam in about a minute. He rushed again, broke through Dave's defense, and closed with him. His great arms crushed into the ribs of his lean opponent. As they swung round and round, Dave gasped for breath. He twisted and squirmed, trying to escape that deadly hug. Somehow he succeeded in tripping his huge foe.

They went down locked together, Dave underneath. The puncher knew that if he had room Miller would hammer his face to a pulp. He drew himself close to the barrel body, arms and legs wound tight like hoops.

Miller gave a yell of pain. Instinctively Dave moved his legs higher and clamped them tighter. The yell rose again, became a scream of agony.

"Lemme loose!" shrieked the man on top. "My Gawd, you're killin' me!"

Dave had not the least idea what was disturbing Miller's peace of mind, but whatever it was moved to his advantage. He clamped tighter, working his heels into another secure position. The big man bellowed with pain. "Take him off! Take him off!" he implored in shrill crescendo.

"What's all this?" demanded an imperious voice.

Miller was torn howling from the arms and legs that bound him and Dave found himself jerked roughly to his feet. The big rawboned foreman was glaring at him above his large hook nose. The trail boss had been out at the remuda with the jingler when the trouble began. He had arrived in time to rescue his fat friend.

"What's eatin' you, Sanders?" he demanded curtly.

"He jumped George!" yelped Miller.

Breathing hard, Dave faced his foe warily. He was in a better strategic position than he had been, for he had pulled the revolver of the fat man from its holster just as they were dragged apart. It was in his right hand now, pressed close to his hip, ready for instant use if need be. He could see without looking that Doble was still struggling ineffectively in the grip of Russell.

"Dave stumbled and spilt some coffee on George; then George he tried to gun him. Miller mixed in then," explained Hart.

The foreman glared. "None of this stuff while you're on the trail with my outfit. Get that, Sanders? I won't have it."

"Dave he couldn't hardly he'p hisse'f," Buck Byington broke in. "They was runnin' on him considerable, Dug."

"I ain't askin' for excuses. I'm tellin' you boys what's what," retorted the road boss. "Sanders, give him his gun."

The cowpuncher took a step backward. He had no inten-

18

tion of handing a loaded gun to Miller while the gambler was in his present frame of mind. That might be equivalent to suicide. He broke the revolver, turned the cylinder, and shook out the cartridges. The empty weapon he tossed on the ground.

"He ripped me with his spurs," Miller said sullenly. "That's howcome I had to turn him loose."

Dave looked down at the man's legs. His trousers were torn to shreds. Blood trickled down the lacerated calves where the spurs had roweled the flesh cruelly. No wonder Miller had suddenly lost interest in the fight. The vaquero thanked his lucky stars that he had not taken off his spurs and left them with the saddle.

The first thing that Dave did was to strike straight for the wagon where his roll of bedding was. He untied the rope, flung open the blankets, and took from inside the forty-five he carried to shoot rattlesnakes. This he shoved down inside his shirt and trousers where it would be handy for use in case of need. His roll he brought back with him as a justification for the trip to the wagon. He had no intention of starting anything. All he wanted was not to be caught at a disadvantage a second time.

Miller and the two Dobles were standing a little way apart talking together in low tones. The fat man, his foot on the spoke of a wagon wheel, was tying up one of his bleeding calves with a bandanna handkerchief. Dave gathered that his contribution to the conversation consisted mainly of fervent and almost tearful profanity.

The brothers appeared to be debating some point with heat. George insisted, and the foreman gave up with a lift of his big shoulders.

"Have it yore own way. I hate to have you leave us after I tell you there'll be no more trouble, but if that's how you feel about it I got nothin' to say. What I want understood is this" —Dug Doble raised his voice for all to hear—"that I'm boss of this outfit and won't stand for any rough stuff. If the boys, or any one of 'em, can't lose their money without bellyachin', they can get their time pronto."

The two gamblers packed their race-horse, saddled, and rode away without a word to any of the range-riders. The men round the fire gave no sign that they knew the confidence men were on the map until after they had gone. Then tongues began to wag, the foreman having gone to the edge of the camp with them.

"Well, my feelin's ain't hurt one li'l' bit because they won't play with us no more," Steve Russell said, smiling broadly.

"Can you blame that fat guy for not wantin' to play with Dave here?" asked Hart, and he beamed at the memory of what he had seen. "Son, you ce'tainly gave him one surprise party when yore rowels dug in."

"Wonder to me he didn't stampede the cows, way he hollered," grinned a third. "I don't grudge him my ten plunks. Not none. Dave he give me my money's worth that last round."

"I had a little luck," admitted Dave modestly.

"Betcha," agreed Steve. "I was just startin' over to haul the fat guy off Dave when he began bleatin' for us to come help him turn loose the bear. I kinda took my time then."

"Onct I went to a play called 'All's Well That Ends Well,'" said Byington reminiscently. "At the Tabor Grand the-á-ter, in Denver."

"Did it tell how a freckled cow-punch rode a fat tinhorn on his spurs?" asked Hart.

"Bet he wears stovepipes on his laigs next time he mixes it with Dave," suggested one coffee-brown youth. "Well, looks like the show's over for to-night. I'm gonna roll in." Motion carried unanimously.

CHAPTER IV

THE PAINT HOSS DISAPPEARS

Wakened by the gong, Dave lay luxuriously in the warmth of his blankets. It was not for several moments that he remembered the fight or the circumstances leading to it. The grin that lit his boyish face at thought of its unexpected conclusion was a fleeting one, for he discovered that it hurt his face to smile. Briskly he rose, and grunted "Ouch!" His sides were sore from the rib squeezing of Miller's powerful arms.

Byington walked out to the remuda with him. "How's the man-tamer this glad mo'nin'?" he asked of Dave.

"Fine and dandy, old lizard."

"You sure got the deadwood on him when yore spurs got into action. A man's like a watermelon. You cayn't tell how good he is till you thump him. Miller is right biggity, and they say he's sudden death with a gun. But when it come down to cases he hadn't the guts to go through and stand the gaff."

"He's been livin' soft too long, don't you reckon?"

"No, sir. He just didn't have the sand in his craw to hang on and finish you off whilst you was rippin' up his laigs."

Dave roped his mount and rode out to meet Chiquito. The pinto was an aristocrat in his way. He preferred to choose his company, was a little disdainful of the cowpony that had no accomplishments. Usually he grazed a short distance from the remuda, together with one of Bob Hart's string. The two ponies had been brought up in the same bunch.

This morning Dave's whistle brought no nicker of joy, no thud of hoofs galloping out of the darkness to him. He rode deeper into the desert. No answer came to his calls. At a canter he cut across the plain to the wrangler. That young man had seen nothing of Chiquito since the evening before, but this was not at all unusual.

The cowpuncher returned to camp for breakfast and got permission of the foreman to look for the missing horses.

Beyond the flats was a country creased with draws and dry arroyos. From one to another of these Dave went without finding a trace of the animals. All day he pushed through cactus and mesquite heavy with gray dust. In the late afternoon he gave up for the time and struck back to the flats. It was possible that the lost broncos had rejoined the remuda of their own accord or had been found by some of the riders gathering up strays.

Dave struck the herd trail and followed it toward the new camp. A horseman came out of the golden west of the sunset to meet him. For a long time he saw the figure rising and falling in the saddle, the pony moving in the even fox-trot of the cattle country.

The man was Bob Hart.

"Found 'em?" shouted Dave when he was close enough to be heard.

"No, and we won't—not this side of Malapi. Those scalawags didn't make camp last night. They kep' travelin'. If you ask me, they're movin' yet, and they've got our broncs with 'em."

This had already occurred to Dave as a possibility. "Any proof?" he asked quietly.

"A-plenty. I been ridin' on the point all day. Three-four times we cut trail of five horses. Two of the five are bein' ridden. My Four-Bits hoss has got a broken front hoof. So has one of the five."

"Movin' fast, are they?"

"You're damn whistlin'. They're hivin' off for parts unknown. Malapi first off, looks like. They got friends there."

"Steelman and his outfit will protect them while they hunt cover and make a getaway. Miller mentioned Denver before the race—said he was figurin' on goin' there. Maybe—"

"He was probably lyin'. You can't tell. Point is, we've got to get busy. My notion is we'd better make a bee-line for Malapi right away," proposed Bob.

"We'll travel all night. No use wastin' any more time."

Dug Doble received their decision sourly. "It don't tickle me a heap to be left short-handed because you two boys have got an excuse to get to town quicker."

Hart looked him straight in the eye. "Call it an excuse if you want to. We're after a pair of shorthorn crooks that stole our horses."

The foreman flushed angrily. "Don't come bellyachin' to me about yore broomtails. I ain't got 'em."

"We know who's got 'em," said Dave evenly. "What we want is a wage check so as we can cash it at Malapi."

"You don't get it," returned the big foreman bluntly. "We pay off when we reach the end of the drive."

"I notice you paid yore brother and Miller when we gave an order for it," Hart retorted with heat.

"A different proposition. They hadn't signed up for this drive like you boys did. You'll get what's comin' to you when I pay off the others. You'll not get it before."

The two riders retired sulkily. They felt it was not fair, but on the trail the foreman is an autocrat. From the other riders they borrowed a few dollars and gave in exchange orders on their pay checks.

Within an hour they were on the road. Fresh horses had been roped from the remuda and were carrying them at an even Spanish jog-trot through the night. The stars came out, clear and steady above a ghostly world at sleep. The desert was a place of mystery, of vast space peopled by strange and misty shapes.

The plain stretched vaguely before them. Far away was the thin outline of the range which enclosed the valley. The riders held their course by means of that trained sixth sense of direction their occupation had developed.

They spoke little. Once a coyote howled dismally from the edge of the mesa. For the most part there was no sound except the chuffing of the horses' movements and the occasional ring of a hoof on the baked ground.

The gray dawn, sifting into the sky, found them still traveling. The mountains came closer, grew more definite. The desert flamed again, dry, lifeless, torrid beneath a sky of turquoise. Dust eddies whirled in inverted cones, wind devils playing in spirals across the sand. Tablelands, mesas, wide plains, desolate lava stretches. Each in turn was traversed by these lean, grim, bronzed riders.

They reached the foothills and left behind the desert shimmering in the dancing heat. In a deep gorge, where the hill creases gave them shade, the punchers threw off the trail, unsaddled, hobbled their horses, and stole a few hours' sleep.

In the late afternoon they rode back to the trail through a draw, the ponies wading fetlock deep in yellow, red, blue, and purple flowers. The mountains across the valley looked in the dry heat as though made of *papier-mâchè*. Closer at hand the undulations of sand hills stretched toward the pass for which they were making.

A mule deer started out of a dry wash and fled into the sunset light. The long, stratified faces of rock escarpments caught the glow of the sliding sun and became battlemented towers of ancient story.

The riders climbed steadily now, no longer engulfed in the ground swell of land waves. They breathed an air like wine, strong, pure, bracing. Presently their way led them into a hill pocket, which ran into a gorge of piñons stretching toward Gunsight Pass.

The stars were out again when they looked down from the other side of the pass upon the lights of Malapi.

CHAPTER V

SUPPER AT DELMONICO'S INTERRUPTED

The two D Bar Lazy R punchers ate supper at Delmonico's. The restaurant was owned by Wong Chung. A Cantonese celestial did the cooking and another waited on table. The price of a meal was twenty-five cents, regardless of what one ordered.

Hop Lee, the waiter, grinned at the frolicsome youths with the serenity of a world-old wisdom.

"Bleef steak, plork chop, lamb chop, hlam'neggs, clorn bleef hash, Splanish stew," he chanted, reciting the bill of fare.

"Yes," murmured Bob.

The waiter said his piece again.

"Listens good to me," agreed Dave. "Lead it to us."

"You takee two—bleef steak and hlam'neggs mebbe," suggested Hop helpfully.

"Tha's right. Two orders of everything on the mean-you, Charlie."

Hop did not argue with them. He never argued with a customer. If they stormed at him he took refuge in a suddenly acquired lack of understanding of English. If they called him Charlie or John or One Lung, he accepted the name cheerfully and laid it to a racial mental deficiency of the 'melicans. Now he decided to make a selection himself.

"Vely well. Bleef steak and hlam'neggs."

"Fried potatoes done brown, John."

"Flied plotatoes. Tea or cloffee?"

"Coffee," decided Dave for both of them. "Warm mine."

"And custard pie," added Bob. "Made from this year's crop."

"Aigs sunny side up," directed his friend.

"Fry mine one on one side and one on the other," Hart continued facetiously.

"Vely well." Hop Lee's impassive face betrayed no perplexity as he departed. In the course of a season he waited on hundreds of wild men from the hills, drunk and sober.

Dave helped himself to bread from a plate stacked high with thick slices. He buttered it and began to eat. Hart did the same. At Delmonico's nobody ever waited till the meal was served. Just about to attack a second slice, Dave stopped to stare at his companion. Hart was looking past his shoulder with alert intentness. Dave turned his head. Two men, leaving the restaurant, were paying the cashier.

"They just stepped outa that booth to the right," whispered Bob.

The men were George Doble and a cowpuncher known as Shorty, a broad, heavy-set little man who worked for Bradley Steelman, owner of the Rocking Horse Ranch, what time he was not engaged on nefarious business of his own. He was wearing a Chihuahua hat and leather chaps with silver conchas.

At this moment Hop Lee arrived with dinner.

Dave sighed as he grinned at his friend. "I need that supper in my system. I sure do, but I reckon I don't get it."

"You do not, old lizard," agreed Hart. "I'll say Doble's the most inconsiderate guy I ever did trail. Why couldn't he 'a' showed up a half-hour later, dad gum his ornery hide?"

They paid their bill and passed into the street. Immediately the sound of a clear, high voice arrested their attention. It vibrated indignation and dread.

"What have you done with my father?" came sharply to them on the wings of the soft night wind.

A young woman was speaking. She was in a buggy and was talking to two men on the sidewalk—the two men who had preceded the range-riders out of the restaurant.

"Why, Miss, we ain't done a thing to him—nothin' a-tall." The man Shorty was speaking, and in a tone of honeyed conciliation. It was quite plain he did not want a scene on the street.

"That's a lie." The voice of the girl broke for an instant to a sob. "Do you think I don't know you're Brad Steelman's handy man, that you do his meanness for him when he snaps his fingers?"

"You sure do click yore heels mighty loud, Miss." Dave

caught in that soft answer the purr of malice. He remembered now hearing from Buck Byington that years ago Emerson Crawford had rounded up evidence to send Shorty to the penitentiary for rebranding through a blanket. "I reckon you come by it honest. Em always acted like he was God Almighty."

"Where is he? What's become of him?" she cried.

"Is yore paw missin'? I'm right sorry to hear that," the cowpuncher countered with suave irony. He was eager to be gone. His glance followed Doble, who was moving slowly down the street.

The girl's face, white and shining in the moonlight, leaned out of the buggy toward the retreating vaquero. "Don't you dare hurt my father! Don't you dare!" she warned. The words choked in her tense throat.

Shorty continued to back away. "You're excited, Miss. You go home an' think it over reasonable. You'll be sorry you talked this away to me," he said with unctuous virtue. Then, swiftly, he turned and went straddling down the walk, his spurs jingling music as he moved.

Quickly Dave gave directions to his friend. "Duck back into the restaurant, Bob. Get a pocketful of dry rice from the Chink. Trail those birds to their nest and find where they roost. Then stick around like a burr. Scatter rice behind you, and I'll drift along later. First off, I got to stay and talk with Miss Joyce. And, say, take along a rope. Might need it."

A moment later Hart was in the restaurant commandeering rice and Sanders was lifting his dusty hat to the young woman in the buggy.

"If I can he'p you any, Miss Joyce," he said.

Beneath dark and delicate brows she frowned at him. "Who are you?"

"Dave Sanders my name is. I reckon you never heard tell of me. I punch cows for yore father."

Her luminous, hazel-brown eyes steadied in his, read the honesty of his simple, boyish heart.

"You heard what I said to that man?"

"Part of it."

"Well, it's true. I know it is, but I can't prove it."

Hart, moving swiftly down the street, waved a hand at his friend as he passed. Without turning his attention from Joyce Crawford, Dave acknowledged the signal.

"How do you know it?"

"Steelman's men have been watching our house. They were

26

hanging around at different times day before yesterday. This man Shorty was one."

"Any special reason for the feud to break out right now?"

"Father was going to prove up on a claim this week—the one that takes in the Tularosa water-holes. You know the trouble they've had about it—how they kept breaking our fences to water their sheep and cattle. Don't you think maybe they're trying to keep him from proving up?"

"Maybeso. When did you see him last?"

Her lip trembled. "Night before last. After supper he started for the Cattleman's Club, but he never got there."

"Sure he wasn't called out to one of the ranches unexpected?"

"I sent out to make sure. He hasn't been seen there."

"Looks like some of Brad Steelman's smooth work," admitted Dave. "If he could work yore father to sign a relinquishment—"

Fire flickered in her eye. "He'd ought to know Dad better."

"Tha's right too. But Brad needs them water-holes in his business bad. Without 'em he loses the whole Round Top range. He might take a crack at turning the screws on yore father."

"You don't think—?" She stopped, to fight back a sob that filled her soft throat.

Dave was not sure what he thought, but he answered cheerfully and instantly. "No, I don't reckon they've dry-gulched him or anything. Emerson Crawford is one sure-enough husky citizen. He couldn't either be shot or rough-housed in town without someone hearin' the noise. What's more, it wouldn't be their play to injure him, but to force a relinquishment."

"That's true. You believe that, don't you?" Joyce cried eagerly.

"Sure I do." And Dave discovered that his argument or his hopes had for the moment convinced him. "Now the question is, what's to be done?"

"Yes," she admitted, and the tremor of the lips told him that she depended upon him to work out the problem. His heart swelled with glad pride at the thought.

"That man who jus' passed is my friend," he told her. "He's trailin' that duck Shorty. Like as not we'll find out what's stirrin'."

"I'll go with you," the girl said, vivid lips parted in anticipation.

27

"No, you go home. This is a man's job. Soon as I find out anything I'll let you know."

"You'll come, no matter what time o' night it is," she pleaded.

"Yes," he promised.

Her firm little hand rested a moment in his brown palm. "I'm depending on you," she murmured in a whisper lifted to a low wail by a stress of emotion.

CHAPTER VI

BY WAY OF A WINDOW

The trail of rice led down Mission Street, turned at Junipero, crossed into an alley, and trickled along a dusty road to the outskirts of the frontier town.

The responsibility Joyce had put upon him uplifted Dave. He had followed the horse-race gamblers to town on a purely selfish undertaking. But he had been caught in a cross-current of fate and was being swept into dangerous waters for the sake of another.

Doble and Miller were small fish in the swirl of this more desperate venture. He knew Brad Steelman by sight and by reputation. The man's coffee-brown, hatchet face, his restless, black eyes, the high, narrow shoulders, the slope of nose and chin, combined somehow to give him the look of a wily and predacious wolf. The boy had never met any one who so impressed him with a sense of ruthless rapacity. He was audacious and deadly in attack, but always he covered his tracks cunningly. Suspected of many crimes, he had been proved guilty of none. It was a safe bet that now he had a line of retreat worked out in case his plans went awry.

A soft, low whistle stayed his feet. From behind a greasewood bush Bob rose and beckoned him. Dave tiptoed to him. Both of them crouched behind cover while they whispered.

"The 'dobe house over to the right," said Bob. "I been up and tried to look in, but they got curtains drawn. I would've like to 've seen how many gents are present. Nothin' doin'. It's a strictly private party."

Dave told him what he had learned from the daughter of Emerson Crawford.

"Might make a gather of boys and raid the joint," suggested Hart.

"Bad medicine, Bob. Our work's got to be smoother than that. How do we know they got the old man a prisoner there? What excuse we got for attackin' a peaceable house? A friend of mine's brother onct got shot up makin' a similar mistake. Maybe Crawford's there. Maybe he ain't. Say he is. All right. There's some gun-play back and forth like as not. A b'ilin' of men pour outa the place. We go in and find the old man with a bullet right spang through his forehead. Well, ain't that too bad! In the rookus his own punchers must 'a' gunned him accidental. How would that story listen in court?"

"It wouldn't listen good to me. Howcome Crawford to be a prisoner there, I'd want to know."

"Sure you would, and Steelman would have witnesses aplenty to swear the old man had just drapped in to see if they couldn't talk things over and make a settlement of their troubles."

"All right. What's yore programme, then?" asked Bob.

"Darned if I know. Say we scout the ground over first."

They made a wide circuit and approached the house from the rear, worming their way through the Indian grass toward the back door. Dave crept forward and tried the door. It was locked. The window was latched and the blind lowered. He drew back and rejoined his companion.

"No chance there," he whispered.

"How about the roof?" asked Hart.

It was an eight-roomed house. From the roof two dormers jutted. No light issued from either of them.

Dave's eyes lit.

"What's the matter with takin' a whirl at it?" his partner continued. "You're tophand with a rope."

"Suits me fine."

The young puncher arranged the coils carefully and whirled the loop around his head to get the feel of the throw.

29

It would not do to miss the first cast and let the rope fall dragging down the roof. Some one might hear and come out to investigate.

The rope snaked forward and up, settled gracefully over the chimney, and tightened round it close to the shingles.

"Good enough. Now me for the climb," murmured Hart.

"Don't pull yore picket-pin, Bob. Me first."

"All right. We ain't no time to debate. Shag up, old scout."

Dave slipped off his high-heeled boots and went up hand over hand, using his feet against the rough adobe walls to help in the ascent. When he came to the eaves he threw a leg up and clambered to the roof. In another moment he was huddled against the chimney waiting for his companion.

As soon as Hart had joined him he pulled up the rope and wound it round the chimney.

"You stay here while I see what's doin'," Dave proposed.

"I never did see such a fellow for hoggin' all the fun," objected Bob. "Ain't you goin' to leave me trail along?"

"Got to play a lone hand till we find out where we're at, Bob. Doubles the chances of being bumped into if we both go."

"Then you roost on the roof and lemme look the range over for the old man."

"Didn't Miss Joyce tell me to find her paw? What's eatin' you, pard?"

"You pore plugged nickel!" derided Hart. "Think she picked you special for this job, do you?"

"Be reasonable, Bob," pleaded Dave.

His friend gave way. "Cut yore stick, then. Holler for me when I'm wanted."

Dave moved down the roof to the nearest dormer. The house, he judged, had originally belonged to a well-to-do Mexican family and had later been rebuilt upon American ideas. The thick adobe walls had come down from the earlier owners, but the roof had been put on as a substitute for the flat one of its first incarnation.

The range-rider was wearing plain shiny leather chaps with a gun in an open holster tied at the bottom to facilitate quick action. He drew out the revolver, tested it noiselessly, and restored it carefully to its place. If he needed the six-shooter at all, he would need it badly and suddenly.

Gingerly he tested the window of the dormer, working at it from the side so that his body would not be visible to anybody

30

who happened to be watching from within. Apparently it was latched. He crept across the roof to the other dormer.

It was a casement window, and at the touch of the hand it gave way. The heart of the cowpuncher beat fast with excitement. In the shadowy darkness of that room death might be lurking, its hand already outstretched toward him. He peered in, accustoming his eyes to the blackness. A prickling of the skin ran over him. The tiny cold feet of mice pattered up and down his spine. For he knew that, though he could not yet make out the objects inside the room, his face must be like a framed portrait to anybody there.

He made out presently that it was a bedroom with sloping ceiling. A bunk with blankets thrown back just as the sleeper had left them filled one side of the chamber. There were two chairs, a washstand, a six-inch by ten looking-glass, and a chromo or two on the wall. A sawed-off shotgun was standing in a corner. Here and there were scattered soiled clothing and stained boots. The door was ajar, but nobody was in the room.

Dave eased himself over the sill and waited for a moment while he listened, the revolver in his hand. It seemed to him that he could hear a faint murmur of voices, but he was not sure. He moved across the bare plank floor, slid through the door, and again stopped to take stock of his surroundings.

He was at the head of a stairway which ran down to the first floor and lost itself in the darkness of the hall. Leaning over the banister, he listened intently for any sign of life below. He was sure now that he heard the sound of low voices behind a closed door.

The cowpuncher hesitated. Should he stop to explore the upper story? Or should he go down at once and try to find out what those voices might tell him? It might be that time was of the essence of his contract to discover what had become of Emerson Crawford. He decided to look for his information on the first floor.

Never before had Dave noticed that stairs creaked and groaned so loudly beneath the pressure of a soft footstep. They seemed to shout his approach, though he took every step with elaborate precautions. A door slammed somewhere, and his heart jumped at the sound of it. He did not hide the truth from himself. If Steelman or his men found him here looking for Crawford he would never leave the house alive. His foot left the last tread and found the uncarpeted floor. He

31

crept, hand outstretched, toward the door behind which he heard men talking. As he moved forward his stomach muscles tightened. At any moment some one might come out of the room and walk into him.

He put his eye to the keyhole, and through it saw a narrow segment of the room. Ad Miller was sitting a-straddle a chair, his elbows on the back. Another man, one not visible to the cowpuncher, was announcing a decision and giving an order.

"Hook up the horses, Shorty. He's got his neck bowed and he won't sign. All right. I'll get the durn fool up in the hills and show him whether he will or won't."

"I could 'a' told you he had sand in his craw." Shorty was speaking. He too was beyond the range of Dave's vision. "Em Crawford won't sign unless he's a mind to."

"Take my advice, Brad. Collect the kid, an' you'll sure have Em hogtied. He sets the world an' all by her. Y'betcha he'll talk turkey then," predicted Miller.

"Are we fightin' kids?" the squat puncher wanted to know.

"Did I ask your advice, Shorty?" inquired Steelman acidly.

The range-rider grumbled an indistinct answer. Dave did not make out the words, and his interest in the conversation abruptly ceased.

For from upstairs there came the sudden sounds of trampling feet, of bodies thrashing to and fro in conflict. A revolver shot barked its sinister menace.

Dave rose to go. At the same time the door in front of him was jerked open. He pushed his forty-five into Miller's fat ribs.

"What's yore hurry? Stick up yore hands—stick 'em up!"

The boy was backing along the passage as he spoke. He reached the newel post in that second while Miller was being flung aside by an eruption of men from the room. Like a frightened rabbit Dave leaped for the stairs, taking them three at a time. Halfway up he collided with a man flying down. They came together with the heavy impact of fast-moving bodies. The two collapsed and rolled down, one over the other.

Sanders rose like a rubber ball. The other man lay still. He had been put out cold. Dave's head had struck him in the solar plexus and knocked the breath out of him. The young cowpuncher found himself the active center of a cyclone. His own revolver was gone. He grappled with a man, seizing him by the wrist to prevent the use of a long-barreled Colt's. The trigger fell, a bullet flying through the ceiling.

32

Other men pressed about him, trying to reach him with their fists and to strike him with their weapons. Their high heels crushed cruelly the flesh of his stockinged feet. The darkness befriended Dave. In the massed mêlée they dared not shoot for fear of hitting the wrong mark. Nor could they always be sure which shifting figure was the enemy.

Dave clung close to the man he had seized, using him as a shield against the others. The pack swayed down the hall into the wedge of light thrown by the lamp in the room.

Across the head of the man next him Shorty reached and raised his arm. Dave saw the blue barrel of the revolver sweeping down, but could not free a hand to protect himself. A jagged pain shot through his head. The power went out of his legs. He sagged at the hinges of his knees. He stumbled and went down. Heavy boots kicked at him where he lay. It seemed to him that bolts of lightning were zigzagging through him.

The pain ceased and he floated away into a sea of space.

CHAPTER VII

BOB HART TAKES A HAND

Bob Hart waited till his friend had disappeared into the house before he moved.

"Thought he'd run it over me, so I'd roost here on the roof, did he? Well, I'm after the ol' horn-toad full jump," the puncher murmured, a gay grin on his good-looking face.

He, too, examined his gun before he followed Dave through the dormer window and passed into the frowsy bed-chamber. None of the details of it escaped his cool, keen gaze, least of all the sawed-off shotgun in the corner.

"That scatter gun might come handy. Reckon I'll move it so's I'll know just where it's at when I need it," he said to himself, and carried the gun to the bed, where he covered it with a quilt.

At the top of the stairs Bob also hesitated before passing down. Why not be sure of his line of communications with the roof before going too far? He did not want to be in such a hurry that his retreat would be cut off.

With as little noise as possible Bob explored the upper story. The first room in which he found himself was empty of all furniture except a pair of broken-backed chairs. One casual glance was enough here.

He was about to try a second door when some one spoke. He recognized the voice. It belonged to the man who wrote his pay checks, and it came from an adjoining room.

"Always knew you was crooked as a dog's hind laig, Doble. Never liked you a lick in the road. I'll say this. Some day I'll certainly hang yore hide up to dry for yore treachery."

"No use to get on the peck, Em. It don't do you no good to make me sore. Maybe you'll need a friend before you're shet of Brad."

"It relieves my mind some to tell you what a yellow coyote you are," explained the cattleman. "You got about as much sand as a brush rabbit and I'd trust you as far as I would a rattler, you damned sidewinder."

Bob tried the door. The knob turned in his hand and the door slowly opened inward.

The rattle of the latch brought George Doble's sly, shifty eye round. He was expecting to see one of his friends from below. A stare of blank astonishment gave way to a leaping flicker of fear. The crook jumped to his feet, tugging at his gun. Before he could fire, the range-rider had closed with him.

The plunging attack drove Doble back against the table, a flimsy, round-topped affair which gave way beneath this assault upon it. The two men went down in the wreck. Doble squirmed away like a cat, but before he could turn to use his revolver Bob was on him again. The puncher caught his right arm, in time and in no more than time. The deflected bullet pinged through a looking-glass on a dresser near the foot of the bed.

"Go to it, son! Grab the gun and bust his haid wide open!" an excited voice encouraged Hart.

But Doble clung to his weapon as a lost cow does to a 'dobe water-hole in the desert. Bob got a grip on his arm and twisted till he screamed with pain. He did a head spin and escaped. One hundred and sixty pounds of steel-muscled cow-puncher landed on his midriff and the six-shooter went clattering away to a far corner of the room.

Bob dived for the revolver, Doble for the door. A moment, and Hart had the gun. But whereas there had been three in the room there were now but two.

A voice from the bed spoke in curt command. "Cut me loose." Bob had heard that voice on more than one round-up. It was that of Emerson Crawford.

The range-rider's sharp knife cut the ropes that tied the hands and feet of his employer. He worked in the dark and it took time.

"Who are you? Howcome you here?" demanded the cattleman.

"I'm Bob Hart. It's quite a story. Miss Joyce sent me and Dave Sanders," answered the young man, still busy with the ropes.

From below came the sound of a shot, the shuffling of many feet.

"Must be him downstairs."

"I reckon. They's a muley gun in the hall."

Crawford stretched his cramped muscles, flexing and reflexing his arms and legs. "Get it, son. We'll drift down and sit in."

When Bob returned he found the big cattleman examining Doble's revolver. He broke the shotgun to make sure it was loaded.

Then, "We'll travel," he said coolly.

The battle sounds below had died away. From the landing they looked down into the hall and saw a bar of light that came through a partly open door. Voices were lifted in excitement.

"One of Em Crawford's riders," some one was saying. "A whole passel of 'em must be round the place."

Came the thud of a boot on something soft. "Put the damn spy outa business, I say," broke in another angrily.

Hart's gorge rose. "Tha's Miller," he whispered to his chief. "He's kickin' Dave now he's down 'cause Dave whaled him good."

Softly the two men padded down the stair treads and moved along the passage.

"Who's that?" demanded Shorty, thrusting his head into the hall. "Stay right there or I'll shoot."

"Oh, no, you won't," answered the cattleman evenly. "I'm

comin' into that room to have a settlement. There'll be no shootin'—unless I do it."

His step did not falter. He moved forward, brushed Shorty aside, and strode into the midst of his enemies.

Dave lay on the floor. His hair was clotted with blood and a thin stream of it dripped from his head. The men grouped round his body had their eyes focused on the man who had just pushed his way in. All of them were armed, but not one of them made a move to attack.

For there is something about a strong man unafraid more potent than a company of troopers. Such a man was Emerson Crawford now. His life might be hanging in the balance of his enemies' fears, but he gave no sign of uncertainty. His steady gray eyes swept the circle, rested on each worried face, and fastened on Brad Steelman.

The two had been enemies for years, rivals for control of the range and for leadership in the community. Before that, as young men, they had been candidates for the hand of the girl that the better one had won. The sheepman was shrewd and cunning, but he had no such force of character as Crawford. At the bottom of his heart, though he seethed with hatred, he quailed before that level gaze. Did his foe have the house surrounded with his range-riders? Did he mean to make him pay with his life for the thing he had done?

Steelman laughed uneasily. An option lay before him. He could fight or he could throw up the hand he had dealt himself from a stacked deck. If he let his enemy walk away scot free, some day he would probably have to pay Crawford with interest. His choice was a characteristic one.

"Well, I reckon you've kinda upset my plans, Em. 'Course I was a-coddin' you. I didn't aim to hurt you none, though I'd 'a' liked to have talked you outa the water-holes."

The big cattleman ignored this absolutely. "Have a team hitched right away. Shorty will 'tend to that. Bob, tie up yore friend's haid with a handkerchief."

Without an instant's hesitation Hart thrust his revolver back into its holster. He was willing to trust Crawford to dominate this group of lawless foes, every one of whom held some deep grudge against him. One he had sent to the penitentiary. Another he had actually kicked out of his employ. A third was in his debt for many injuries received. Almost any of them would have shot him in the back on a dark night, but none had the cold nerve to meet him in the open. For even in a land which bred men there were few to match Emerson Crawford.

Shorty looked at Steelman. "I'm waitin', Brad," he said.

The sheepman nodded sullenly. "You done heard your orders, Shorty."

The ex-convict reached for his steeple hat, thrust his revolver back into its holster, and went jingling from the room. He looked insolently at Crawford as he passed.

"Different here. If it was my say-so I'd go through."

Hart administered first aid to his friend. "I'm servin' notice, Miller, that some day I'll bust you wide and handsome for this," he said, looking straight at the fat gambler. "You have give Dave a raw deal, and you'll not get away with it."

"I pack a gun. Come a-shootin' when you're ready," retorted Miller.

"Tha's liable to be right soon, you damn horsethief. We've rid 'most a hundred miles to have a li'l' talk with you and yore pardner there."

"Shoutin' about that race yet, are you? If I wasn't a better loser than you—"

"Don't bluff, Miller. You know why we trailed you."

Doble edged into the talk. He was still short of wind, but to his thick wits a denial seemed necessary. "We ain't got yore broncs."

"Who mentioned our broncs?" Hart demanded swiftly.

"Called Ad a horsethief, didn't you?"

"So he is. You, too. You've got our ponies. Not in yore vest pockets, but hid out in the brush somewheres. I'm servin' notice right now that Dave and me have come to collect."

Dave opened his eyes upon a world which danced hazily before him. He had a splitting headache.

"Wha's the matter?" he asked.

"You had a run-in with a bunch of sheep wranglers," Bob told him. "They're going to be plumb sorry they got gay."

Presently Shorty returned. "That team's hooked up," he told the world at large.

"You'll drive us, Steelman," announced Crawford.

"Me!" screamed the leader of the other faction. "You got the most nerve I ever did see."

"Sure. Drive him home, Brad," advised Shorty with bitter sarcasm. "Black his boots. Wait on him good. Step lively when yore new boss whistles." He cackled with splenetic laughter.

"I dunno as I need to drive you home," Steelman said slowly, feeling his way to a decision. "You know the way better 'n I do."

The eyes of the two leaders met.

"You'll drive," the cattleman repeated steadily.

The weak spot in Steelman's leadership was that he was personally not game. Crawford had a pungent personality. He was dynamic, strong, master of himself in any emergency. The sheepman's will melted before his insistence. He dared not face a showdown.

"Oh, well, what's it matter? We can talk things over on the way. Me, I'm not lookin' for trouble none," he said, his small black eyes moving restlessly to watch the effect of this on his men.

Bob helped his partner out of the house and into the surrey. The cattleman took the seat beside Steelman, across his knees the sawed-off shotgun. He had brought his enemy along for two reasons. One was to weaken his prestige with his own men. The other was to prevent them from shooting at the rig as they drove away.

Steelman drove in silence. His heart was filled with surging hatred. During that ride was born a determination to have nothing less than the life of his enemy when the time should be ripe.

At the door of his house Crawford dismissed him contemptuously. "Get out."

The man with the reins spoke softly, venomously, from a dry throat. "One o' these days you'll crawl on your hands and knees to me for this."

He whipped up the team and rattled away furiously into the night.

CHAPTER VIII

THE D BAR LAZY R BOYS
MEET AN ANGEL

Joyce came flying to her father's arms. The white lace of a nightgown showed beneath the dressing-robe she had hurriedly donned. A plait of dark hair hung across her shoulder far below the waist. She threw herself at Crawford with a moaning little sob.

"Oh Dad . . . Dad . . . Dad!" she cried, and her slender arms went round his neck.

" 'T's all right, sweetheart. Yore old dad's not even powder-burnt. You been worryin' a heap, I reckon." His voice was full of rough tenderness.

She began to cry.

He patted her shoulder and caressed her dark head, drawing it close to his shoulder. "Now—now—now, sweetheart, don't you cry. It's all right, li'l' honeybug."

"You're not . . . hurt," she begged through her tears.

"Not none. Never was huskier. But I got a boy out here that's beat up some. Come in, Dave—and you, Bob. They're good boys, Joy. I want you to meet 'em both."

The girl had thought her father alone. She flung one startled glance into the night, clutched the dressing-gown closer round her throat, and fled her barefoot way into the darkness of the house. To the boys, hanging back awkwardly at the gate, the slim child-woman was a vision wonderful. Their starved eyes found in her white loveliness a glimpse of heaven.

Her father laughed. "Joy ain't dressed for callers. Come in, boys."

He lit a lamp and drew Dave to a lounge. "Lemme look at yore haid, son. Bob, you hotfoot it for Doc Green."

39

"It's nothin' a-tall to make a fuss about," Dave apologized. "Only a love tap, compliments of Shorty, and some kicks in the slats, kindness of Mr. Miller."

In spite of his debonair manner Dave still had a bad headache and was so sore around the body that he could scarcely move without groaning. He kept his teeth clamped on the pain because he had been brought up in the outdoor code of the West which demands of a man that he grin and stand the gaff.

While the doctor was attending to his injuries, Dave caught sight once or twice of Joyce at the door, clad now in a summer frock of white with a blue sash. She was busy supplying, in a brisk, competent way, the demands of the doctor for hot and cold water and clean linen.

Meanwhile Crawford told his story. "I was right close to the club when Doble met me. He pulled a story of how his brother Dug had had trouble with Steelman and got shot up. I swallowed it hook, bait, and sinker. Soon as I got into the house they swarmed over me like bees. I didn't even get my six-gun out. Brad wanted me to sign a relinquishment. I told him where he could head in at."

"What would have happened if the boys hadn't dropped along?" asked Dr. Green as he repacked his medicine case.

The cattleman looked at him, and his eyes were hard and bleak. "Why, Doc, yore guess is as good as mine." he said.

"Mine is, you'd have been among the missing, Em. Well, I'm leaving a sleeping-powder for the patient in case he needs it in an hour or two. In the morning I'll drop round again," the doctor said.

He did, and found Dave much improved. The clean outdoors of the rough-riding West builds blood that is red. A city man might have kept his bed a week, but Dave was up and ready to say good-bye within forty-eight hours. He was still a bit under par, a trifle washed-out, but he wanted to take the road in pursuit of Miller and Doble, who had again decamped in a hurry with the two horses they had stolen.

"They had the broncs hid up Frio Cañon way, I reckon," explained Hart. "But they didn't take no chances. When they left that 'dobe house they lit a-runnin' and clumb for the high hills on the jump. And they didn't leave no address neither. We'll be followin' a cold trail. We're not liable to find them after they hole up in some mountain pocket."

"Might. Never can tell. Le's take a whirl at it anyhow," urged Dave.

"Hate to give up yore paint hoss, don't you?" said Bob with his friendly grin. "Ain't blamin' you none whatever. I'd sleep on those fellows' trail if Chiquito was mine. What say we outfit in the mornin' and pull our freights? Maybeso we'll meet up with the thieves at that. *Yo no se* (I don't know)."

When Joyce was in the room where Dave lay on the lounge, the young man never looked at her, but he saw nobody else. Brought up in a saddle on the range, he had never before met a girl like her. It was not only that she was beautiful and fragrant as apple-blossoms, a mystery of maidenhood whose presence awed his simple soul. It was not only that she seemed so delicately precious, a princess of the blood royal set apart by reason of her buoyant grace, the soft rustle of her skirts, the fine texture of the satiny skin. What took him by the throat was her goodness. She was enshrined in his heart as a young saint. He would have thought it sacrilege to think of her as a wide-awake young woman subject to all the vanities of her sex. And he could have cited evidence. The sweetness of her affection for rough Em Crawford, the dear, maternal tenderness with which she ruled her three-year-old brother Keith, motherless since the week of his birth, the kindness of the luminous brown eyes to the uncouth stranger thrown upon her hospitality: Dave treasured them all as signs of angelic grace, and they played upon his heartstrings disturbingly.

Joyce brought Keith in to say good-bye to Dave and his friend before they left. The little fellow ran across the room to his new pal, who had busied himself weaving horsehair playthings for the youngster.

"You tum back and make me a bwidle, Dave," he cried.

"I'll sure come or else send you one," the cowpuncher promised, rising to meet Joyce.

She carried her slender figure across the room with perfect ease and rhythm, head beautifully poised, young seventeen as self-possessed as thirty. As much could not be said for her guests. They were all legs and gangling arms, red ears and dusty boots.

"Yes, we all want you to come back," she said with a charming smile. "I think you saved Father's life. We can't tell you how much we owe you. Can we, Keith?"

"Nope. When will you send the bwidle?" he demanded.

"Soon," the restored patient said to the boy, and to her: "That wasn't nothin' a-tall. From where I come from we always been use to standin' by our boss."

41

He shifted awkwardly to the other foot, flushing to the hair while he buried her soft little hand in his big freckled one. The girl showed no shyness. Seventeen is sometimes so much older than twenty.

"Tha's what us D Bar Lazy R boys are ridin' with yore paw's outfit for, Miss—to be handy when he needs us," Bob added in his turn. "We're sure tickled we got a chanct to go to Brad Steelman's party. I'm ce'tainly glad to 'a' met you, Miss Joyce." He ducked his head and scraped back a foot in what was meant to be a bow.

Emerson Crawford sauntered in, big and bluff and easygoing. "Hittin' the trail, boys? Good enough. Hope you find the thieves. If you do, play yore cards close. They're treacherous devils. Don't take no chances with 'em. I left an order at the store for you to draw on me for another pair of boots in place of those you lost in the brush, Dave. Get a good pair, son. They're on me. Well, so long. Luck, boys. I'll look for you-all back with the D Bar Lazy R when you've finished this job."

The punchers rode away without looking back, but many times in the days that followed their hearts turned to that roof which had given the word home a new meaning to them both.

CHAPTER IX

GUNSIGHT PASS

The pursuit took the riders across a wide, undulating plain above which danced the dry heat of the desert. Lizards sunned themselves on flat rocks. A rattlesnake slid toward the cover of a prickly pear. The bleached bones of a cow shone white beside the trail.

The throats of the cowpunchers filled with alkali dust and

their eyes grew red and sore from it. Magnificent mirages unfolded themselves: lakes cool and limpid, stretching to the horizon, with inviting forests in the distance; an oasis of lush green fields that covered miles; mesquite distorted to the size of giant trees and cattle transformed into dinosaurs. The great gray desert took on freakish shapes of erosion. Always, hour after hour beneath a copper sky, they rode in palpitating heat through sand drifts, among the salt bushes and the creosote, into cowbacked hills beyond which the stark mountains rose.

Out of the fiery furnace of the plain they came in late afternoon to the uplands, plunging into a land of deep gorges and great chasms. Here manzanita grew and liveoaks flourished. They sent a whitetail buck crashing through the brush into a cañon.

When night fell they built a fire of niggerheads and after they had eaten found its glow grateful. For they were well up in the hills now and the night air was sharp.

In the sandy desert they had followed easily the trail of the thieves, but as they had got into the hills the tracks had become fainter and fewer. The young men discussed this while they lay in their blankets in a water-gutted gulch not too near the fire they had built.

"Like huntin' for a needle in a haystack," said Bob. "Their trail's done petered out. They might be in any one of a hundred pockets right close, or they may have bore 'way off to the right. All they got to do is hole up and not build any fires."

"Fat chance we got," admitted Dave. "Unless they build a fire like we done. Say, I'd a heap rather be sleepin' here than by that niggerhead blaze to-night. They might creep up and try to gun us."

Before they had been in the saddle an hour next day the trail of the thieves was lost. The pursuers spent till sunset trying to pick it up again. The third day was wasted in aimless drifting among the defiles of the mountains.

"No use, Bob," said his friend while they were cooking supper. "They've made their getaway. Might as well drift back to Malapi, don't you reckon?"

"Looks like. We're only wastin' our time here."

Long before day broke they started.

The cañons below were filled with mist as they rode down out of the mountains toward the crystal dawn that already flooded the plain. The court-house clock at Malapi said the time was midnight when the dust-covered men and horses drew into the town.

The tired men slept till noon. At the Delmonico Restaurant they found Buck Byington and Steve Russell. The trail herd had been driven in an hour before.

"How's old Alkali?" asked Dave of his friend Buck, thumping him on the back.

"Jes' tolable," answered the old-timer equably, making great play with knife and fork. "A man or a hawss don't either one amount to much after they onct been stove up. Since that bronc piled me at Willow Creek I been mighty stiff, you might say."

"Dug's payin' off to-day, boys," Russell told me. "You'll find him round to the Boston Emporium."

The foreman settled first with Hart, after which he turned to the page in his pocket notebook that held the account of Sanders.

"You've drew one month's pay. That leaves you three months, less the week you've fooled away after the pinto."

"C'rect," admitted Dave.

"I'll dock you seven and a half for that. Three times thirty 's ninety. Take seven and a half from that leaves eighty-two fifty."

"Hold on!" objected Dave. "My pay's thirty-five a month."

"First I knew of it," said the foreman, eyes bleak and harsh. "Thirty 's what you're gettin'."

"I came in as top hand at thirty-five."

"You did not," denied Doble flatly.

The young man flushed. "You can't run that on me, Dug. I'll not stand for it."

"Eighty-two fifty is what you get," answered the other dogmatically. "You can take it or go to hell."

He began to sort out a number of small checks with which to pay the puncher. At that time the currency of the country consisted largely of cattlemen's checks which passed from hand to hand till they were grimy with dirt. Often these were not cashed for months later.

"We'll see what the old man says about that," retorted Dave hotly. It was in his mind to say that he did not intend to be robbed by both the Doble brothers, but he wisely repressed the impulse. Dug would as soon fight as eat, and the young rider knew he would not have a chance in the world against him.

"All right," sneered the foreman. "Run with yore tale of

44

grief to Crawford. Tell him I been pickin' on you. I hear you've got to be quite a pet of his."

This brought Dave up with a short turn. He could not take advantage of the service he had done the owner of the D Bar Lazy R to ask him to interfere in his behalf with the foreman. Doble might be cynically defrauding him of part of what was due him in wages. Dave would have to fight that out with him for himself. The worst of it was that he had no redress. Unless he appealed to the cattleman he would have to accept what the foreman offered.

Moreover, his pride was touched. He was young enough to be sensitive on the subject of his ability to look out for himself.

"I'm no pet of anybody," he flung out. "Gimme that money. It ain't a square deal, but I reckon I can stand it."

"I reckon you'll have to. It's neck meat or nothin',", grunted the foreman.

Doble counted him out eighty dollars in cattlemen's checks and paid him two-fifty in cash. While Dave signed a receipt the hook-nosed foreman, broad shoulders thrown back and thumbs hitched in the arm-holes of his vest, sat at ease in a tilted chair and grinned maliciously at his victim. He was "puttin' somethin' over on him," and he wanted Dave to know it. Dug had no affection for his half-brother, but he resented the fact that Sanders publicly and openly despised him as a crook. He took it as a personal reflection on himself.

Still smouldering with anger at this high-handed proceeding, Dave went down to the Longhorn Corral and saddled his horse. He had promised Byington to help water the herd.

This done, he rode back to town, hitched the horse back of a barber shop, and went in for a shave. Presently he was stretched in a chair, his boots thrown across the foot rest in front of him.

The barber lathered his face and murmured gossip in his ear. "George Doble and Miller claim they're goin' to Denver to run some skin game at a street fair. They're sure slick guys."

Dave offered no comment.

"You notice they didn't steal any of Em Crawford's stock. No, sirree! They knew better. Hopped away with broncs belongin' to you boys because they knew it'd be safe."

"Picked easy marks, did they?" asked the puncher sardonically.

The man with the razor tilted the chin of his customer and

began to scrape. "Well, o' course you're only boys. They took advantage of that and done you a meanness."

Dug Doble came into the shop, very grim about the mouth. He stopped to look down sarcastically at the new boots Sanders was wearing.

"I see you've bought you a new pair of boots," he said in a heavy, domineering voice.

Dave waited without answering, his eyes meeting steadily those of the foreman.

The big fellow laid a paper on the breast of the cow-puncher. "Here's a bill for a pair of boots you charged to the old man's account—eighteen dollars. I got it just now at the store. You'll dig up."

It was the custom for riders who came to town to have the supplies they needed charged to their employers against wages due them. Doble took it for granted that Sanders had done this, which was contrary to the orders he had given his outfit. He did not know the young man had lost his boots while rescuing Crawford and had been authorized by him to get another pair in place of them.

Nor did Dave intend to tell him. Here was a chance to even the score against the foreman. Already he had a plan simmering in his mind that would take him out of this part of the country for a time. He could no longer work for Doble without friction, and he had business of his own to attend to. The way to solve the immediate difficulty flashed through his brain instantly, every detail clear.

It was scarcely a moment before he drawled an answer. "I'll 'tend to it soon as I'm out of the chair."

"I gave orders for none of you fellows to charge goods to the old man," said Doble harshly.

"Did you?" Dave's voice was light and careless.

"You can go hunt a job somewheres else. You're through with me."

"I'll hate to part with you."

"Don't get heavy, young fellow."

"No," answered Dave with mock meekness.

Doble sat down in a chair to wait. He had no intention of leaving until Dave had settled.

After the barber had finished with him the puncher stepped across to a looking-glass and adjusted carefully the silk handkerchief worn knotted loosely round the throat.

"Get a move on you!" urged the foreman. His patience, of

46

which he never had a large supply to draw from, was nearly exhausted. "I'm not goin' to spend all day on this."

"I'm ready."

Dave followed Doble out of the shop. Apparently he did not hear the gentle reminder of the barber, who was forced to come to the door and repeat his question.

"Want that shave charged?"

"Oh! Clean forgot." Sanders turned back, feeling in his pocket for change.

He pushed past the barber into the shop, slapped a quarter down on the cigar-case, and ran out through the back door. A moment later he pulled the slip-knot of his bridle from the hitching-bar, swung to the saddle, and spurred his horse to a gallop. In a cloud of dust he swept round the building to the road and waved a hand derisively toward Doble.

"See you later!" he shouted.

The foreman wasted no breath in futile rage. He strode to the nearest hitching-post and flung himself astride leather. The horse's hoofs pounded down the road in pursuit.

Sanders was riding the same bronco he had used to follow the horsethieves. It had been under a saddle most of the time for a week and was far from fresh. Before he had gone a mile he knew that the foreman would catch up with him.

He was riding for Gunsight Pass. It was necessary to get there before Doble reached him. Otherwise he would have to surrender or fight, and neither of these fitted in with his plans.

Once he had heard Emerson Crawford give a piece of advice to a hotheaded and unwise puncher. "Never call for a gun-play on a bluff, son. There's no easier way to commit suicide than to pull a six-shooter you ain't willin' to use." Dug Doble was what Byington called "bull-haided." He had forced a situation which could not be met without a showdown. This meant that the young range-rider would either have to take a thrashing or draw his forty-five and use it. Neither of these alternatives seemed worth while in view of the small stakes at issue. Because he was not ready to kill or be killed, Dave was flying for the hills.

The fugitive had to use his quirt to get there in time. The steepness of the road made heavy going. As he neared the summit the grade grew worse. The bronco labored heavily in its stride as its feet reached for the road ahead.

But here Dave had the advantage. Doble was a much heavier man than he, and his mount took the shoulder of the ridge

47

slower. By the time the foreman showed in silhouette against the skyline at the entrance to the pass the younger man had disappeared.

The D Bar Lazy R foreman found out at once what had become of him. A crisp voice gave clear directions.

"That'll be far enough. Stop right where you're at or you'll notice trouble pop. And don't reach for yore gun unless you want to hear the band begin to play a funeral piece."

The words came, it seemed to Doble, out of the air. He looked up. Two great boulders lay edge to edge beside the path. Through a narrow rift the blue nose of a forty-five protruded. Back of it glittered a pair of steady, steely eyes.

The foreman did not at all like the look of things. Sanders was a good shot. From where he lay, almost entirely protected, all he had to do was to pick his opponent off at his leisure. If his hand were forced he would do it. And the law would let him go scot free, since Doble was a fighting man and had been seen to start in pursuit of the boy.

"Come outa there and shell out that eighteen dollars," demanded Doble.

"Nothin' doin', Dug."

"Don't run on the rope with me, young fellow. You'll sure be huntin' trouble."

"What's the use o' beefin'? I've got the deadwood on you. Better hit the dust back to town and explain to the boys how yore bronc went lame," advised Dave.

"Come down and I'll wallop the tar outa you."

"Much obliged. I'm right comfortable here."

"I've a mind to come up and dig you out."

"Please yoreself, Dug. We'll find out then which one of us goes to hell."

The foreman cursed, fluently, expertly, passionately. Not in a long time had he had the turn called on him so adroitly. He promised Dave sudden death in various forms whenever he could lay hands upon him.

"You're sure doin' yoreself proud, Dug," the young man told him evenly. "I'll write the boys how you spilled language so thorough."

"If I could only lay my hands on you!" the raw-boned cattleman stormed.

"I'll bet you'd massacree me proper," admitted Dave quite cheerfully.

Suddenly Doble gave up. He wheeled his horse and began

48

to descend the steep slope. Steadily he jogged on to town, not once turning to look back. His soul was filled with chagrin and fury at the defeat this stripling had given him. He was ready to pick a quarrel with the first man who asked him a question about what had taken place at the pass.

Nobody asked a question. Men looked at him, read the menace of his sullen, angry face, and side-stepped his rage. They did not need to be told that his ride had been a failure. His manner advertised it. Whatever had taken place had not redounded to the glory of Dug Doble.

Later in the day the foreman met the owner of the D Bar Lazy R brand to make a detailed statement of the cost of the drive. He took peculiar pleasure in mentioning one item.

"That young scalawag Sanders beat you outa eighteen dollars," he said with a sneer of triumph.

Doble had heard the story of what Dave and Bob had done for Crawford and of how the wounded boy had been taken to the cattleman's home and nursed there. It pleased him now to score off what he chose to think was the soft-headedness of his chief.

The cattleman showed interest. "That so, Dug? Sorry. I took a fancy to that boy. What did he do?"

"You know how vaqueros are always comin' in and chargin' goods against the boss. I give out the word they was to quit it. Sanders he gets a pair of eighteen-dollar boots, then jumps the town before I find out about it."

Crawford started to speak, but Doble finished his story.

"I took out after him, but my bronc went lame from a stone in its hoof. You'll never see that eighteen plunks, Em. It don't do to pet cowhands."

"Too bad you took all that trouble, Dug," the old cattleman began mildly. "The fact is—"

"Trouble. Say, I'd ride to Tombstone to get a crack at that young smart Aleck. I told him what I'd do to him if I ever got my fists on him."

"So you *did* catch up with him."

Dug drew back sulkily within himself. He did not intend to tell all he knew about the Gunsight Pass episode. "I didn't say *when* I told him."

"Tha's so. You didn't. Well, I'm right sorry you took so blamed much trouble to find him. Funny, though, he didn't tell you I gave him the boots."

"You—what?" The foreman snapped the question out with angry incredulity.

The ranchman took the cigar from his mouth and leaned back easily. He was smiling now frankly.

"Why, yes. I told him to buy the boots and have 'em charged to my account. And the blamed little rooster never told you, eh?"

Doble choked for words with which to express himself. He glared at his employer as though Crawford had actually insulted him.

In an easy, conversational tone the cattleman continued, but now there was a touch of frost in his eyes. "It was thisaway, Dug. When he and Bob knocked Steelman's plans hell west and crooked after that yellow skunk George Doble betrayed me to Brad, the boy lost his boots in the brush. 'Course I said to get another pair at the store and charge 'em to me. I reckon he was havin' some fun joshin' you."

The foreman was furious. He sputtered with the rage that boiled inside him. But some instinct warned him that unless he wanted to break with Crawford completely he must restrain his impulse to rip loose.

"All right," he mumbled. "If you told him to get 'em, 'nough said."

CHAPTER X

THE CATTLE TRAIN

Dave stood on the fence of one of the shipping pens at the Albuquerque stockyards and used a prod-pole to guide the bawling cattle below. The Fifty-Four Quarter Circle was loading a train of beef steers and cows for Denver. Just how he was going to manage it Dave did not know, but he intended to be aboard that freight when it pulled out for the mile-high town in Colorado.

He had reached Albuquerque by a strange and devious route of zigzags and back-trackings. His weary bronco he had long since sold for ten dollars at a cow town where he had sacked his saddle to be held at a livery stable until sent for. By blind baggage he had ridden a night and part of a day. For a hundred miles he had actually paid his fare. The next leg of the journey had been more exciting. He had elected to travel by freight. For many hours he and a husky brakeman had held different opinions about this. Dave had been chased from the rods into an empty and out of the box car to the roof. He had been ditched half a dozen times during the night, but each time he had managed to hook on before the train had gathered headway. The brakeman enlisted the rest of the crew in the hunt, with the result that the range-rider found himself stranded on the desert ten miles from a station. He walked the ties in his high-heeled boots, and before he reached the yards his feet were sending messages of pain at every step. Reluctantly he bought a ticket to Albuquerque. Here he had picked up a temporary job ten minutes after his arrival.

A raw-boned inspector kept tally at the chute while the cattle passed up into the car.

"Fifteen, sixteen—prod 'em up, you Arizona—seventeen, eighteen—jab that whiteface along—nineteen—hustle 'em in."

The air was heavy with the dust raised by the milling cattle. Calves stretched their necks and blatted for their mothers, which kept up in turn a steady bawling for their strayed offspring. They were conscious that something unusual was in progress, something that threatened their security and comfort, and they resented it in the only way they knew.

Car after car was jammed full of the frightened creatures as the men moved from pen to pen, threw open and shut the big gates, and hustled the stock up the chutes. Dave had begun work at six in the morning. A glance at his watch showed him that it was now ten o'clock.

A middle-aged man in wrinkled corduroys and a pinched-in white hat drove up to the fence. "How're they coming, Sam?" he asked of the foreman in charge.

"We'd ought to be movin' by noon, Mr. West."

"Fine. I've decided to send Garrison in charge. He can pick one of the boys to take along. We can't right well spare any of 'em now. If I knew where to find a good man—"

51

The lean Arizona-born youth slid from the fence on his prod-pole and stepped forward till he stood beside the buckboard of the cattleman.

"I'm the man you're lookin' for, Mr. West."

The owner of the Fifty-Four Quarter Circle brand looked him over with keen eyes around which nets of little wrinkles spread.

"What man?" he asked.

"The one to help Mr. Garrison take the cattle to Denver."

"Recommend yoreself, can you?" asked West with a hint of humor.

"Yes, sir."

"Who are you?"

"Dave Sanders—from Arizona, first off."

"Been punchin' long?"

"Since I was a kid. Worked for the D Bar Lazy R last."

"Ever go on a cattle train?"

"Twice—to Kansas City."

"Hmp!" That grunt told Dave just what the difficulty was. It said, "I don't know you. Why should I trust you to help take a trainload of my cattle through?"

"You can wire to Mr. Crawford at Malapi and ask him about me," the young fellow suggested.

"How long you ride for him?"

"Three years comin' grass."

"How do I know you're the man you say you are?"

"One of yore boys knows me—Bud Holway."

West grunted again. He knew Emerson Crawford well. He was a level-headed cowman and his word was as good as his bond. If Em said this young man was trustworthy, the shipper was willing to take a chance on him. The honest eye, the open face, the straightforward manner of the youth recommended his ability and integrity. The shipper was badly in need of a man. He made up his mind to wire.

"Let you know later," he said, and for the moment dropped Dave out of the conversation.

But before noon he sent for him.

"I've heard from Crawford," he said, and mentioned terms.

"Whatever's fair," agreed Dave.

An hour later he was in the caboose of a cattle train rolling eastward. He was second in command of a shipment consigned to the Denver Terminal Stockyards Company. Most of them were shipped by the West Cattle Company. An odd car

52

was a jackpot bunch of pickups composed of various brands. All the cars were packed to the door, as was the custom of those days.

After the train had settled down to the chant of the rails Garrison sent Dave on a tour of the cars. The young man reported all well and returned to the caboose. The train crew was playing poker for small stakes. Garrison had joined them. For a time Dave watched, then read a four-day-old newspaper through to the last advertisement. The hum of the wheels made him drowsy. He stretched out comfortably on the seat with his coat for a pillow.

When he awoke it was beginning to get dark. Garrison had left the caboose, evidently to have a look at the stock. Dave ate some crackers and cheese, climbed to the roof, and with a lantern hanging on his arm moved forward.

Already a few of the calves, yielding to the pressure in the heavily laden cars, had tried to escape it by lying down. With his prod Dave drove back the nearest animal. Then he used the nail in the pole to twist the tails of the calves and force them to their feet. In those days of crowded cars almost the most important thing in transit was to keep the cattle on their legs to prevent any from being trampled and smothered to death.

As the night grew older both men were busier. With their lanterns and prod-poles they went from car to car relieving the pressure wherever it was greatest. The weaker animals began to give way, worn out by the heavy lurching and the jam of heavy bodies against them. They had to be defended against their own weakness.

Dave was crossing from the top of one car to another when he heard his name called. He knew the voice belonged to Garrison and he listened to make sure from which car it came. Presently he heard it a second time and localized the sound as just below him. He entered the car by the end door near the roof.

"Hello! Call me?" he asked.

"Yep. I done fell and bust my laig. Can you get me outa here?"

"Bad, is it?"

"Broken."

"I'll get some of the train hands. Will you be all right till I get back?" the young man asked.

"I reckon. Hop along lively. I'm right in the jam here."

53

The conductor stopped the train. With the help of the crew Dave got Garrison back to the caboose. There was no doubt that the leg was broken. It was decided to put the injured man off at the next station, send him back by the up train, and wire West that Dave would see the cattle got through all right. This was done.

Dave got no more sleep that night. He had never been busier in his life. Before morning broke half the calves were unable to keep their feet. The only thing to do was to reload.

He went to the conductor and asked for a siding. The man running the train was annoyed, but he did not say so. He played for time.

"All right. We'll come to one after a while and I'll put you on it," he promised.

Half an hour later the train rumbled merrily past a siding without stopping. Dave walked back along the roof to the caboose.

"We've just passed a siding," he told the trainman.

"Couldn't stop there. A freight behind us has orders to take that to let the Limited pass," he said glibly.

Dave suspected he was lying, but he could not prove it. He asked where the next siding was.

"A little ways down," said a brakeman.

The puncher saw his left eyelid droop in a wink to the conductor. He knew now that they were "stalling" for time. The end of their run lay only thirty miles away. They had no intention of losing two or three hours time while the cattle were reloaded. After the train reached the division point another conductor and crew would have to wrestle with the problem.

Young Sanders felt keenly his inexperience. They were taking advantage of him because he was a boy. He did not know what to do. He had a right to insist on a siding, but it was not his business to decide which one.

The train rolled past another siding and into the yards of the division town. At once Dave hurried to the station. The conductor about to take charge of the train was talking with the one just leaving. The range-rider saw them look at him and laugh as he approached. His blood began to warm.

"I want you to run this train onto a siding," he said at once.

"You the train dispatcher?" asked the new man satirically.

"You know who I am. I'll say right now that the cattle on this train are suffering. Some won't last another hour. I'm goin' to reload."

"Are you? I guess not. This train's going out soon as we've changed engines, and that'll be in about seven minutes."

"I'll not go with it."

"Suit yourself," said the officer jauntily, and turned away to talk with the other man.

Dave walked to the dispatcher's office. The cowpuncher stated his case.

"Fix that up with the train conductor," said the dispatcher. "He can have a siding whenever he wants it."

"But he won't gimme one."

"Not my business."

"Whose business is it?"

The dispatcher got busy over his charts. Dave became aware that he was going to get no satisfaction here.

He tramped back to the platform.

"All aboard," sang out the conductor.

Dave, not knowing what else to do, swung on to the caboose as it passed. He sat down on the steps and put his brains at work. There must be a way out, if he could only find what it was. The next station was fifteen miles down the line. Before the train stopped there Dave knew exactly what he meant to do. He wrote out two messages. One was to the division superintendent. The other was to Henry B. West.

He had swung from the steps of the caboose and was in the station before the conductor.

"I want to send two telegrams," he told the agent. "Here they are all ready. Rush 'em through. I want an answer here to the one to the superintendent."

The wire to the railroad official read:

Conductor freight number 17 refuses me siding to reload stock in my charge. Cattle down and dying. Serve notice herewith I put responsibility for all loss on railroad. Will leave cars in charge of train crew.

DAVID SANDERS
Representing West Cattle Company

The other message was just as direct.

Conductor refuses me siding to reload. Cattle suffering and dying. Have wired division superintendent. Will refuse responsibility and leave train unless siding given me.

DAVE SANDERS

The conductor caught the eye of the agent.

"I'll send the wires when I get time," said the latter to the cowboy.

"You'll send 'em now—right now," announced Dave.

"Say, are you the president of the road?" bristled the agent.

"You'll lose yore job within forty-eight hours if you don't send them telegrams *now*. I'll see to that personal." Dave leaned forward and looked at him steadily.

The conductor spoke to the agent, nodding his head insolently toward Dave. "Young-man-heap-swelled-head," he introduced him.

But the agent had had a scare. It was his job at stake, not the conductor's. He sat down sulkily and sent the messages.

The conductor read his orders and walked to the door.

"Number 17 leaving. All aboard," he called back insolently.

"I'm stayin' here till I hear from the superintendent," answered Dave flatly. "You leave an' you've got them cattle to look out for. They'll be in yore care."

The conductor swaggered out and gave the signal to go. The train drew out from the station and disappeared around a curve in the track. Five minutes later it backed in again. The conductor was furious.

"Get aboard here, you hayseed, if you're goin' to ride with me!" he yelled.

Dave was sitting on the platform whittling a stick. His back was comfortably resting against a truck. Apparently he had not heard.

The conductor strode up to him and looked down at the lank boy. "Say, are you comin' or ain't you?" he shouted, as though he had been fifty yards away instead of four feet.

"Talkin' to me?" Dave looked up with amiable surprise. "Why, no, not if you're in a hurry. I'm waitin' to hear from the superintendent."

"If you think any boob can come along and hold my train up till I lose my right of way you've got another guess comin'. I ain't goin' to be sidetracked by every train on the division."

"That's the company's business, not mine. I'm interested only in my cattle."

The conductor had a reputation as a bully. He had intended to override this young fellow by weight of age, authority, and personality. That he had failed filled him with rage.

"Say, for half a cent I'd kick you into the middle of next week," he said, between clamped teeth.

The cowpuncher's steel-blue eyes met his steadily. "Do you reckon that would be quite safe?" he asked mildly.

That was a question the conductor had been asking himself. He did not know. A good many cowboys carried six-shooters tucked away on their ample persons. It was very likely this one had not set out on his long journey without one.

"You're more obstinate than a Missouri mule," the railroad man exploded. "I don't have to put up with you, and I won't!"

"No?"

The agent came out from the station waving two slips of paper. "Heard from the super," he called.

One wire was addressed to Dave, the other to the conductor. Dave read:

Am instructing conductor to put you on siding and place train crew under your orders to reload.

Beneath was the signature of the superintendent.

The conductor flushed purple as he read the orders sent by his superior.

"Well," he stormed at Dave. "What do you want? Spit it out!"

"Run me on the siding. I'm gonna take the calves out of the cars and tie 'em on the feed-racks above."

"How're you goin' to get 'em up?"

"Elbow grease."

"If you think I'll turn my crew into freight elevators because some fool cattleman didn't know how to load right—"

"Maybe you've got a kick comin'. I'll not say you haven't. But this is an emergency. I'm willin' to pay good money for the time they help me." Dave made no reference to the telegram in his hand. He was giving the conductor a chance to save his face.

"Oh, well, that's different. I'll put it up to the boys."

Three hours later the wheels were once more moving eastward. Dave had had the calves roped down to the feed-racks above the cars.

CHAPTER XI

THE NIGHT CLERK GETS BUSY PRONTO

The stars were out long before Dave's train drew into the suburbs of Denver. It crawled interminably through squalid residence sections, warehouses, and small manufactories, coming to a halt at last in a wilderness of tracks on the border of a small, narrow stream flowing sluggishly between wide banks cut in the clay.

Dave swung down from the caboose and looked round in the dim light for the stockyards engine that was to pick up his cars and run them to the unloading pens. He moved forward through the mud, searching the semi-darkness for the switch engine. It was nowhere to be seen.

He returned to the caboose. The conductor and brakemen were just leaving.

"My engine's not here. Some one must'a' slipped up on his job, looks like. Where are the stockyards?" Sanders asked.

The conductor was a small, middle-aged man who made it his business to get along with everybody he could. He had distinctly refused to pick up his predecessor's quarrel with Dave. Now he stopped and scratched his head.

"Too bad. Can't you go uptown and 'phone out to the stockyards? Or if you want to take a street-car out there you'll have time to hop one at Stout Street. Last one goes about midnight."

In those days the telephone was not a universal necessity. Dave had never used one and did not know how to get his connection. He spent several minutes ringing up, shouting at the operator, and trying to understand what she told him. He did not shout at the girl because he was annoyed. His idea

58

was that he would have to speak loud to have his voice carry. At last he gave up, hot and perspiring from the mental exertion.

Outside the drug-store he just had time to catch the last stockyards car. His watch told him that it was two minutes past twelve.

He stepped forty-five minutes later into an office in which sat two men with their feet on a desk. The one in his shirt-sleeves was a smug, baldish young man with clothes cut in the latest mode. He was rather heavy-set and looked flabby. The other man appeared to be a visitor.

"This the office of the Denver Terminal Stockyards Company?" asked Dave.

The clerk looked the raw Arizonan over from head to foot and back again. The judgment that he passed was indicated by the tone of his voice.

"Name's on the door, ain't it?" he asked superciliously.

"You in charge here?"

The clerk was amused, or at least took the trouble to seem so. "You might think so, mightn't you?"

"Are you in charge?" asked Dave evenly.

"Maybeso. What you want?"

"I asked you if you was runnin' this office."

"Hell, yes! What're your eyes for?"

The clerk's visitor sniggered.

"I've got a train of cattle on the edge of town," explained Dave. "The stockyards engine didn't show up."

"Consigned to us?"

"To the Denver Terminal Stockyards Company."

"Name of shipper?"

"West Cattle Company and Henry B. West."

"All right. I'll take care of 'em." The clerk turned back to his friend. His manner dismissed the cowpuncher. "And she says to me, 'I'd love to go with you, Mr. Edmonds; you dance like an angel.' Then I says—"

"When?" interrupted Dave calmly, but those who knew him might have guessed his voice was a little too gentle.

"I says, 'You're some little kidder,' and—"

"When?"

The man who danced like an angel turned halfway round, and looked at the cowboy over his shoulder. He was irritated.

"When what?" he snapped.

"When you goin' to onload my stock?"

59

"In the morning."

"No, sir. You'll have it done right now. That stock has been more'n two days without water."

"I'm not responsible for that."

"No, but you'll be responsible if the train ain't onloaded now," said Dave.

"It won't hurt 'em to wait till morning."

"That's where you're wrong. They're sufferin'. All of 'em are alive now, but they won't all be by mo'nin' if they ain't 'tended to."

"Guess I'll take a chance on that, since you say it's my responsibility," replied the clerk impudently.

"Not none," announced the man from Arizona. "You'll get busy pronto."

"Say, is this my business or yours?"

"Mine and yours both."

"I guess I can run it. If I need any help from you I'll ask for it. Watch me worry about your old cows. I have guys coming in here every day with hurry-up tales about how their cattle won't live unless I get a wiggle on me. I notice they all are able to take a little nourishment next day all right, all right."

Dave caught at the gate of the railing which was between him and the night clerk. He could not find the combination to open it and therefore vaulted over. He caught the clerk back of the neck by the collar and jounced him up and down hard in his chair.

"You're asleep," he explained. "I got to waken you up before you can sabe plain talk."

The clerk looked up out of a white, frightened face. "Say, don't do that. I got heart trouble," he said in a voice dry as a whisper.

"What about that onloadin' proposition?" asked the Arizonan.

"I'll see to it right away."

Presently the clerk, with a lantern in his hand, was going across to the railroad tracks in front of Dave. He had quite got over the idea that this lank youth was a safe person to make sport of.

They found the switch crew in the engine of the cab playing seven-up.

"Got a job for you. Train of cattle out at the junction," the clerk said, swinging up to the cab.

The men finished the hand and settled up, but within a few minutes the engine was running out to the freight train.

Day was breaking before Dave tumbled into bed. He had left a call with the clerk to be wakened at noon. When the bell rang, it seemed to him that he had not been asleep five minutes.

After he had eaten at the stockyards hotel he went out to have a look at his stock. He found that on the whole the cattle had stood the trip well. While he was still inspecting them a voice boomed at him a question.

"Well, young fellow, are you satisfied with all the trouble you've made me?"

He turned, to see standing before him the owner of the Fifty-Four Quarter Circle brand. The boy's surprise fairly leaped from his eyes.

"Didn't expect to see me here, I reckon," the cattleman went on. "Well, I hopped a train soon as I got yore first wire. Spill yore story, young man."

Dave told his tale, while the ranchman listened in grim silence. When Sanders had finished, the owner of the stock brought a heavy hand down on his shoulder approvingly.

"You can ship cattle for me long as you've a mind to, boy. You fought for that stock like as if it had been yore own. You'll do to take along."

Dave flushed with boyish pleasure. He had not known whether the cattleman would approve what he had done, and after the long strain of the trip this endorsement of his actions was more to him than food or drink.

"They say I'm kinda stubborn. I didn't aim to lie down and let those guys run one over me," he said.

"Yore stubbornness is money in my pocket. Do you want to go back and ride for the Fifty-Four Quarter Circle?"

"Maybe, after a while, Mr. West. I got business in Denver for a few days."

The cattleman smiled. "Most of my boys have when they hit town, I notice."

"Mine ain't that kind. I reckon it's some more stubbornness," explained Dave.

"All right. When you've finished that business I can use you."

If Dave could have looked into the future he would have known that the days would stretch into months and the months to years before his face would turn toward ranch life again.

CHAPTER XII

THE LAW PUZZLES DAVE

Dave knew he was stubborn. Not many men would have come on such a wild-goose chase to Denver in the hope of getting back a favorite horse worth so little in actual cash. But he meant to move to his end intelligently.

If Miller and Doble were in the city they would be hanging out at some saloon or gambling-house. Once or twice Dave dropped in to Chuck Weaver's place, where the sporting men from all over the continent inevitably drifted when in Denver. But he had little expectation of finding the men he wanted there. These two rats of the underworld would not attempt to fleece keen-eyed professionals. They would prey on the unsophisticated.

His knowledge of their habits took him to that part of town below Lawrence Street. While he chatted with his foot on the rail, a glass of beer in front of him, he made inconspicuous inquiries of bartenders. It did not take him long to strike the trail.

"Two fellows I knew in the cattle country said they were comin' to Denver. Wonder if they did. One of 'em's a big fat guy name o' Miller—kinda rolls when he walks. Other's small and has a glass eye. Called himself George Doble when I knew him."

"Come in here 'most every day—both of 'em. Waitin' for the Festival of Mountain and Plain to open up. Got some kinda concession. They look to yours truly like—"

The bartender pulled himself up short and began polishing the top of the bar vigorously. He was a gossipy soul, and more than once his tongue had got him into trouble.

"You was sayin'—" suggested the cowboy.

"—that they're good spenders, as the fellow says," amended the bartender, to be on the safe side.

"When I usta know 'em they had a mighty cute little trick pony—name was Chiquito, seems to me. Ever hear 'em mention it?"

"They was fussin' about that horse to-day. Seems they got an offer for him and Doble wants to sell. Miller he says no."

"Yes?"

"I'll tell 'em a friend asked for 'em. What name?"

"Yes, do. Jim Smith."

"The fat old gobbler's liable to drop in any time now."

This seemed a good reason to Mr. Jim Smith, *alias* David Sanders, for dropping out. He did not care to have Miller know just yet who the kind friend was that had inquired for him.

But just as he was turning away a word held him for a moment. The discretion of the man in the apron was not quite proof against his habit of talk.

"They been quarrelin' a good deal together. I expect the combination is about ready to bust up," he whispered confidentially.

"Quarrelin'? What about?"

"Oh, I dunno. They act like they're sore as a boil at each other. Honest, I thought they was goin' to mix it yesterday. I breezed up wit' a bottle an' they kinda cooled off."

"Doble drunk?"

"Nope. Fact is, they'd trimmed a Greeley boob and was rowin' about the split. Miller he claimed Doble held out on him. I'll bet he did too."

Dave did not care how much they quarreled or how soon they parted after he had got back his horse. Until that time he preferred that they would give him only one trail to follow instead of two.

The cowpuncher made it his business to loaf on Larimer Street for the rest of the day. His beat was between Fifteenth and Sixteenth Streets, usually on the other side of the road from the Klondike Saloon.

About four o'clock his patience was rewarded. Miller came rolling along in a sort of sailor fashion characteristic of him. Dave had just time to dive into a pawnbroker's shop unnoticed.

A black-haired, black-eyed salesman came forward to wait on him. The puncher cast an eye helplessly about him. It fell on a suitcase.

63

"How much?" he asked.

"Seven dollars. Dirt sheap, my frient."

"Got any telescope grips?"

The salesman produced one. Dave bought it because he did not know how to escape without.

He carried it with him while he lounged up and down the sidewalk waiting for Miller to come out of the Klondike. When the fat gambler reappeared, the range-rider fell in behind him unobserved and followed uptown past the Tabor Opera House as far as California Street. Here they swung to the left to Fourteenth, where Miller disappeared into a rooming-house.

The amateur detective turned back toward the business section. On the way he dropped guiltily the telescope grip into a delivery wagon standing in front of a grocery. He had no use for it, and he had already come to feel it a white elephant on his hands.

With the aid of a city directory Dave located the livery stables within walking distance of the house where Miller was staying. Inspired perhaps by the nickel detective stories he had read, the cowboy bought a pair of blue goggles and a "store" collar. In this last, substituted for the handkerchief he usually wore loosely round his throat, the sleuth nearly strangled himself for lack of air. His inquiries at such stables as he found brought no satisfaction. Neither Miller nor the pinto had been seen at any of them.

Later in the evening he met Henry B. West at the St. James Hotel.

"How's that business of yore's gettin' along, boy?" asked the cattleman with a smile.

"Don' know yet. Say, Mr. West, if I find a hawss that's been stole from me, how can I get it back?"

"Some one steal a hawss from you?"

Dave told his story. West listened to a finish.

"I know a lawyer here. We'll ask him what to do," the ranchman said.

They found the lawyer at the Athletic Club. West stated the case.

"Your remedy is to replevin. If they fight, you'll have to bring witnesses to prove ownership."

"Bring witnesses from Malapi! Why, I can't do that," said Dave, staggered. "I ain't got the money. Why can't I just take the hawss? It's mine."

"The law doesn't know it's yours."

64

Dave left much depressed. Of course the thieves would go to a lawyer, and of course he would tell them to fight. The law was a darned queer thing. It made the recovery of his property so costly that the crooks who stole it could laugh at him.

"Looks like the law's made to protect scalawags instead of honest folks," Dave told West.

"I don't reckon it is, but it acts that way sometimes," admitted the cattleman. "You can see yoreself it wouldn't do for the law to say a fellow could get property from another man by just sayin' it was his. Sorry, Sanders. After all, a bronc's only a bronc. I'll give you yore pick of two hundred if you come back with me to the ranch."

"Much obliged, seh. Maybe I will later."

The cowpuncher walked the streets while he thought it over. He had no intention whatever of giving up Chiquito if he could find the horse. So far as the law went he was in a blind alley. He was tied hand and foot. That possession was nine points before the courts he had heard before.

The way to recover flashed to his brain like a wave of light. He must get possession. All he had to do was to steal his own horse and make for the hills. If the thieves found him later—and the chances were that they would not even attempt pursuit if he let them know who he was—he would force them to the expense of going to law for Chiquito. What was sauce for the goose must be for the gander too.

Dave's tramp had carried him across the Platte into North Denver. On his way back he passed a corral close to the railroad tracks. He turned in to look over the horses.

The first one his eyes fell on was Chiquito.

CHAPTER XIII

FOR MURDER

Dave whistled. The pony pricked up its ears, looked round, and came straight to him. The young man laid his face against the soft, silky nose, fondled it, whispered endearments to his pet. He put the bronco through its tricks for the benefit of the corral attendant.

"Well, I'll be doggoned," that youth commented. "The little pinto sure is a wonder. Acts like he knows you mighty well."

"Ought to. I trained him. Had him before Miller got him."

"Bet you hated to sell him."

"You *know* it." Dave moved forward to his end, the intention to get possession of the horse. He spoke in a voice easy and casual. "Saw Miller a while ago. They're talkin' about sellin' the paint hawss, him and his pardner Doble. I'm to saddle up and show what Chiquito can do."

"Say, that's a good notion. If I was a buyer I'd pay ten bucks more after you'd put him through that circus stuff."

"Which is Miller's saddle?" When it was pointed out to him, Dave examined it and pretended to disapprove. "Too heavy. Lend me a lighter one, can't you?"

"Sure. Here's three or four. Help yourself."

The wrangler moved into the stable to attend to his work.

Dave cinched, swung to the saddle, and rode to the gate of the corral. Two men were coming in, and by the sound of their voices were quarreling. They stepped aside to let him pass, one on each side of the gate, so that it was necessary to ride between them.

They recognized the pinto at the same moment Dave did them. On the heels of that recognition came another.

Doble ripped out an oath and a shout of warning. "It's Sanders!"

A gun flashed as the pony jumped to a gallop. The silent night grew noisy with shots, voices, the clatter of hoofs. Twice Dave fired answers to the challenges which leaped out of the darkness at him. He raced across the bridge spanning the Platte and for a moment drew up on the other side to listen for sounds which might tell him whether he would be pursued. One last solitary revolver shot disturbed the stillness.

The rider grinned. "Think he'd know better than to shoot at me this far."

He broke his revolver, extracted the empty shells, and dropped them to the street. Then he rode up the long hill toward Highlands, passed through that suburb of the city, and went along the dark and dusty road to the shadows of the Rockies silhouetted in the night sky.

His flight had no definite objective except to put as much distance between himself and Denver as possible. He knew nothing about the geography of Colorado, except that a large part of the Rocky Mountains and a delectable city called Denver lived there. His train trip to it had told him that one of its neighbors was New Mexico, which was in turn adjacent to Arizona. Therefore he meant to get to New Mexico as quickly as Chiquito could quite comfortably travel.

Unfortunately Dave was going west instead of south. Every step of the pony was carrying him nearer the roof of the continent, nearer the passes of the front range which lead, by divers valleys and higher mountains beyond, to the snowclad regions of eternal white.

Up in this altitude it was too cold to camp out without a fire and blankets.

"I reckon we'll keep goin', old pal," the young man told his horse. "I've noticed roads mostly lead somewheres."

Day broke over valleys of swirling mist far below the rider. The sun rose and dried the moisture. Dave looked down on a town scattered up and down a gulch.

He met an ore team and asked the driver what town it was. The man looked curiously at him.

"Why, it's Idaho Springs," he said. "Where you come from?"

Dave eased himself in the saddle. "From the Southwest."

"You're quite a ways from home. I reckon your hills ain't so uncurried down there, are they?"

The cowpuncher looked over the mountains. He was among the summits, aglow in the amber light of day with the many blended colors of wild flowers. "We got some down there, too, that don't fit a lady's boodwar. Say, if I keep movin' where'll this road take me?"

The man with the ore team gave information. It struck Dave that he had run into a blind alley.

"If you're after a job, I reckon you can find one at some of the mines. They're needin' hands," the teamster added.

Perhaps this was the best immediate solution of the problem. The puncher nodded farewell and rode down into the town.

He left Chiquito at a livery barn, after having personally fed and watered the pinto, and went himself to a hotel. Here he registered, not under his own name, ate breakfast, and lay down for a few hours' sleep. When he awakened he wrote a note with the stub of a pencil to Bob Hart. It read:

Well, Bob, I done got Chiquito back though it sure looked like I wasnt going to but you never can tell and as old Buck Byington says its a hell of a long road without no bend in it and which you can bet your boots the old alkali is right at that. Well I found the little pie-eater in Denver O K but so gaunt he wont hardly throw a shadow and what can you expect of scalawags like Miller and Doble who dont know how to treat a horse. Well I run Chiquito off right under their noses and we had a little gun play and made my getaway and I reckon I will stay a spell and work here. Well good luck to all the boys till I see them again in the sweet by and by.

DAVE

P.S. Get this money order cashed old-timer and pay the boys what I borrowed when we hit the trail after Miller and Doble. I lit out to sudden to settle. Five to Steve and five to Buck. Well so long.

DAVE

The puncher went to the post-office, got a money order, and mailed the letter, after which he returned to the hotel. He intended to eat dinner and then look for work.

Three or four men were standing on the steps of the hotel talking with the proprietor. Dave was quite close before the Boniface saw him.

"That's him," the hotel-keeper said in an excited whisper.

68

A brown-faced man without a coat turned quickly and looked at Sanders. He wore a belt with cartridges and a revolver.

"What's your name?" he demanded.

Dave knew at once this man was an officer of the law. He knew, too, the futility of trying to escape under the pseudonym he had written on the register.

"Sanders—Dave Sanders."

"I want you."

"So? Who are you?"

"Sheriff of the county."

"Whadjawant me for?"

"Murder."

Dave gasped. His heart beat fast with a prescience of impending disaster. "Murder," he repeated dully.

"You're charged with the murder of George Doble last night in Denver."

The boy stared at him with horror-stricken eyes. "Doble? My God, did I kill him?" He clutched at a porch post to steady himself. The hills were sliding queerly up into the sky.

CHAPTER XIV

TEN YEARS

All the way back to Denver, while the train ran down through the narrow, crooked cañon, Dave's mind dwelt in a penumbra of horror. It was impossible he could have killed Doble, he kept telling himself. He had fired back into the night without aim. He had not even tried to hit the men who were shooting at him. It must be some ghastly joke.

None the less he knew by the dull ache in his heart that this awful thing had fastened on him and that he would have to pay the penalty. He had killed a man, snuffed out his life wantonly as a result of taking the law into his own hands. The knowledge of what he had done shook him to the soul.

It remained with him, in the background of his mind, up to and through his trial. What shook his nerve was the fact that he had taken a life, not the certainty of the punishment that must follow.

West called to see him at the jail, and to the cattleman Dave told the story exactly as it had happened. The owner of the Fifty-Four Quarter Circle walked up and down the cell rumpling his hair.

"Boy, why didn't you let on to me what you was figurin' on pullin' off? I knew you was some bull-haided, but I thought you had a lick o' sense left."

"Wisht I had," said Dave miserably.

"Well, what's done's done. No use cryin' over the bust-up. We'd better fix up whatever's left from the smash. First off, we'll get a lawyer, I reckon."

"I gotta li'l' money left—twenty-six dollars," spoke up Dave timidly. "Maybe that's all he'll want."

West smiled at this babe in the woods. "It'll last as long as a snowball in you-know-where if he's like some lawyers I've met up with."

It did not take the lawyer whom West engaged long to decide on the line the defense must take. "We'll show that Miller and Doble were crooks and that they had wronged Sanders. That will count a lot with a jury," he told West. "We'll admit the killing and claim self-defense."

The day before the trial Dave was sitting in his cell cheerlessly reading a newspaper when visitors were announced. At sight of Emerson Crawford and Bob Hart he choked in his throat. Tears brimmed in his eyes. Nobody could have been kinder to him than West had been, but these were home folks. He had known them many years. Their kindness in coming melted his heart.

He gripped their hands, but found himself unable to say anything in answer to their greetings. He was afraid to trust his voice, and he was ashamed of his emotion.

"The boys are for you strong, Dave. We all figure you done right. Steve he says he wouldn't worry none if you'd got Miller too," Bob breezed on.

"Tha's no way to talk, son," reproved Crawford. "It's bad enough right as it is without you boys wantin' it any worse. But don't you get downhearted, Dave. We're allowin' to stand by you to a finish. It ain't as if you'd got a good man. Doble was a mean-hearted scoundrel if ever I met up with one. He's no loss to society. We're goin' to show the jury that too."

They did. By the time Crawford, Hart, and a pair of victims who had been trapped by the sharpers had testified about Miller and Doble, these worthies had no shred of reputation left with the jury. It was shown that they had robbed the defendant of the horse he had trained and that he had gone to a lawyer and found no legal redress within his means.

But Dave was unable to prove self-defense. Miller stuck doggedly to his story. The cowpuncher had fired the first shot. He had continued to fire, though he must have seen Doble sink to the ground immediately. Moreover, the testimony of the doctor showed that the fatal shot had taken effect at close range.

Just prior to this time there had been an unusual number of killings in Denver. The newspapers had stirred up a public sentiment for stricter enforcement of law. They had claimed that both judges and juries were too easy on the gunmen who committed these crimes. Now they asked if this cowboy killer was going to be allowed to escape. Dave was tried when this wave of feeling was at its height and he was a victim of it.

The jury found him guilty of murder in the second degree. The judge sentenced him to ten years in the penitentiary.

When Bob Hart came to say good-bye before Dave was removed to Cañon City, the young range-rider almost broke down. He was greatly distressed at the misfortune that had befallen his friend.

"We're gonna stay with this, Dave. You know Crawford. He goes through when he starts. Soon as there's a chance we'll hit the Governor for a pardon. It's a damn shame, old pal. That's what it is."

Dave nodded. A lump in his throat interfered with speech.

"The ol' man lent me money to buy Chiquito, and I'm gonna keep the pinto till you get out. That'll help pay yore lawyer," continued Bob. "One thing more. You're not the only one that's liable to be sent up. Miller's on the way back to Malapi. If he don't get a term for hawss-stealin', I'm a liar. We got a dead open-and-shut case against him."

The guard who was to take Dave to the penitentiary bustled in cheerfully. "All right, boys. If you're ready we'll be movin' down to the depot."

The friends shook hands again.

CHAPTER XV

IN DENVER

The warden handed him a ticket back to Denver, and with it a stereotyped little lecture of platitudes.

"Your future lies before you to be made or marred by yourself, Sanders. You owe it to the Governor who has granted this parole and to the good friends who have worked so hard for it that you be honest and industrious and temperate. If you do this the world will in time forget your past mistakes and give you the right hand of fellowship, as I do now."

The paroled man took the fat hand proffered him because he knew the warden was a sincere humanitarian. He meant exactly what he said. Perhaps he could not help the touch of condescension. But patronage, no matter how kindly meant, was one thing this tall, straight convict would not stand. He was quite civil, but the hard, cynical eyes made the warden uncomfortable. Once or twice before he had known prisoners like this, quiet, silent men who were never insolent, but whose eyes told him that the iron had seared their souls.

The voice of the warden dropped briskly to business. "Seen the bookkeeper? Everything all right, I suppose."

"Yes, sir."

"Good. Well, wish you luck."

"Thanks."

The convict turned away, grave, unsmiling.

The prison officer's eyes followed him a little wistfully. His function, as he understood it, was to win these men back to fitness for service to the society which had shut them up for their misdeeds. They were not wild beasts. They were human beings who had made a misstep. Sometimes he had been able to influence men strongly, but he felt that it had not been true of this puncher from the cow country.

Sanders walked slowly out of the office and through the door in the wall that led back to life. He was free. To-morrow was his. All the to-morrows of all the years of his life were waiting for him. But the fact stirred in him no emotion. As he stood in the dry Colorado sunshine his heart was quite dead.

In the earlier days of his imprisonment it had not been so. He had dreamed often of this hour. At night, in the darkness of his cell, imagination had projected picture after picture of it, vivid, colorful, set to music. But his parole had come too late. The years had taken their toll of him. The shadow of the prison had left its chill, had done something to him that had made him a different David Sanders from the boy who had entered. He wondered if he would ever learn to laugh again, if he would ever run to meet life eagerly as that other David Sanders had a thousand years ago.

He followed the road down to the little station and took a through train that came puffing out of the Royal Gorge on its way to the plains. Through the crowd at the Denver depot he passed into the city, moving up Seventeenth Street without definite aim or purpose. His parole had come unexpectedly, so that none of his friends could meet him even if they had wanted to do so. He was glad of this. He preferred to be alone, especially during these first days of freedom. It was his intention to go back to Malapi, to the country he knew and loved, but he wished to pick up a job in the city for a month or two until he had settled into a frame of mind in which liberty had become a habit.

Early next morning he began his search for work. It carried him to a lumber yard adjoining the railroad yards.

"We need a night watchman," the superintendent said. "Where'd you work last?"

"At Cañon City."

The lumberman looked at him quickly, a question in his glance.

"Yes," Dave went on doggedly. "In the penitentiary."

A moment's awkward embarrassment ensued.

"What were you in for?"

"Killing a man."

"Too bad. I'm afraid—"

"He had stolen my horse and I was trying to get it back. I had no intention of hitting him when I fired."

73

"I'd take you in a minute so far as I'm concerned personally, but our board of directors—afraid they wouldn't like it. That's one trouble in working for a corporation."

Sanders turned away. The superintendent hesitated, then called after him.

"If you're up against it and need a dollar—"

"Thanks. I don't. I'm looking for work, not charity," the applicant said stiffly.

Wherever he went it was the same. As soon as he mentioned the prison, doors of opportunity closed to him. Nobody wanted to employ a man tarred with that pitch. It did not matter why he had gone, under what provocation he had erred. The thing that damned him was that he had been there. It was a taint, a corrosion.

He could have picked up a job easily enough if he had been willing to lie about his past. But he had made up his mind to tell the truth. In the long run he could not conceal it. Better start with the slate clean.

When he got a job it was to unload cars of fruit for a commission house. A man was wanted in a hurry and the employer did not ask any questions. At the end of an hour he was satisfied.

"Fellow hustles peaches like he'd been at it all his life," the commission man told his partner.

A few days later came the question that Sanders had been expecting. "Where'd you work before you came to us?"

"At the penitentiary."

"A guard?" asked the merchant, taken aback.

"No. I was a convict." The big lithe man in overalls spoke quietly, his eyes meeting those of the Market Street man with unwavering steadiness.

"What was the trouble?"

Dave explained. The merchant made no comment, but when he paid off the men Saturday night he said with careful casualness, "Sorry, Sanders. The work will be slack next week. I'll have to lay you off."

The man from Cañon City understood. He looked for another place, was rebuffed a dozen times, and at last was given work by an employer who had vision enough to know the truth that the bad men do not all go to prison and that some who go may be better than those who do not.

In this place Sanders lasted three weeks. He was doing concrete work on a viaduct job for a contractor employed by the city.

This time it was a fellow-workman who learned of the Arizonan's record. A letter from Emerson Crawford, forwarded by the warden of the penitentiary, dropped out of Dave's coat pocket where it hung across a plank.

The man who picked it up read the letter before returning it to the pocket. He began at once to whisper the news. The subject was discussed back and forth among the men on the quiet. Sanders guessed they had discovered who he was, but he waited for them to move. His years in prison had given him at least the strength of patience. He could bide his time.

They went to the contractor. He reasoned with them.

"Does his work all right, doesn't he? Treats you all civilly. Doesn't force himself on you. I don't see any harm in him."

"We ain't workin' with no jail bird," announced the spokesman.

"He told me the story and I've looked it up since. Talked with the lawyer that defended him. He says the man Sanders killed was a bad lot and had stolen his horse from him. Sanders was trying to get it back. He claimed self-defense, but couldn't prove it."

"Don't make no difference. The jury said he was guilty, didn't it?"

"Suppose he was. We've got to give him a chance when he comes out, haven't we?"

Some of the men began to weaken. They were not cruel, but they were children of impulse, easily led by those who had force enough to push to the front.

"I won't mix cement with no convict," the self-appointed leader announced flatly. "That goes."

The contractor met him eye to eye. "You don't have to, Reynolds. You can get your time."

"Meanin' that you keep him on the job and let me go?"

"That's it exactly. Long as he does his work well I'll not ask him to quit."

A shadow darkened the doorway of the temporary office. The Arizonan stepped in with his easy, swinging stride, a lithe, straight-backed Hermes showing strength of character back of every movement.

"I'm leaving to-day, Mr. Shields." His voice carried the quiet power of reserve force.

"Not because I want you to, Sanders."

"Because I'm not going to stay and make you trouble."

"I don't think it will come to that. I'm talking it over with the boys now. Your work stands up. I've no criticism."

75

"I'll not stay now, Mr. Shields. Since they've complained to you I'd better go."

The ex-convict looked around, the eyes in his sardonic face hard and bitter. If he could have read the thoughts of the men it would have been different. Most of them were ashamed of their protest. They would have liked to have drawn back, but they did not know how to say so. Therefore they stood awkwardly silent. Afterward, when it was too late, they talked it over freely enough and blamed each other.

From one job to another Dave drifted. His stubborn pride, due in part to a native honesty that would not let him live under false pretenses, in part to a bitterness that had become dogged defiance, kept him out of good places and forced him to do heavy, unskilled labor that brought the poorest pay.

Yet he saved money, bought himself good, cheap clothes, and found energy to attend night school where he studied stationary and mechanical engineering. He lived wholly within himself, his mental reactions tinged with morose scorn. He found little comfort either in himself or in the external world, in spite of the fact that he had determined with all his stubborn will to get ahead.

The library he patronized a good deal, but he gave no time to general literature. His reading was of a highly specialized nature. He studied everything that he could find about the oil fields of America.

The stigma of his disgrace continued to raise its head. One of the concrete workers was married to the sister of the woman from whom he rented his room. The quiet, upstanding man who never complained or asked any privileges had been a favorite of hers, but she was a timid, conventional soul. Visions of her roomers departing in a flock when they found out about the man in the second floor back began to haunt her dreams. Perhaps he might rob them all at night. In a moment of nerve tension, summoning all her courage, she asked the killer from the cattle country if he would mind leaving.

He smiled grimly and began to pack. For several days he had seen it coming. When he left, the expressman took his trunk to the station. The ticket which Sanders bought showed Malapi as his destination.

CHAPTER XVI

DAVE MEETS TWO FRIENDS AND A FOE

In the early morning Dave turned to rest his cramped limbs. He was in a day coach, and his sleep through the night had been broken. The light coming from the window woke him. He looked out on the opalescent dawn of the desert, and his blood quickened at sight of the enchanted mesa. To him came that joyous thrill of one who comes home to his own after years of exile.

Presently he saw the silvery sheen of the mesquite when the sun is streaming westward. Dust eddies whirled across the barranca. The prickly pear and the palo verde flashed past, green splashes against a background of drab. The pudgy creosote, the buffalo grass, the undulation of sand hills were an old story, but to-day his eyes devoured them hungrily. The wonderful effect of space and light, the cloud skeins drawn out as by some invisible hand, the brown ribbon of road that wandered over the hill: they brought to him an emotion poignant and surprising.

The train slid into a narrow valley bounded by hills freakishly eroded to fantastic shapes. Piñon trees fled to the rear. A sheep corral fenced with brush and twisted roots, in which were long, shallow feed troughs and flat-roofed sheds, leaped out of nowhere, was for a few moments, and vanished like a scene in a moving picture. A dim, gray mass of color on a hillside was agitated like a sea wave. It was a flock of sheep moving toward the corral. For an instant Dave caught a glimpse of a dog circling the huddled pack; then dog and sheep were out of sight together.

The pictures stirred memories of the acrid smoke of hill camp-fires, of nights under a tarp with the rain beating down

77

on him, and still others of a road herd bawling for water, of winter camps when the ropes were frozen stiff and the snow slid from trees in small avalanches.

At the junction he took the stage for Malapi. Already he could see that he was going into a new world, one altogether different from that he had last seen here. These men were not cattlemen. They talked the vocabulary of oil. They had the shrewd, keen look of the driller and the wildcatter. They were full of nervous energy that oozed out in constant conversation.

"Jackpot Number Three lost a string o' tools yesterday. While they're fishin', Steelman'll be drillin' hella-mile. You got to sit up all night to beat that Coal Oil Johnny," one wrinkled little man said.

A big man in boots laced over corduroy trousers nodded. "He's smooth as a pump plunger, and he sure has luck. He can buy up a dry hole any old time and it'll be a gusher in a week. He'll bust Em Crawford high and dry before he finishes with him. Em had ought to 'a' stuck to cattle. That's one game he knows from hoof to hide."

"Sure. Em's got no business in oil. Say, do you know when they're expectin' Shiloh Number Two in?"

"She's into the sand now, but still dry as a cork leg. That's liable to put a crimp in Em's bank roll, don't you reckon?"

"Yep. Old Man Hard Luck's campin' on his trail sure enough. The banks'll be shakin' their heads at his paper soon."

The stage had stopped to take on a mailsack. Now it started again, and the rest of the talk was lost to Dave. But he had heard enough to guess that the old feud between Crawford and Steelman had taken on a new phase, one in which his friend was likely to get the worst of it.

At Malapi Dave descended from the stage into a town he hardly knew. It had the same wide main street, but the business section extended five blocks instead of one. Everywhere oil dominated the place. Hotels, restaurants, and hardware stores jostled saloons and gambling-houses. Tents had been set up in vacant lots beside frame buildings, and in them stores, rooming-houses, and lunch-counters were doing business. Everybody was in a hurry. The street was filled with men who had to sleep with one eye open lest they miss the news of some new discovery.

The town was having growing-pains. One contractor was putting down sidewalks in the same street where another laid sewer pipe and a third put in telephone poles. A branch line

78

of a trans-continental railroad was moving across the desert to tap the new oil field. Houses rose overnight. Mule teams jingled in and out freighting supplies to Malapi and from there to the fields. On all sides were rustle, energy, and optimism, signs of the new West in the making.

Up the street a team of half-broken broncos came on the gallop, weaving among the traffic with a certainty that showed a skilled pair of hands at the reins. From the buckboard stepped lightly a straight-backed, well-muscled young fellow. He let out a moment later a surprised shout of welcome and fell upon Sanders with two brown fists.

"Dave! Where in Mexico you been, old alkali? We been lookin' for you everywhere."

"In Denver, Bob."

Sanders spoke quietly. His eyes went straight into those of Bob Hart to see what was written there. He found only a glad and joyous welcome, neither embarrassment nor any sign of shame.

"But why didn't you write and let us know?" Bob grew mildly profane in his warmth. He was as easy as though his friend had come back from a week in the hills on a deer hunt. "We didn't know when the Governor was goin' to act. Or we'd 'a' been right at the gate, me or Em Crawford one. Whyn't you answer our letters, you darned old scalawag? Dawggone, but I'm glad to see you."

Dave's heart warmed to this fine loyalty. He knew that both Hart and Crawford had worked in season and out of season for a parole or a pardon. But it's one thing to appear before a pardon board for a convict in whom you are interested and quite another to welcome him to your heart when he stands before you. Bob would do to tie to, Sanders told himself with a rush of gratitude. None of this feeling showed in his dry voice.

"Thanks, Bob."

Hart knew already that Dave had come back a changed man. He had gone in a boy, wild, turbulent, untamed. He had come out tempered by the fires of experience and discipline. The steel-gray eyes were no longer frank and gentle. They judged warily and inscrutably. He talked little and mostly in monosyllables. It was a safe guess that he was master of his impulses. In his manner was a cold reticence entirely foreign to the Dave Sanders his friend had known and frolicked with. Bob felt in him a quality of dangerous strength as hard and cold as hammered iron.

79

"Where's yore trunk? I'll take it right up to my shack," Hart said.

"I've rented a room."

"Well, you can onrent it. You're stayin' with me."

"No, Bob. I reckon I won't do that. I'll live alone awhile."

"No, sir. What do you take me for? We'll load yore things up on the buckboard."

Dave shook his head. "I'm much obliged, but I'd rather not yet. Got to feel out my way while I learn the range here."

To this Bob did not consent without a stiff protest, but Sanders was inflexible.

"All right. Suit yoreself. You always was stubborn as a Missouri mule," Hart said with a grin. "Anyhow, you'll eat supper with me. Le's go to the Delmonico for ol' times' sake. We'll see if Hop Lee knows you. I'll bet he does."

Hart had come in to see a contractor about building a derrick for a well. "I got to see him now, Dave. Go along with me," he urged.

"No, see you later. Want to get my trunk from the depot."

They arranged an hour of meeting at the restaurant.

In front of the post-office Bob met Joyce Crawford. The young woman had fulfilled the promise of her girlhood. As she moved down the street, tall and slender, there was a light, joyous freedom in her step. So Ellen Terry walked in her resilient prime.

"Miss Joyce, he's here," Bob said.

"Who—Dave?"

She and her father and Bob had more than once met as a committee of three to discuss the interests of Sanders both before and since his release. The week after he left Cañon City letters of thanks had reached both Hart and Crawford, but these had given no address. Their letters to him had remained unanswered nor had a detective agency been able to find him.

"Yes, ma'am, Dave! He's right here in town. Met him half an hour ago."

"I'm glad. How does he look?"

"He's grown older, a heap older. And he's different. You know what an easy-goin' kid he was, always friendly and happy as a half-grown pup. Well, he ain't thataway now. Looks like he never would laugh again real cheerful. I don't reckon he ever will. He's done got the prison brand on him for good. I couldn't see my old Dave in him a-tall. He's hard as nails—and bitter."

80

The brown eyes softened. "He would be, of course. How could he help it?"

"And he kinda holds you off. He's been hurt bad and ain't takin' no chances whatever, don't you reckon?"

"Do you mean he's broken?"

"Not a bit. He's strong, and he looks at you straight and hard. But they've crushed all the kid outa him. He was a mighty nice boy, Dave was. I hate to lose him."

"When can I see him?" she asked.

Bob looked at his watch. "I got an appointment to meet him at Delmonico's right now. Maybe I can get him to come up to the house afterward."

Joyce was a young woman who made swift decisions. "I'll go with you now," she said.

Sanders was standing in front of the restaurant, but he was faced in the other direction. His flat, muscular back was rigid. In his attitude was a certain tenseness, as though his body was a bundle of steel springs ready to be released.

Bob's eye traveled swiftly past him to a fat man rolling up the street on the opposite sidewalk. "It's Ad Miller, back from the pen. I heard he got out this week," he told the girl in a low voice.

Joyce Crawford felt the blood ebb from her face. It was as though her heart had been drenched with ice water. What was going to take place between these men? Were they armed? Would the gambler recognize his old enemy?

She knew that each was responsible for the other's prison sentence. Sanders had followed the thieves to Denver and found them with his horse. The fat crook had lied Dave into the penitentiary by swearing that the boy had fired the first shots. Now they were meeting for the first time since.

Miller had been drinking. The stiff precision of his gait showed that. For a moment it seemed that he would pass without noticing the man across the road. Then, by some twist of chance, he decided to take the sidewalk on the other side. The sign of the Delmonico had caught his eye and he remembered that he was hungry.

He took one step—and stopped. He had recognized Sanders. His eyes narrowed. The head on his short, red neck was thrust forward.

"Goddlemighty!" he screamed, and next moment was plucking a revolver from under his left armpit.

Bob caught Joyce and swept her behind him, covering her with his body as best he could. At the same time Sanders

81

plunged forward, arrow-straight and swift. The revolver cracked. It spat fire a second time, a third. The tiger-man, head low, his whole splendid body vibrant with energy, hurled himself across the road as though he had been flung from a catapult. A streak of fire ripped through his shoulder. Another shot boomed almost simultaneously. He thudded hard into the fat paunch of the gunman. They went down together.

The fingers of Dave's left hand closed on the fat wrist of the gambler. His other hand tore the revolver away from the slack grasp. The gun rose and fell. Miller went into unconsciousness without even a groan. The corrugated butt of the gun had crashed down on his forehead.

Dizzily Sanders rose. He leaned against a telephone pole for support. The haze cleared to show him the white, anxious face of a young woman.

"Are you hurt?" she asked.

Dave looked at Joyce, wondering at her presence here. "He's the one that's hurt," he answered quietly.

"I thought—I was afraid—" Her voice died away. She felt her knees grow weak. To her this man had appeared to be plunging straight to death.

No excitement in him reached the surface. His remarkably steady eyes still held their grim, hard tenseness, but otherwise his self-control was perfect. He was absolutely imperturbable.

"He was shootin' wild. Sorry you were here, Miss Crawford." His eyes swept the gathering crowd. "You'd better go, don't you reckon?"

"Yes. . . . You come too, please." The girl's voice broke.

"Don't worry. It's all over." He turned to the crowd. "He began shootin' at me. I was unarmed. He shot four times before I got to him."

"Tha's right. I saw it from up street," a stranger volunteered. "Where do you take out yore insurance, friend? I'd like to get some of the same."

"I'll be in town here if I'm wanted," Dave announced before he came back to where Bob and Joyce were standing. "Now we'll move, Miss Crawford."

At the second street corner he stopped, evidently intending to go no farther. "I'll say good-bye, for this time. I'll want to see Mr. Crawford right soon. How is little Keith comin' on?"

She had mentioned that the boy frequently spoke of him.

"Can you come up to see Father to-night? Or he'll go to your room if you'd rather."

"Maybe to-morrow—"

82

"He'll be anxious to see you. I want you and Bob to come to dinner Sunday."

"Don't hardly think I'll be here Sunday. My plans aren't settled. Thank you just the same, Miss Crawford."

She took his words as a direct rebuff. There was a little lump in her throat that she had to get rid of before she spoke again.

"Sorry. Perhaps some other time." Joyce gave him her hand. "I'm mighty glad to have seen you again, Mr. Sanders."

He bowed. "Thank you."

After she had gone, Dave turned swiftly to his friend. "Where's the nearest doctor's office? Miller got me in the shoulder."

CHAPTER XVII

OIL

"I'll take off my hat to Dave," said Hart warmly. "He's chain lightnin'. I never did see anything like the way he took that street in two jumps. And game? Did you ever hear tell of an unarmed man chargin' a guy with a gun spittin' at him?"

"I always knew he had sand in his craw. What does Doc Green say?" asked Crawford, lighting a corncob pipe.

"Says nothin' to worry about. A flesh wound in the shoulder. Ought to heal up in a few days."

Miss Joyce speaking, with an indignant tremor of the voice: "It was the most cowardly thing I ever saw. He was unarmed, and he hadn't lifted a finger when that ruffian began to shoot. I was sure he would be . . . killed."

"He'll take a heap o' killin', that boy," her father reassured. "In a way it's a good thing this happened now. His enemies have showed their hand. They tried to gun him, before witnesses, while he was unarmed. Whatever happens now, Dave's got public sentiment on his side. I'm always glad to have my enemy declare himself. Then I can take measures."

"What measures can Dave take?" asked Joyce.

A faint, grim smile flitted across the old cattleman's face. "Well, one measure he'll take pronto will be a good six-shooter on his hip. One I'll take will be to send Miller back to the pen, where he belongs, 'soon as I can get court action. He's out on parole, like Dave is. All the State has got to do is to reach out and haul him back again."

"If it can find him," added Bob dryly. "I'll bet it can't. He's headed for the hills or the border right now."

Crawford rose. "Well, I'll run down with you to his room and see the boy, Bob. Wisht he would come up and stay with us. Maybe he will."

To the cattleman Dave made light of his wound. He would be all right in a few days, he said. It was only a scratch.

"Tha's good, son," Crawford answered. "Well, now, what are you aimin' to do? I got a job for you on the ranch if tha's what you want. Or I can use you in the oil business. It's for you to say which."

"Oil," said Dave without a moment of hesitation. "I want to learn that business from the ground up. I've been reading all I could get on the subject."

"Good enough, but don't you go to playin' geology too strong, Dave. Oil is where it's at. The formation don't amount to a damn. You'll find it where you find it."

"Mr. Crawford ain't strong for the scientific sharps since a college professor got him to drill a nice straight hole on Round Top plumb halfway to China," drawled Bob with a grin.

"I suppose it's a gamble," agreed Sanders.

"Worse'n the cattle market, and no livin' man can guess that," said the owner of the D Bar Lazy R dogmatically. "Bob, you better put Dave with the crew of that wildcat you're spuddin' in, don't you reckon?"

"I'll put him on afternoon tower in place of that fellow Scott. I've been intendin' to fire him soon as I could get a good man."

"Much obliged to you both. Hope you've found that good man," said Sanders.

"We have. Ain't either of us worryin' about that." With a quizzical smile Crawford raised a point that was in his mind. "Say, son, you talk a heap more like a book than you used to. You didn't slip one over on us and go to college, did you?"

"I went to school in the penitentiary," Dave said.

He had been immured in a place of furtive, obscene whisperings, but he had found there not only vice. There was the chance of an education. He had accepted it at first because he dared not let himself be idle in his spare time. That way lay degeneration and the loss of his manhood. He had studied under competent instructors English, mathematics, the Spanish grammar, and mechanical drawing, as well as surveying and stationary engineering. He had read some of the world's best literature. He had waded through a good many histories. If his education in books was lopsided, it was in some respects more thorough than that of many a college boy.

Dave did not explain all this. He let his simple statement of fact stand without enlarging on it. His life of late years had tended to make him reticent.

"Heard from Burns yet about that fishin' job on Jackpot Number Three?" Bob asked Crawford.

"Only that he thinks he hooked the tools and lost 'em again. Wisht you'd run out in the mo'nin', son, and see what's doin'. I got to go out to the ranch."

"I'll drive out to-night and take Dave with me if he feels up to it. Then we'll know the foreman keeps humpin'."

"Fine and dandy." The cattleman turned to Sanders. "But I reckon you better stay right here and rest up. Time enough for you to go to work when yore shoulder's all right."

"Won't hurt me a bit to drive out with Bob. This thing's going to keep me awake anyhow. I'd rather be outdoors."

They drove out in the buckboard behind the half-broken colts. The young broncos went out of town to a flying start. They raced across the plain as hard as they could tear, the light rig swaying behind them as the wheels hit the high spots. Not till they had worn out their first wild energy was conversation possible.

Bob told of his change of occupation.

"Started dressin' tools on a wildcat test for Crawford two years ago when he first begun to plunge in oil. Built derricks for a while. Ran a drill. Dug sump holes. Shot a coupla wells. Went in with a fellow on a star rig as pardner. Went busted and took Crawford's offer to be handy man for him. Tha's about all, except that I own stock in two-three dead ones and some that ain't come to life yet."

The road was full of chuck holes and very dusty, both faults due to the heavy travel that went over it day and night. They were in the oil field now and gaunt derricks tapered to the sky to right and left of them. Occasionally Dave could hear the kick of an engine or could see a big beam pumping.

"I suppose most of the D Bar Lazy R boys have got into oil some," suggested Sanders.

"Every man, woman, and kid around is in oil neck deep," Bob answered. "Malapi's gone oil crazy. Folks are tradin' and speculatin' in stock and royalty rights that never could amount to a hill o' beans. Slick promoters are gettin' rich. I've known photographers to fake gushers in their darkrooms. The country's full of abandoned wells of busted companies. Oil is a big man's game. It takes capital to operate. I'll bet it ain't onct in a dozen times an investor gets a square run for his white alley, at that."

"There are crooks in every game."

"Sure, but oil's so darned temptin' to a crook. All the suckers are shovin' money at a promoter. They don't ask his capitalization or investigate his field. Lots o' promoters would hate like Sam Hill to strike oil. If they did they'd have to take care of it. That's a lot of trouble. They can make more organizin' a new company and rakin' in money from new investors."

Bob swung the team from the main road and put it at a long rise.

"There ain't nothin' easier than to drop money into a hole in the ground and call it an oil well," he went on. "Even if the proposition is absolutely on the level, the chances are all against the investor. It's a fifty-to-one shot. Tools are lost, the casin' collapses, the cable breaks, money gives out, shootin' is badly done, water filters in, or oil ain't there in payin' quantities. In a coupla years you can buy a deskful of no-good stock for a dollar Mex."

"Then why is everybody in it?"

"We've all been bit by this get-rich-quick bug. If you hit it right in oil you can wear all the diamonds you've a mind to. That's part of it, but it ain't all. The West always did like to take a chance, I reckon. Well, this is gamblin' on a big scale and it gets into a fellow's blood. We're all crazy, but we'd hate to be cured."

The driver stopped at the location of Jackpot Number Three and invited his friend to get out.

"Make yoreself to home, Dave. I reckon you ain't sorry that fool team has quit joltin' yore shoulder."

Sanders was not, but he did not say so. He could stand the

pain of his wound easily enough, but there was enough of it to remind him pretty constantly that he had been in a fight.

The fishing for the string of lost tools was going on by lamplight. With a good deal of interest Dave examined the big hooks that had been sent down in an unsuccessful attempt to draw out the drill. It was a slow business and a not very interesting one. The tools seemed as hard to hook as a wily old trout. Presently Sanders wandered to the bunkhouse and sat down on the front step. He thought perhaps he had not been wise to come out with Hart. His shoulder throbbed a good deal.

After a time Bob joined him. Faintly there came to them the sound of an engine thumping.

"Steelman's outfit," said Hart gloomily. "His li'l' old engine goes right on kickin' all the darned time. If he gets to oil first we lose. Man who makes first discovery on a claim wins out in this country."

"How's that? Didn't you locate properly?"

"Had no time to do the assessment work after we located. Dug a sump hole, maybe. Brad jumps in when the field here began to look up. Company that shows oil first will sure win out."

"How deep has he drilled?"

"We're a li'l' deeper—not much. Both must be close to the sands. We were showin' driller's smut when we lost our string." Bob reached into his hip pocket and drew out "the makings." He rolled his cigarette and lit it. "I reckon Steelman's a millionaire now—on paper, anyhow. He was about busted when he got busy in oil. He was lucky right off, and he's crooked as a dawg's hind laig—don't care how he gets his, so he gets it. He sure trimmed the suckers a-plenty."

"He and Crawford are still unfriendly," Dave suggested, the inflection of his voice making the statement a question.

"Onfriendly!" drawled Bob, leaning back against the step and letting a smoke ring curl up. "Well, tha's a good, nice parlor word. Yes, I reckon you could call them onfriendly." Presently he went on, in explanation: "Brad's goin' to put Crawford down and out if it can be done by hook or crook. He's a big man in the country now. We haven't been lucky, like he has. Besides, the ol' man's company's on the square. This business ain't like cows. It takes big money to swing. You make or break mighty sudden."

"Yes."

"And Steelman won't stick at a thing. Wouldn't trust him or any one of his crowd any further than I could sling a bull by the tail. He'd blow Crawford and me sky high if he thought he could get away with it."

Sanders nodded agreement. He hadn't a doubt of it.

With a thumb jerk toward the beating engine, Bob took up again his story. "Got a bunch of thugs over there right now ready for business if necessary. Imported plug-uglies and genuwine blown-in-the-bottle home talent. Shorty's still one of the gang, and our old friend Dug Doble is boss of the rodeo. I'm lookin' for trouble if we win out and get to oil first."

"You think they'll attack."

A gay light of cool recklessness danced in the eyes of the young oilman. "I've a kinda notion they'll drap over and pay us a visit one o' these nights, say in the dark of the moon. If they do—well, we certainly aim to welcome them proper."

CHAPTER XVIII

DOBLE PAYS A VISIT

"Hello, the Jackpot!"

Out of the night the call came to the men at the bunk-house.

Bob looked at his companion and grinned. "Seems to me I recognize that melojious voice."

A man stepped from the gloom with masterful, arrogant strides.

" 'Lo, Hart," he said. "Can you lend me a reamer?"

Bob knew he had come to spy out the land and not to borrow tools.

"Don't seem to me we've hardly got any reamers to spare, Dug," drawled the young man sitting on the porch floor. "What's the trouble? Got a kink in yore casin'?"

"Not so you could notice it, but you never can tell when you're goin' to run into bad luck, can you?" He sat down on the porch and took a cigar from his vest pocket. "What with losin' tools and one thing an' 'nother, this oil game sure is hell. By the way, how's yore fishin' job comin' on?"

"Fine, Dug. We ain't hooked our big fish yet, but we're hopeful."

Dave was sitting in the shadow. Doble nodded carelessly to him without recognition. It was characteristic of his audacity that Dug had walked over impudently to spy out the camp of the enemy. Bob knew why he had come, and he knew that Bob knew. Yet both ignored the fact that he was not welcome.

"I've known fellows angle a right long time for a trout and not catch him," said Doble, stretching his long legs comfortably.

"Yes," agreed Bob. "Wish I could hire you to throw a monkey wrench in that engine over there. Its chuggin' keeps me awake."

"I'll bet it does. Well, young fellow, you can't hire me or anybody else to stop it," retorted Doble, an edge to his voice.

"Well, I just mentioned it," murmured Hart. "I don't aim to rile yore feelin's. We'll talk of somethin' else. . . . Hope you enjoyed that reunion this week with yore old friend, absent far, but dear to memory ever."

"Referrin' to?" demanded Doble with sharp hostility.

"Why, Ad Miller, Dug."

"Is he a friend of mine?"

"Ain't he?"

"Not that I ever heard tell of."

"Glad of that. You won't miss him now he's lit out."

"Oh, he's lit out, has he?"

"A li'l' bird whispered to me he had."

"When?"

"This evenin', I understand."

"Where'd he go?"

"He didn't leave any address. Called away on sudden business."

"Did he mention the business?"

"Not to me." Bob turned to his friend. "Did he say anything to you about that, Dave?"

In the silence one might have heard a watch tick. Doble leaned forward, his body rigid, danger written large in his burning eyes and clenched fist.

"So you're back," he said at last in a low, harsh voice.

"I'm back."

"It would 'a' pleased me if they had put a rope round yore neck, Mr. Convict."

Dave made no comment. Nobody could have guessed from his stillness how fierce was the blood pressure at his temples.

"It's a difference of opinion makes horse-races, Dug," said Bob lightly.

The big ex-foreman rose, snarling. "For half a cent I'd gun you here and now like you did George."

Sanders looked at him steadily, his hands hanging loosely by his sides.

"I wouldn't try that, Dug," warned Hart. "Dave ain't armed, but I am. My hand's on my six-shooter right this minute. Don't make a mistake."

The ex-foreman glared at him. Doble was a strong, reckless devil of a fellow who feared neither God nor man. A primeval savagery burned in his blood, but like most "bad" men he had that vein of caution in his make-up which seeks to find its victim at disadvantage. He knew Hart too well to doubt his word. One cannot ride the range with a man year in, year out, without knowing whether the iron is in his arteries.

"Declarin' yoreself in on this, are you?" he demanded ominously, showing his teeth.

"I've always been in on it, Dug. Took a hand at the first deal, the day of the race. If you're lookin' for trouble with Dave you'll find it goes double."

"Not able to play his own hand, eh?"

"Not when you've got a six-shooter and he hasn't. Not after he has just been wounded by another gunman he cleaned up with his bare hands. You and yore friends are lookin' for things too easy."

"Easy, hell! I'll fight you and him both, with or without guns. Any time. Any place."

Doble backed away till his figure grew vague in the darkness. Came the crack of a revolver. A bullet tore a splinter from the wall of the shack in front of which Dave was standing. A jeering laugh floated to the two men, carried on the light night breeze.

Bob whipped out his revolver, but he did not fire. He and his friend slipped quietly to the far end of the house and found shelter round the corner.

"Ain't that like Dug, the damned double-crosser?" whispered Bob. "I reckon he didn't try awful hard to hit you. Just sent his compliments kinda casual to show good-will."

"I reckon he didn't try very hard to miss me either," said Dave dryly. "The bullet came within a foot of my head."

"He's one bad citizen, if you ask me," admitted Hart, without reluctance. "Know how he came to break with the old man? He had the nerve to start beauin' Miss Joyce. She wouldn't have it a minute. He stayed right with it—tried to ride over her. Crawford took a hand and kicked him out. Since then Dug has been one bitter enemy of the old man."

"Then Crawford had better look out. If Doble isn't a killer, I've never met one."

"I've got a fool notion that he ain't aimin' to kill him; that maybe he wants to help Steelman bust him so as he can turn the screws on him and get Miss Joyce. Dug must 'a' been makin' money fast in Brad's company. He's on the inside."

Dave made no comment.

"I expect you was some surprised when I told Dug who was roostin' on the step so clost to him," Hart went on. "Well, I had a reason. He was due to find it out anyhow in about a minute, so I thought I'd let him know we wasn't tryin' to keep him from knowin' who his neighbor was; also that I was good and ready for him if he got red-haided like Miller done."

"I understood, Bob," said his friend quietly.

CHAPTER XIX

AN INVOLUNTARY BATH

Jackpot Number Three hooked its tools the second day after Sanders's visit to that location. A few hours later its engine was thumping merrily and the cable rising and falling monotonously in the casing. On the afternoon of the third day Bob Hart rode up to the wildcat well where Dave was building a sump hole with a gang of Mexicans.

He drew Sanders to one side. "Trouble to-night, Dave, looks like. At Jackpot Number Three. We're in a layer of soft shale just above the oil-bearin' sand. Soon we'll know where we're at. Word has reached me that Doble means to rush the night tower and wreck the engine."

"You'll stand his crowd off?"

"You're whistlin'."

"Sure your information is right?"

"It's c'rect." Bob added, after a momentary hesitation: "We got a spy in his camp."

Sanders did not ask whether the affair was to be a pitched battle. He waited, sure that Bob would tell him when he was ready. That young man came to the subject indirectly.

"How's yore shoulder, Dave?"

"Doesn't trouble me any unless something is slammed against it."

"Interfere with you usin' a six-shooter?"

"No."

"Like to take a ride with me over to the Jackpot?"

"Yes."

"Good enough. I want you to look the ground over with me. Looks now as if it would come to fireworks. But we don't want any Fourth-of-July stuff if we can help it. Can we? That's the point."

At the Jackpot the friends walked over the ground together. Back of the location and to the west of it an arroyo ran from a cañon above.

"Follow it down and it'll take you right into the location where Steelman is drillin'," explained Bob. "Dug's gonna lead his gang up the arroyo to the mesquite here, sneak down on us, and take our camp with a rush. At least, that's what he aims to do. You can't always tell, as the fellow says."

"What's up above?"

"A dam. Steelman owns the ground up there. He's got several acres of water backed up there for irrigation purposes."

"Let's go up and look it over."

Bob showed a mild surprise. "Why, yes, if you want to take some exercise. This is my busy day, but—"

Sanders ignored the hint. He led the way up a stiff trail that took them to the mouth of the cañon. Across the face of this a dam stretched. They climbed to the top of it. The water rose to within about six feet from the rim of the curved wall.

"Some view," commented Bob with a grin, looking across the plains that spread fanlike from the mouth of the gorge. "But I ain't much interested in scenery today somehow."

"When were you expectin' to shoot the well, Bob?"

"Some time to-morrow. Don't know just when. Why?"

"Got the nitro here yet?"

"Brought it up this mo'nin' myself."

"How much?"

"Twelve quarts."

"Any dynamite in camp?"

"Yes. A dozen sticks, maybe."

"And three gallons of nitro, you say."

"Yep."

"That's enough to do the job," Sanders said, as though talking aloud to himself.

"Yep. Tha's what we usually use."

"I'm speaking of another job. Let's get down from here. We might be seen."

"They couldn't hit us from the Steelman location. Too far," said Bob. "And I don't reckon any one would try to do that."

"No, but they might get to wondering what we're doing up here."

"I'm wonderin' that myself," drawled Hart. "Most generally when I take a pasear it's on the back of a bronc. I ain't one of them that believes the good Lord made human laigs to be walked on, not so long as any broomtails are left to straddle."

Screened by the heavy mesquite below, Sanders unfolded his proposed plan of operations. Bob listened, and as Dave talked there came into Hart's eyes dancing imps of deviltry. He gave a subdued whoop of delight, slapped his dusty white hat on his thigh, and vented his enthusiasm in murmurs of admiring profanity.

"It may not work out," suggested his friend. "But if your information is correct and they come up the arroyo—"

"It's c'rect enough. Lemme ask you a question. If you was attackin' us, wouldn't you come that way?"

"Yes."

"Sure. It's the logical way. Dug figures to capture our camp without firin' a shot. And he'd 'a' done it, too, if we hadn't had warnin'."

Sanders frowned, his mind busy over the plan. "It ought to work, unless something upsets it," he said.

"Sure it'll work. You darned old fox, I never did see yore beat. Say, if we pull this off right, Dug's gonna pretty near be laughed outa the country."

"Keep it quiet. Only three of us need to know it. You stay at the well to keep Doble's gang back if we slip up. I'll give the signal, and the third man will fire the fuse."

"Buck Byington will be here pretty soon. I'll get him to set off the Fourth-of-July celebration. He's a regular clam—won't ever say a word about this."

"When you hear her go off, you'd better bring the men down on the jump."

Byington came up the road half an hour later at a cow-puncher's jog-trot. He slid from the saddle and came forward chewing tobacco. His impassive, leathery face expressed no emotion whatever. Carelessly and casually he shook hands. "How, Dave?"

"How, Buck?" answered Sanders.

The old puncher had always liked Dave Sanders. The boy had begun work on the range as a protégé of his. He had taught him how to read sign and how to throw a rope. They had ridden out a blizzard together, and the old-timer had cared for him like a father. The boy had repaid him with a warm, ingenuous affection, an engaging sweetness of outward respect. A certain fineness in the eager face had lingered as an inheritance from his clean youth. No playful pup could have been more friendly. Now Buck shook hands with a grim-faced man, one a thousand years old in bitter experience. The eyes let no warmth escape. In the younger man's consciousness rose the memory of a hundred kindnesses flowing from Buck to him. Yet he could not let himself go. It was as though the prison chill had encased his heart in ice which held his impulses fast.

After dusk had fallen they made their preparations. The three men slipped away from the bunkhouse into the chaparral. Bob carried a bulging gunnysack, Dave a lantern, a pick, a drill, and a hammer. None of them talked till they had reached the entrance to the cañon.

"We'd better get busy before it's too dark," Bob said. "We picked this spot, Buck. Suit you?"

Byington had been a hard-rock Colorado miner in his youth. He examined the dam and came back to the place chosen. After taking off his coat he picked up the hammer. "Le's start. The sooner the quicker."

Dave soaked the gunnysack in water and folded it over the

top of the drill to deaden the sound. Buck wielded the hammer and Bob held the drill.

After it grew dark they worked by the light of the lantern. Dave and Bob relieved Buck at the hammer. They drilled two holes, put in the dynamite charges, tamped them down, and filled in again the holes. The nitroglycerine, too, was prepared and set for explosion.

Hart straightened stiffly and looked at his watch. "Time to move back to camp, Dave. Business may get brisk soon now. Maybe Dug may get in a hurry and start things earlier than he intended."

"Don't miss my signal, Buck. Two shots, one right after another," said Dave.

"I'll promise you to send back two shots a heap louder. You sure won't miss 'em," answered Buck with a grin.

The younger men left him at the dam and went back down the trail to their camp.

"No report yet from the lads watchin' the arroyo. I expect Dug's waitin' till he thinks we're all asleep except the night tower," whispered the man who had been left in charge by Hart.

"Dave, you better relieve the boys at the arroyo," suggested Bob. "Fireworks soon now, I expect."

Sanders crept through the heavy chaparral to the liveoaks above the arroyo, snaking his way among cactus and mesquite over the sand. A watcher jumped up at his approach. Dave raised his hand and moved it above his head from right to left. The guard disappeared in the darkness toward the Jackpot. Presently his companion followed him. Dave was left alone.

It seemed to him that the multitudinous small voices of the night had never been more active. A faint trickle of water came up from the bed of the stream. He knew this was caused by leakage from the reservoir in the gulch. A tiny rustle stirred the dry grass close to his hand. His peering into the thick brush did not avail to tell him what form of animal life was palpitating there. Far away a mocking-bird throbbed out a note or two, grew quiet, and again became tunefully clamorous. A night owl hooted. The sound of a soft footfall rolling a pebble brought him to taut alertness. Eyes and ears became automatic detectives keyed to finest service.

A twig snapped in the arroyo. Indistinctly movements of blurred masses were visible. The figure of a man detached itself from the gloom and crept along the sandy wash. A second and a third took shape. The dry bed became filled with vague motion. Sanders waited no longer. He crawled back from the lip of the ravine a dozen yards, drew his revolver, and fired twice.

His guess had been that the attacking party, startled at the shots, would hesitate and draw together for a whispered conference. This was exactly what occurred.

An explosion tore to shreds the stillness of the night. Before the first had died away a second one boomed out. Dave heard a shower of falling rock and concrete. He heard, too, a roar growing every moment in volume. It swept down the walled gorge like a railroad train making up lost time.

Sanders stepped forward. The gully, lately a wash of dry sand and baked adobe, was full of a fury of rushing water. Above the noise of it he caught the echo of a despairing scream. Swiftly he ran, dodging among the catclaw and the prickly pear like a half-back carrying the ball through a broken field. His objective was the place where the arroyo opened to a draw. At this precise spot Steelman had located his derrick.

The tower no longer tapered gauntly to the sky. The rush of waters released from the dam had swept it from its foundation, torn apart the timbers, and scattered them far and wide. With it had gone the wheel, dragging from the casing the cable. The string of tools, jerked from their socket, probably lay at the bottom of the well two thousand feet down.

Dave heard a groan. He moved toward the sound. A man lay on a sand hummock, washed up by the tide.

"Badly hurt?" asked Dave.

"I've been drowned intirely, swallowed by a flood and knocked galley-west for Sunday. I don't know yit am I dead or not. Mither o' Moses, phwat was it hit us?"

"The dam must have broke."

"Was the Mississippi corked up in the dom cañon?"

Bob bore down upon the scene at the head of the Jackpot contingent. He gave a whoop at sight of the wrecked derrick and engine. "Kindlin' wood and junk," was his verdict. "Where's Dug and his gang?"

Dave relieved the half-drowned man of his revolver. "Here's one. The rest must be either in the arroyo or out in the draw."

"Scatter, boys, and find 'em. Look out for them if they're hurt. Collect their hardware first off."

The water by this time had subsided. Released from the

96

walls of the arroyo, it had spread over the desert. The supply in the reservoir was probably exhausted, for the stream no longer poured down in a torrent. Instead, it came in jets, weakly and with spent energy.

Hart called. "Come here and meet an old friend, Dave."

Sanders made his way, ankle deep in water, to the spot from which that irrepressibly gay voice had come. He was still carrying the revolver he had taken from the Irishman.

"Meet Shorty, Dave. Don't mind his not risin' to shake. He's just been wrastlin' with a waterspout and he's some wore out."

The squat puncher glared at his tormentor. "I done bust my laig," he said at last sullenly.

He was wet to the skin. His lank, black hair fell in front of his tough, unshaven face. One hand nursed the lacerated leg. The other was hooked by the thumb into the band of his trousers.

"That worries us a heap, Shorty," answered Hart callously. "I'd say you got it comin' to you."

The hand hitched in the trouser band moved slightly. Bob, aware too late of the man's intention, reached for his six-shooter. Something flew past him straight and hard.

Shorty threw up his hands with a yelp and collapsed. He had been struck in the head by a heavy revolver.

"Some throwin', Dave. Much obliged," said Hart. "We'll disarm this bird and pack him back to the derrick." They did. Shorty almost wept with rage and pain and impotent malice. He cursed steadily and fluently. He might as well have saved his breath, for his captors paid not the least attention to his spleen.

Weak as a drowned rat, Doble came limping out of the ravine. He sat down on a timber, very sick at the stomach from too much water swallowed in haste. After he had relieved himself, he looked up wanly and recognized Hart, who was searching him for a hidden six-shooter.

"Must 'a' lost yore forty-five whilst you was in swimmin', Dug. Was the water good this evenin'? I'll bet you and yore lads pulled off a lot o' fancy stunts when the water come down from Lodore or wherever they had it corralled." Dancing imps of mischief lit the eyes of the ex-cowpuncher. "Well, I'll bet the boys in town get a great laugh at yore comedy stuff. You ce'tainly did a good turn. Oh, you've sure earned yore laugh."

If hatred could have killed with a look Bob would have been a dead man. "You blew up the dam," charged Doble.

"Me! Why, it ain't my dam. Didn't Brad give you orders to open the sluices to make you a swimmin' hole?"

The searchers began to straggle in, bringing with them a sadly drenched and battered lot of gunmen. Not one but looked as though he had been through the wars. An inventory of wounds showed a sprained ankle, a broken shoulder blade, a cut head, and various other minor wounds. Nearly every member of Doble's army was exceedingly nauseated. The men sat down or leaned up against the wreckage of the plant and drooped wretchedly. There was not an ounce of fight left in any of them.

"They must 'a' blew the dam up. Them shots we heard!" one ventured without spirit.

"Who blew it up?" demanded one of the Jackpot men belligerently. "If you say we did, you're a liar."

He was speaking the truth so far as he knew. The man who had been through the waters did not take up the challenge. Officers in the army say that men will not fight on an empty stomach, and his was very empty.

"I'll remember this, Hart," Doble said, and his face was a thing ill to look upon. The lips were drawn back so that his big teeth were bared like tusks. The eyes were yellow with malignity.

"Y'betcha! The boys'll look after that, Dug," retorted Bob lightly. "Every time you hook yore heel over the bar rail at the Gusher, you'll know they're laughin' at you up their sleeves. Sure, you'll remember it."

"Some day I'll make yore whole damned outfit sorry for this," the big hook-nosed man threatened blackly. "No livin' man can laugh at me and get away with it."

"I'm laughin' at you, Dug. We all are. Wish you could see yoreself as we see you. A little water takes a lot o' tuck outa some men who are feelin' real biggity."

Byington, at this moment, sauntered into the assembly. He looked around in simulated surprise. "Must be bath night over at you-all's camp, Dug. You look kinda drookid yore own self, as you might say."

Doble swore savagely. He pointed with a shaking finger at Sanders, who was standing silently in the background. "Tha's the man who's responsible for this. Think I don't know? That jail bird! That convict! That killer!" His voice trembled with fury. "You'd never a-thought of it in a thousand years, Hart.

98

Nor you, Buck, you old fathead. Wait. Tha's what I say. Wait. It'll be me or him one day. Soon, too."

The paroled man said nothing, but no words could have been more effective than the silence of this lean, powerful man with the close-clamped jaw whose hard eyes watched his enemy so steadily. He gave out an impression of great vitality and reserve force. Even these hired thugs, dull and unimaginative though they were, understood that he was dangerous beyond most fighting men. A laugh snapped the tension. The Jackpot engineer pointed to a figure emerging from the arroyo. The man who came dejectedly into view was large and fat and dripping. He was weeping curses and trying to pick cactus burrs from his anatomy. Dismal groans punctuated his profanity.

"It stranded me right on top of a big prickly pear," he complained. "I like never to 'a' got off, and a million spines are stickin' into me."

Bob whooped. "Look who's among us. If it ain't our old friend Ad Miller, the human pincushion. Seein' as he drapped in, we'll collect him right now and find out if the sheriff ain't lookin' for him to take a trip on the choo-choo cars."

The fat convict looked to Doble in vain for help. His friend was staring at the ground sourly in a huge disgust at life and all that it contained. Miller limped painfully to the Jackpot in front of Hart. Two days later he took the train back to the penitentiary. Emerson Crawford made it a point to see to that.

CHAPTER XX

THE LITTLE MOTHER FREES HER MIND

If some one had made Emerson Crawford a present of a carload of Herefords he could not have been more pleased than he was at the result of the Jackpot crew's night adventure with the Steelman forces. The news came to him at an opportune moment, for he had just been served notice by the president of the Malapi First National Bank that Crawford must prepare to meet at once a call note for $10,000. A few hours earlier in the day the cattleman had heard it rumored that Steelman had just bought a controlling interest in the bank. He did not need a lawyer to tell him that the second fact was responsible for the first. In fact the banker, personally friendly to Crawford, had as good as told him so.

Bob rode in with the story of the fracas in time to cheer the drooping spirits of his employer. Emerson walked up and down the parlor waving his cigar while Joyce laughed at him.

"Dawggone my skin, if that don't beat my time! I'm settin' aside five thousand shares in the Jackpot for Dave Sanders right now. Smartest trick ever I did see." The justice of the Jackpot's vengeance on its rival and the completeness of it came home to him as he strode the carpet. "He not only saves my property without havin' to fight for it—and that was a blamed good play itself, for I don't want you boys shootin' up anybody even in self-defense—but he disarms Brad's plug-uglies, humiliates them, makes them plumb sick of the job, and at the same time wipes out Steelman's location lock, stock, and barrel. I'll make that ten thousand shares, by gum! That boy's sure some stemwinder."

"He uses his haid," admitted Bob admiringly.

"I'd give my best pup to have been there," said the cattleman regretfully.

"It was some show," drawled the younger man. "Drowned rats was what they reminded me of. Couldn't get a rise out of any of 'em except Dug. That man's dangerous, if you ask me. He's crazy mad at all of us, but most at Dave."

"Will he hurt him?" asked Joyce quickly.

"Can't tell. He'll try. That's a cinch."

The dark brown eyes of the girl brooded. "That's not fair. We can't let him run into more danger for us, Dad. He's had enough trouble already. We must do something. Can't you send him to the Spring Valley Ranch?"

"Meanin' Dug Doble?" asked Bob.

She flashed a look of half-smiling, half-tender reproach at him. "You know who I mean, Bob. And I'm not going to have him put in danger on our account," she added with naïve dogmatism.

"Joy's right. She's sure right," admitted Crawford.

100

"Maybeso." Hart fell into his humorous drawl. "How do you aim to get him to Spring Valley? You goin' to have him hawg-tied and shipped as freight?"

"I'll talk to him. I'll tell him he must go." Her resolute little face was aglow and eager. "It's time Malapi was civilized. We mustn't give these bad men provocation. It's better to avoid them."

"Yes," admitted Bob dryly. "Well, you tell all that to Dave. Maybe he's the kind o' lad that will pack up and light out because he's afraid of Dug Doble and his outfit. Then again maybe he ain't."

Crawford shook his head. He was a game man himself. He would go through when the call came, and he knew quite well that Sanders would do the same. Nor would any specious plea sidetrack him. At the same time there was substantial justice in the contention of his daughter. Dave had no business getting mixed up in this row. The fact that he was an ex-convict would be in itself a damning thing in case the courts ever had to pass upon the feud's results. The conviction on the records against him would make a second conviction very much easier.

"You're right, Bob. Dave won't let Dug's crowd run him out. But you keep an eye on him. Don't let him go out alone nights. See he packs a gun."

"Packs a gun!" Joyce was sitting in a rocking-chair under the glow of the lamp. She was darning one of Keith's stockings, and to the young man watching her—so wholly winsome girl, so much tender but businesslike little mother—she was the last word in the desirability of woman. "That's the very way to find trouble, Dad. He's been doing his best to keep out of it. He can't, if he stays here. So he must go away. That's all there is to it."

Her father laughed. "Ain't it scandalous the way she bosses us all around, Bob?"

The face of the girl sparkled to a humorous challenge. "Well, some one has got to boss you-all boys, Dad. If you'd do as I say you wouldn't have any trouble with that old Steelman or his gunmen."

"We wouldn't have any oil wells either, would we, honey?"

"They're not worth having if you and Dave Sanders and Bob have to live in danger all the time," she flashed.

"Glad you look at it that way, Joy," Emerson retorted with a rueful smile. "Fact is, we ain't goin' to have any more oil wells than a jackrabbit pretty soon. I'm at the end of my rope

101

right now. The First National promised me another loan on the Arizona ranch, but Brad has got a-holt of it and he's called in my last loan. I'm not quittin'. I'll put up a fight yet, but unless things break for me I'm about done."

"Oh, Dad!" Her impulse of sympathy carried Joyce straight to him. Soft, rounded arms went round his neck with impassioned tenderness. "I didn't dream it was as bad as that. You've been worrying all this time and you never let me know."

He stroked her hair fondly. "You're the blamedest little mother ever I did see—always was. Now don't you fret. It'll work out somehow. Things do."

CHAPTER XXI

THE HOLD-UP

To Sanders, working on afternoon tower at Jackpot Number Three, the lean, tanned driller in charge of operations was wise with an uncanny knowledge the newcomer could not fathom. For eight hours at a stretch he stood on the platform and watched a greasy cable go slipping into the earth. Every quiver of it, every motion of the big walking-beam, every kick of the engine, told him what was taking place down that narrow pipe two thousand feet below the surface. He knew when the tools were in clay and had become gummed up. He could tell just when the drill had cut into hard rock at an acute angle and was running out of the perpendicular to follow the softer stratum. His judgment appeared infallible as to whether he ought to send down a reamer to straighten the kink. All Dave knew was that a string of tools far underground was jerking up and down monotonously.

This spelt romance to Jed Burns, superintendent of operations, though he would never have admitted it. He was a bachelor; always would be one. Hard-working, hard-drinking, at odd times a plunging gambler, he lived for nothing but oil and the atmosphere of oil fields. From one boom to another he drifted, as inevitably as the gamblers, grafters, and organizers of "fake" companies. Several times he had made fortunes, but it was impossible for him to stay rich. He was always ready to back a drilling proposition that looked promising, and no independent speculator can continue to wildcat without going broke.

He was sifting sand through his fingers when Dave came on tower the day after the flood. To Bob Hart, present as Crawford's personal representative, he expressed an opinion.

"Right soon now or never. Sand tastes, feels, looks, and smells like oil. But you can't ever be sure. An oil prospect is like a woman. She will or she won't, you never can tell which. Then, if she does, she's liable to change her mind."

Dave sniffed the pleasing, pungent odor of the crude oil sands. His friend had told him that Crawford's fate hung in the balance. Unless oil flowed very soon in paying quantities he was a ruined man. The control of the Jackpot properties would probably pass into the hands of Steelman. The cattleman would even lose the ranches which had been the substantial basis of his earlier prosperity.

Everybody working on the Jackpot felt the excitement as the drill began to sink into the oil-bearing sands. Most of the men owned stock in the company. Moreover, they were getting a bonus for their services and had been promised an extra one if Number Three struck oil in paying quantities before Steelman's crew did. Even to an outsider there is a fascination in an oil well. It is as absorbing to the drillers as a girl's mind is to her hopeful lover. Dave found it impossible to escape the contagion of this. Moreover, he had ten thousand shares in the Jackpot, stock turned over to him out of the treasury supply by the board of directors in recognition of services which they did not care to specify in the resolution which authorized the transfer. At first he had refused to accept this, but Bob Hart had put the matter to him in such a light that he changed his mind.

"The oil business pays big for expert advice, no matter whether it's legal or technical. What you did was worth fifty times what the board voted you. If we make a big strike you've saved the company. If we don't the stock's not worth a plugged nickel anyhow. You've earned what we voted you. Hang on to it, Dave."

Dave had thanked the board and put the stock in his pocket. Now he felt himself drawn into the drama represented by the thumping engine which continued day and night.

After his shift was over, he rode to town with Bob behind his team of wild broncos.

"Got to look for an engineer for the night tower," Hart explained as he drew up in front of the Gusher Saloon. "Come in with me. It's some gambling-hell, if you ask me."

The place hummed with the turbulent life that drifts to every wild frontier on the boom. Faro dealers from the Klondike, poker dealers from Nome, roulette croupiers from Leadville, were all here to reap the rich harvest to be made from investors, field workers, and operators. Smooth grafters with stock in worthless companies for sale circulated in and out with blue-prints and whispered inside information. The men who were ranged in front of the bar, behind which half a dozen attendants in white aprons busily waited on their wants, usually talked oil and nothing but oil. To-day they had another theme. The same subject engrossed the groups scattered here and there throughout the large hall.

In the rear of the room were the faro layouts, the roulette wheels, and the poker players. Around each of these the shifting crowd surged. Mexicans, Chinese, and even Indians brushed shoulders with white men of many sorts and conditions. The white-faced professional gambler was in evidence, winning the money of big brown men in miner's boots and corduroys. The betting was wild and extravagant, for the spirit of the speculator had carried away the cool judgment of most of these men. They had seen a barber become a millionaire in a day because the company in which he had plunged had struck a gusher. They had seen the same man borrow five dollars three months later to carry him over until he got a job. Riches were pouring out of the ground for the gambler who would take a chance. Thrift was a much-discredited virtue in Malapi. The one unforgivable vice was to be "a piker."

Bob found his man at a faro table. While the cards were being shuffled, he engaged him to come out next evening to the Jackpot properties. As soon as the dealer began to slide the cards out of the case the attention of the engineer went back to his bets.

While Dave was standing close to the wall, ready to leave as soon as Bob returned to him, he caught sight of an old acquaintance. Steve Russell was playing stud poker at a table a few feet from him. The cowpuncher looked up and waved his hand.

"See you in a minute, Dave," he called, and as soon as the pot had been won he said to the man shuffling the cards, "Deal me out this hand."

He rose, stepped across to Sanders, and shook hands with a strong grip. "You darned old son-of-a-gun! I'm sure glad to see you. Heard you was back. Say, you've ce'tainly been goin' some. Suits me. I never did like either Dug or Miller a whole lot. Dug's one sure-enough bad man and Miller's a tinhorn would-be. What you did to both of 'em was a-plenty. But keep yore eye peeled, old-timer. Miller's where he belongs again, but Dug's still on the range, and you can bet he's seein' red these days. He'll gun you if he gets half a chance."

"Yes," said Dave evenly.

"You don't figure to let yoreself get caught again without a six-shooter." Steve put the statement with the rising inflection.

"No."

"Tha's right. Don't let him get the drop on you. He's sudden death with a gun."

Bob joined them. After a moment's conversation Russell drew them to a corner of the room that for the moment was almost deserted.

"Say, you heard the news, Bob?"

"I can tell you that better after I know what it is," returned Hart with a grin.

"The stage was held up at Cottonwood Bend and robbed of seventeen thousand dollars. The driver was killed."

"When?"

"This mo'nin'. They tried to keep it quiet, but it leaked out."

"Whose money was it?"

"Brad Steelman's pay roll and a shipment of gold for the bank."

"Any idea who did it?"

Steve showed embarrassment. "Why, no, *I* ain't, if that's what you mean."

"Well, anybody else?"

"Tha's what I wanta tell you. Two men were in the job. They're whisperin' that Em Crawford was one."

"Crawford! Some of Steelman's fine work in that rumor, I'll bet. He's crazy if he thinks he can get away with that. Tha's plumb foolish talk. What evidence does he claim?" demanded Hart.

105

"Em deposited ten thousand with the First National to pay off a note he owed the bank. Rode into town right straight to the bank two hours after the stage got in. Then, too, seems one of the hold-ups called the other one Crawford."

"A plant," said Dave promptly.

"Looks like." Bob's voice was rich with sarcasm. "I don't reckon the other one rose up on his hind laigs and said, 'I'm Bob Hart,' did he?"

"They claim the second man was Dave here."

"Hmp! What time d' you say this hold-up took place?"

"Must 'a' been about eleven."

"Lets Dave out. He was fifteen miles away, and we can prove it by at least six witnesses."

"Good. I reckon Em can put in an alibi too."

"I'll bet he can." Hart promised this with conviction.

"Trouble is they say they've got witnesses to show Em was travelin' toward the Bend half an hour before the hold-up. Art Johnson and Clem Purdy met him while they was on their way to town."

"Was Crawford alone?"

"He was then. Yep."

"Any one might 'a' been there. You might. I might. That don't prove a thing."

"Hell, I know Em Crawford's not mixed up in any hold-up, let alone a damned cowardly murder. You don't need to tell *me* that. Point is that evidence is pilin' up. Where did Em get the ten thousand to pay the bank? Two days ago he was tryin' to increase the loan the First National had made him."

Dave spoke. "I don't know where he got it, but unless he's a born fool—and nobody ever claimed that of Crawford—he wouldn't take the money straight to the bank after he had held up the stage and killed the driver. That's a strong point in his favor."

"If he can show where he got the ten thousand," amended Russell. "And of course he can."

"And where he spent that two hours after the hold-up before he came to town. That'll have to be explained too," said Bob.

"Oh, Em he'll be able to explain that all right," decided Steve cheerfully.

"Where is Crawford now?" asked Dave. "He hasn't been arrested, has he?"

"Not yet. But he's bein' watched. Soon as he showed up at the bank the sheriff asked to look at his six-shooter. Two cartridges had been fired. One of the passengers on the stage told me two shots was fired from a six-gun by the boss hold-up. The second one killed old Tim Harrigan."

"Did they accuse Crawford of the killing?"

"Not directly. He was asked to explain. I ain't heard what his story was."

"We'd better go to his house and talk with him," suggested Hart. "Maybe he can give as good an alibi as you, Dave."

"You and I will go straight there," decided Sanders. "Steve, get three saddle horses. We'll ride out to the Bend and see what we can learn on the ground."

"I'll cash my chips, get the broncs, and meet you lads at Crawford's," said Russell promptly.

CHAPTER XXII

NUMBER THREE COMES IN

Joyce opened the door to the knock of the young men. At sight of them her face lit.

"Oh, I'm so glad you've come!" she cried, tears in her voice. She caught her hands together in a convulsive little gesture. "Isn't it dreadful? I've been afraid all the time that something awful would happen—and now it has."

"Don't you worry, Miss Joyce," Bob told her cheerfully. "We ain't gonna let anything happen to yore paw. We aim to get busy right away and run this thing down. Looks like a frame-up. If it is, you betcha we'll get at the truth."

"Will you? Can you?" She turned to Dave in appeal, eyes starlike in a face that was a white and shining oval in the semi-darkness.

"We'll try," he said simply.

Something in the way he said it, in the quiet reticence of his promise, sent courage flowing to her heart. She had called on him once before, and he had answered splendidly and recklessly.

"Where's Mr. Crawford?" asked Bob.

"He's in the sitting-room. Come right in."

Her father was sitting in a big chair, one leg thrown carelessly over the arm. He was smoking a cigar composedly.

"Come in, boys," he called. "Reckon you've heard that I'm a stage rustler and a murderer."

Joyce cried out at this, the wide, mobile mouth trembling.

"Just now. At the Gusher," said Bob. "They didn't arrest you?"

"Not yet. They're watchin' the house. Sit down, and I'll tell it to you."

He had gone out to see a homesteader about doing some work for him. On the way he had met Johnson and Purdy near the Bend, just before he had turned up a draw leading to the place in the hills owned by the man whom he wanted to see. Two hours had been spent riding to the little valley where the nester had built his corrals and his log house, and when Crawford arrived neither he nor his wife was at home. He returned to the road, without having met a soul since he had left it, and from there jogged on back to town. On the way he had fired twice at a rattlesnake.

"You never reached the Bend, then, at all," said Dave.

"No, but I cayn't prove I didn't." The old cattleman looked at the end of his cigar thoughtfully. "Nor I cayn't prove I went out to Dick Grein's place in that three-four hours not accounted for."

"Anyhow, you can show where you got the ten thousand dollars you paid the bank," said Bob hopefully.

A moment of silence; then Crawford spoke. "No, son, I cayn't tell that either."

Faint and breathless with suspense, Joyce looked at her father with dilated eyes. "Why not?"

"Because the money was loaned me on those conditions."

"But—but—don't you see, Dad?—if you don't tell that—"

"They'll think I'm guilty. Well, I reckon they'll have to think it, Joy." The steady gray eyes looked straight into the brown ones of the girl. "I've been in this county boy and man for 'most fifty years. Any one that's willin' to think me a cold-blooded murderer at this date, why, he's welcome to hold any opinion he pleases. I don't give a damn what he thinks."

"But we've got to prove—"

"No, we haven't. They've got to do the proving. The law holds me innocent till I'm found guilty."

"But you don't aim to keep still and let a lot of miscreants blacken yore good name!" suggested Hart.

"You bet I don't, Bob. But I reckon I'll not break my word to a friend either, especially under the circumstances this money was loaned."

"He'll release you when he understands," cried Joyce.

"Don't bank on that, honey," Crawford said slowly. "You ain't to mention this. I'm tellin' you three private. He cayn't come out and tell that he let me have the money. Understand? You don't any of you know a thing about how I come by that ten thousand. I've refused to answer questions about that money. That's my business."

"Oh, but, Dad, you can't do that. You'll have to give an explanation. You'll have to—"

"The best explanation I can give, Joy, is to find out who held up the stage and killed Tim Harrigan. It's the only one that will satisfy me. It's the only one that will satisfy my friends."

"That's true," said Sanders.

"Steve Russell is bringin' hawsses," said Bob. "We'll ride out to the Bend to-night and be ready for business there at the first streak of light. Must be some trail left by the hold-ups."

Crawford shook his head. "Probably not. Applegate had a posse out there right away. You know Applegate. He'd blunder if he had a chance. His boys have milled all over the place and destroyed any trail that was left."

"We'll go out anyhow—Dave and Steve and I. Won't do any harm. We're liable to discover something, don't you reckon?"

"Maybeso. Who's that knockin' on the door, Joy?"

Some one was rapping on the front door imperatively. The girl opened it, to let into the hall a man in greasy overalls.

"Where's Mr. Crawford?" he demanded excitedly.

"Here. In the sitting-room. What's wrong?"

"Wrong! Not a thing!" He talked as he followed Joyce to the door of the room. "Except that Number Three's come in the biggest gusher ever I see. She's knocked the whole superstructure galley-west an' she's rip-r'arin' to beat the Dutch."

Emerson Crawford leaped to his feet, for once visibly excited. "What?" he demanded. "Wha's that?"

"Jus' like I say. The oil's a-spoutin' up a hundred feet like a fan. Before mornin' the sump holes will be full and she'll be runnin' all over the prairie."

"Burns sent you?"

"Yep. Says for you to get men and teams and scrapers and gunnysacks and heavy timbers out there right away. Many as you can send."

Crawford turned to Bob, his face aglow. "Yore job, Bob. Spread the news. Rustle up everybody you can get. Arrange with the railroad grade contractor to let us have all his men, teams, and scrapers till we get her hogtied and harnessed. Big wages and we'll feed the whole outfit free. Hire anybody you can find. Buy a coupla hundred shovels and send 'em out to Number Three. Get Robinson to move his tent-restaurant out there."

Hart nodded. "What about this job at the Bend?" he asked in a low voice.

"Dave and I'll attend to that. You hump on the Jackpot job. Sons, we're rich, all three of us. Point is to keep from losin' that crude on the prairie. Keep three shifts goin' till she's under control."

"We can't do anything at the Bend till morning," said Dave. "We'd better put the night in helping Bob."

"Sure. We've got to get all Malapi busy. A dozen business men have got to come down and open up their stores so's we can get supplies," agreed Emerson.

Joyce, her face flushed and eager, broke in. "Ring the fire bell. That's the quickest way."

"Sure enough. You got a haid on yore shoulders. Dave, you attend to that. Bob, hit the dust for the big saloons and gather men. I'll see O'Connor about the railroad outfit; then I'll come down to the fire-house and talk to the crowd. We'll wake this old town up to-night, sons."

"What about me?" asked the messenger.

"You go back and tell Jed to hold the fort till Hart and his material arrives."

Outside, they met Russell riding down the road, two saddled horses following. With a word of explanation they helped themselves to his mounts while he stared after them in surprise.

"I'll be dawggoned if they-all ain't three gents in a hurry," he murmured to the breezes of the night. "Well, seein' as I been held up, I reckon I'll have to walk back while the hawss-thieves ride."

Five minutes later the fire-bell clanged out its call to Malapi. From roadside tent and gambling-hell, from houses and camp-fires, men and women poured into the streets. For Malapi was a shell-town, tightly packed and inflammable, likely to go up in smoke whenever a fire should get beyond control of the volunteer company. Almost in less time than it takes to tell it, the square was packed with hundreds of lightly clad people and other hundreds just emerging from the night life of the place.

The clangor of the bell died away, but the firemen did not run out the hose and bucket cart. The man tugging the rope had told them why he was summoning the citizens.

"Some one's got to go out and explain to the crowd," said the fire chief to Dave. "If you know about this strike you'll have to tell the boys."

"Crawford said he'd talk," answered Sanders.

"He ain't here. It's up to you. Go ahead. Just tell 'em why you rang the bell."

Dave found himself pushed forward to the steps of the court-house a few yards away. He had never before attempted to speak in public, and he had a queer, dry tightening of the throat. But as soon as he began to talk the words he wanted came easily enough.

"Jackpot Number Three has come in a big gusher," he said, lifting his voice so that it would carry to the edge of the crowd.

Hundreds of men in the crowd owned stock in the Jackpot properties. At Dave's words a roar went up into the night. Men shouted, danced, or merely smiled, according to their temperament. Presently the thirst for news dominated the enthusiasm. Gradually the uproar was stilled.

Again Dave's voice rang out clear as the bell he had been tolling. "The report is that it's one of the biggest strikes ever known in the State. The derrick has been knocked to pieces and the oil's shooting into the air a hundred feet."

A second great shout drowned his words. This was an oil crowd. It dreamed oil, talked oil, thought oil, prayed for oil. A stranger in the town was likely to feel at first that the place was oil mad. What else can be said of a town with derricks built through its front porches and even the graveyard leased to a drilling company?

"The sump holes are filling," went on Sanders. "Soon the oil will be running to waste on the prairie. We need men, teams, tools, wagons, hundreds of slickers, tents, beds, grub. The wages will be one-fifty a day more than the run of wages

111

in the camp until the emergency has been met, and Emerson Crawford will board all the volunteers who come out to dig."

The speaker was lost again, this time in a buzz of voices of excited men. But out of the hubbub Dave's shout became heard.

"All owners of teams and tools, all dealers in hardware and groceries, are asked to step to the right-hand side of the crowd for a talk with Mr. Crawford. Men willing to work till the gusher is under control, please meet Bob Hart in front of the fire-house. I'll see any cooks and restaurant-men alive to a chance to make money fast. Right here at the steps."

"Good medicine, son," boomed Emerson Crawford, slapping him on the shoulder. "Didn't know you was an orator, but you sure got this crowd goin'. Bob here yet?"

"Yes. I saw him a minute ago in the crowd. Sorry I had to make promises for you, but the fire chief wouldn't let me keep the crowd waiting. Some one had to talk."

"Suits me. I'll run you for Congress one o' these days." Then, "I'll send the grocery-men over to you. Tell them to get the grub out to-night. If the restaurant-men don't buy it I'll run my own chuck wagon outfit. See you later, Dave."

For the next twenty-four hours there was no night in Malapi. Streets were filled with shoutings, hurried foot-falls, the creaking of wagons, and the thud of galloping horses. Stores were lit up and filled with buyers. For once the Gusher and the Oil Pool and other resorts held small attraction for the crowds. The town was moving out to see the big new discovery that was to revolutionize its fortunes with the opening of a new and tremendously rich field. Every ancient rig available was pressed into service to haul men or supplies out to the Jackpot location. Scarcely a minute passed, after the time that the first team took the road, without a loaded wagon, packed to the sideboards, moving along the dusty road into the darkness of the desert.

Three travelers on horseback rode in the opposite direction. Their destination was Cottonwood Bend. Two of them were Emerson Crawford and David Sanders. The third was an oil prospector who had been a passenger on the stage when it was robbed.

Micronite filter.
Mild, smooth taste.
For all the right reasons.
Kent.

America's quality cigarette.
King Size or Deluxe 100's.

Micronite filter.
Mild, smooth taste.
For all the right reasons.
Kent.

© Lorillard 1972

Regular or Menthol.

Kings: 17 mg. "tar,"
1.1 mg. nicotine;
100's: 19 mg. "tar,"
1.3 mg. nicotine;
Menthol: 19 mg. "tar,"
1.3 mg. nicotine
av. per cigarette,
FTC Report Aug. '72.

CHAPTER XXIII

THE GUSHER

Jackpot Number Three had come in with a roar that shook the earth for half a mile. Deep below the surface there was a hiss and a crackle, the shock of rending strata giving way to the pressure of the oil pool. From long experience as a driller, Jed Burns knew what was coming. He swept his crew back from the platform, and none too soon to escape disaster. They were still flying across the prairie when the crown box catapulted into the sky and the whole drilling superstructure toppled over. Rocks, clay, and sand were hurled into the air, to come down in a shower that bombarded everything within a radius of several hundred yards.

The landscape next moment was drenched in black petroleum. The fine particles of it filled the air, sprayed the cactus and the greasewood. Rivulets of the viscid stuff began to gather in depressions and to flow in gathering volume, as tributaries joined the stream, into the sump holes prepared for it. The pungent odor of crude oil, as well as the touch and the taste of it, penetrated the atmosphere.

Burns counted noses and discovered that none of his crew had been injured by falling rocks or beams. He knew that his men could not possibly cope with this geyser on a spree. It was a big strike, the biggest in the history of the district, and to control the flow of the gusher would necessitate tremendous efforts on a wholesale plan.

One of his men he sent in to Malapi on horseback with a hurry-up call to Emerson Crawford, president of the company, for tools, machinery, men, and teams. The others he put to salvaging the engine and accessories and to throwing up an earth dike around the sump hole as a barrier against

113

the escaping crude. All through the night he fought impotently against this giant that had burst loose from its prison two thousand feet below the surface of the earth.

With the first faint streaks of day men came galloping across the desert to the Jackpot. They came at first on horseback, singly, and later by twos and threes. A buckboard appeared on the horizon, the driver leaning forward as he urged on his team.

"Hart," decided the driller, "and comin' hell-for-leather."

Other teams followed, buggies, surreys, light wagons, farm wagons, and at last heavily laden lumber wagons. Business in Malapi was "shot to pieces," as one merchant expressed it. Everybody who could possibly get away was out to see the big gusher.

There was an immediate stampede to make locations in the territory adjacent. The wildcatter flourished. Companies were formed in ten minutes and the stock subscribed for in half an hour. From the bootblack at the hotel to the banker, everybody wanted stock in every company drilling within a reasonable distance of Jackpot Number Three. Many legitimate incorporations appeared on the books of the Secretary of State, and along with these were scores of frauds intended only to gull the small investor and separate him from his money. Saloons and gambling-houses, which did business with such childlike candor and stridency, became offices for the sale and exchange of stock. The boom at Malapi got its second wind. Workmen, investors, capitalists, and crooks poured in to take advantage of the inflation field. For the fame of Jackpot Number Three had spread wide. The production guesses ranged all the way from ten to fifty thousand barrels a day, most of which was still going to waste on the desert.

For Burns and Hart had not yet gained control over the flow, though an army of men in overalls and slickers fought the gusher night and day. The flow never ceased for a moment. The well steadily spouted a stream of black liquid into the air from the subterranean chamber into which the underground lake poured.

The attack had two objectives. The first was to check the outrush of oil. The second was to save the wealth emerging from the mouth of the well and streaming over the lip of the reservoir to the sandy desert.

A crew of men, divided into three shifts, worked with pick, shovel, and scraper to dig a second and a third sump hole. The dirt from the excavation was dumped at the edge of the working to build a dam for the fluid. Sacks filled with wet sand reinforced this dirt.

Meanwhile the oil boiled up in the lake and flowed over its edges in streams. As soon as the second reservoir was ready the tarry stuff was siphoned into it from the original sump hole. By the time this was full a third pool was finished, and into it the overflow was diverted. But in spite of the great effort made to save the product of the gusher, the sands absorbed many thousands of dollars' worth of petroleum.

This end of the work was under the direction of Bob Hart. For ten days he did not take off his clothes. When he slept it was in cat naps, an hour snatched now and again from the fight with the rising tide of wealth that threatened to engulf its owners. He was unshaven, unbathed, his clothes slimy with tar and grease. He ate on the job—coffee, beans, bacon, cornbread, whatever the cooks' flunkies brought him—and did not know what he was eating. Gaunt and dominating, with crisp decision and yet unfailing good-humor, he bossed the gangs under him and led them into the fight, holding them at it till flesh and blood revolted with weariness. Of such stuff is the true outdoor Westerner made. He may drop in his tracks from exhaustion after the emergency has been met, but so long as the call for action lasts he will stick to the finish.

At the other end Jed Burns commanded. One after another he tried all the devices he had known to succeed in capping or checking other gushers. The flow was so continuous and powerful that none of these were effective. Some wells flow in jets. They hurl out oil, die down like a geyser, and presently have another hemorrhage. Jackpot Number Three did not pulse as a cut artery does. Its output was steady as the flow of water in a pipe. The heavy timbers with which he tried to stop up the outlet were hurled aside like straws. He could not check the flow long enough to get control.

On the evening of the tenth day Burns put in the cork. He made elaborate preparations in advance and assigned his force to the posts where they were to work. A string of eight-inch pipe sixty feet long was slid forward and derricked over the stream. Above this a large number of steel rails, borrowed from the incoming road, were lashed to the pipe to prevent it from snapping. The pipe had been fitted with valves of various sizes. After it had been fastened to the well's casing, these were gradually reduced to check the flow without causing a blowout in the pipe line.

Six hours later a metropolitan newspaper carried the headline:

BIG GUSHER HARNESSED
AFTER WILD RAMPAGE

Jackpot No. 3 at Malapi Tamed
Long Battle Ended

CHAPTER XXIV

SHORTY

It was a surprise to Dave to discover that the horse Steve had got for him was his own old favorite Chiquito. The pinto knew him. He tested this by putting him through some of his old tricks. The horse refused to dance or play dead, but at the word of command his right foreleg came up to shake hands. He nuzzled his silky nose against the coat of his master just as in the days of old.

Crawford rode a bay, larger than a bronco. The oil prospector was astride a rangy roan. He was no horseman, but as a perpetual-motion conversationalist the old wildcatter broke records. He was a short barrel of a man, with small eyes set close together, and he made a figure of fun perched high up in the saddle. But he permitted no difficulties of travel to interfere with his monologue.

"The boss hold-up wasn't no glad-hand artist," he explained. "He was a sure-enough sulky devil, though o' course we couldn't see his face behind the mask. Blue mask it was, made outa a bandanna handkerchief. Well, rightaway I knew somethin' was liable to pop, for old Harrigan, scared to death, kep' a-goin' just the same. Maybe he hadn't sense enough to stop, as the fellow says. Maybe he didn't want to. Bang-bang!

I reckon Tim was dead before he hit the ground. They lined us up, but they didn't take a thing except the gold and one Chicago fellow's watch. Then they cut the harness and p'int for the hills."

"How do you know they made for the hills?" asked Dave.

"Well, they naturally would. Anyhow, they lit out round the Bend. I hadn't lost 'em none, and I wasn't lookin' to see where they went. Not in this year of our Lord. I'm right careless at times, but not enough so to make inquiries of road agents when they're red from killin'. I been told I got no terminal facilities of speech, but it's a fact I didn't chirp from start to finish of the hold-up. I was plumb reticent."

Light sifted into the sky. The riders saw the colors change in a desert dawn. The hilltops below them were veiled in a silver-blue mist. Far away Malapi rose out of the caldron, its cheapness for once touched to a moment of beauty and significance. In that glorified sunrise it might have been a jeweled city of dreams.

The prospector's words flowed on. Crystal dawns might come and go, succeeding mist scarfs of rose and lilac, but a great poet has said that speech is silver.

"No, sir. When a man has got the drop on me I don't aim to argue with him. Not none. Tim Harrigan had notions. Different here. I've done some rough-housin'. When a guy puts up his dukes I'm there. Onct down in Sonora I slammed a fellow so hard he woke up among strangers. Fact. I don't make claims, but up at Carbondale they say I'm some rip-snorter when I get goin' good. I'm quiet. I don't go around with a chip on my shoulder. It's the quiet boys you want to look out for. Am I right?"

Crawford gave a little snort of laughter and covered it hastily with a cough.

"You know it," went on the quiet man who was a rip-snorter when he got going. "In regards to that, I'll say my observation is that when you meet a small man with a steady gray eye it don't do a bit of harm to spend a lot of time leavin' him alone. He may be good-natured, but he won't stand no devilin', take it from me."

The small man with the gray eye eased himself in the saddle and moistened his tongue for a fresh start. "But I'm not one o' these foolhardy idiots who have to have wooden suits made for 'em because they don't know when to stay mum. You cattlemen have lived a quiet life in the hills, but I've been right where the tough ones crowd for years. I'll tell you

117

there's a time to talk and a time to keep still, as the old sayin' is."

"Yes," agreed Crawford.

"Another thing. I got an instinct that tells me when folks are interested in what I say. I've seen talkers that went right on borin' people and never caught on. They'd talk yore arm off without gettin' wise to it that you'd had a-plenty. That kind of talker ain't fit for nothin' but to wrangle Mary's little lamb 'way off from every human bein'.'"

In front of the riders a group of cottonwoods lifted their branches at a sharp bend in the road. Just before they reached this turn a bridge crossed a dry irrigating lateral.

"After Harrigan had been shot I came to the ditch for some water, but she was dry as a whistle. Ever notice how things are that way? A fellow wants water; none there. It's rainin' rivers; the ditch is runnin' strong. There's a sermon for a preacher," said the prospector.

The cattleman nodded to Dave. "I noticed she was dry when I crossed higher up on my way out. But she was full up with water when I saw her after I had been up to Dick Grein's."

"Funny," commented Sanders. "Nobody would want water to irrigate at this season. Who turned the water in? And why?"

"Beats me," answered Crawford. "But it don't worry me any. I've got troubles of my own."

They reached the cottonwoods, and the oil prospector pointed out to them just where the stage had been when the bandits first appeared. He showed them the bushes from behind which the robbers had stepped, the place occupied by the passengers after they had been lined up, and the course taken by the hold-ups after the robbery.

The road ran up a long, slow incline to the Bend, which was the crest of the hill. Beyond it the wheel tracks went down again with a sharp dip. The stage had been stopped just beyond the crest, just at the beginning of the down grade.

"The coach must have just started to move downhill when the robbers jumped out from the bushes," suggested Dave.

"Sure enough. That's probably howcome Tim to make a mistake. He figured he could give the horses the whip and make a getaway. The hold-up saw that. He had to shoot to kill or lose the gold. Bein' as he was a cold-blooded killer he shot." There were pinpoints of light in Emerson Crawford's eyes. He knew now the kind of man they were hunting. He was an assassin of a deadly type, not a wild cowboy who had fired in excitement because his nerves had betrayed him.

"Yes. Tim knew what he was doing. He took a chance the hold-ups wouldn't shoot to kill. Most of 'em won't. That was his mistake. If he'd seen the face behind that mask he would have known better," said Dave.

Crawford quartered over the ground. "Just like I thought, Dave. Applegate and his posse have been here and stomped out any tracks the robbers left. No way of tellin' which of all these footprints belonged to them. Likely none of 'em. If I didn't know better I'd think some one had been givin' a dance here, the way the ground is cut up."

They made a wide circle to try to pick up the trail wanted, and again a still larger one. Both of these attempts failed.

"Looks to me like they flew away," the cattleman said at last. "Horses have got hoofs and hoofs make tracks. I see plenty of these, but I don't find any place where the animals waited while this thing was bein' pulled off."

"The sheriff's posse has milled over the whole ground so thoroughly we can't be sure. But there's a point in what you say. Maybe they left their horses farther up the hill and walked back to them," Dave hazarded.

"No-o, son. This job was planned careful. Now the hold-ups didn't know whether they'd have to make a quick getaway or not. They would have their horses handy, but out of sight."

"Why not in the dry ditch back of the cottonwoods?" asked Dave with a flash of light.

Crawford stared at him, but at last shook his head. "I reckon not. In the sand and clay there the hoofs would show too plain."

"What if the hold-ups knew the ditch was going to be filled before the pursuit got started?"

"You mean—?"

"I mean they might have arranged to have the water turned into the lateral to wipe out their tracks."

"I'll be dawged if you ain't on a warm trail, son," murmured Crawford. "And if they knew that, why wouldn't they ride either up or down the ditch and leave no tracks a-tall?"

"They would—for a way, anyhow. Up or down, which?"

"Down, so as to reach Malapi and get into the Gusher before word came of the hold-up," guessed Crawford.

"Up, because in the hills there's less chance of being seen," differed Dave. "Crooks like them can fix up an alibi when
119

they need one. They had to get away unseen, in a hurry, and to get rid of the gold soon in case they should be seen."

"You've rung the bell, son. Up it is. It's an instinct of an outlaw to make for the hills where he can hole up when in trouble."

The prospector had been out of the conversation long enough.

"Depends who did this," he said. "If they come from the town, they'd want to get back there in a hurry. If not, they'd steer clear of folks. Onct, when I was in Oklahoma, a nigger went into a house and shot a white man he claimed owed him money. He made his getaway, looked like, and the whole town hunted for him for fifty miles. They found him two days later in the cellar of the man he had killed."

"Well, you can go look in Tim Harrigan's cellar if you've a mind to. Dave and I are goin' up the ditch," said the old cattleman, smiling.

"I'll tag along, seein' as I've been drug in this far. All I'll say is that when we get to the bottom of this, we'll find it was done by fellows you'd never suspect. I know human nature. My guess is no drunken cowboy pulled this off. No, sir. I'd look higher for the men."

"How about Parson Brown and the school superintendent?" asked Crawford.

"You can laugh. All right. Wait and see. Somehow I don't make mistakes. I'm lucky that way. Use my judgment, I reckon. Anyhow, I always guess right on presidential elections and prize fights. You got to know men, in my line of business. I study 'em. Hardly ever peg 'em wrong. Fellow said to me one day, 'How's it come, Thomas, you most always call the turn?' I give him an answer in one word—psycho-ology."

The trailers scanned closely the edge of the irrigation ditch. Here, too, they failed to get results. There were tracks enough close to the lateral, but apparently none of them led down into the bed of it. The outlaws no doubt had carefully obliterated their tracks at this place in order to give no starting-point for the pursuit.

"I'll go up on the left-hand side, you take the right, Dave," said Crawford. "We've got to find where they left the ditch."

The prospector took the sandy bed of the dry canal as his path. He chose it for two reasons. There was less brush to obstruct his progress, and he could reach the ears of both his auditors better as he burbled his comments on affairs in general and the wisdom of Mr. Thomas in particular.

The ditch was climbing into the hills, zigzagging up draws in order to find the most even grade. The three men traveled slowly, for Sanders and Crawford had to read sign on every foot of the way.

"Chances are they didn't leave the ditch till they heard the water comin'," the cattleman said. "These fellows knew their business, and they were playin' safe."

Dave pulled up. He went down on his knees and studied the ground, then jumped down into the ditch and examined the bank.

"Here's where they got out," he announced.

Thomas pressed forward. With one outstretched hand the young man held him back.

"Just a minute. I want Mr. Crawford to see this before it's touched."

The old cattleman examined the side of the canal. The clay showed where a sharp hoof had reached for a footing, missed, and pawed down the bank. Higher up was the faint mark of a shoe on the loose rubble at the edge.

"Looks like," he assented.

Study of the ground above showed the trail of two horses striking off at a right angle from the ditch toward the mouth of a box cañon about a mile distant. The horses were both larger than broncos. One of them was shod. One of the front shoes, badly worn, was broken and part of it gone on the left side. The riders were taking no pains apparently to hide their course. No doubt they relied on the full ditch to blot out pursuit.

The trail led through the cañon, over a divide beyond, and down into a small grassy valley.

At the summit Crawford gave strict orders. "No talkin', Mr. Thomas. This is serious business now. We're in enemy country and have got to soft-foot it."

The foothills were bristling with chaparral. Behind any scrub oak or cedar, under cover of an aspen thicket or even of a clump of gray sage, an enemy with murder in his heart might be lurking. Here an ambush was much more likely than in the sun-scorched plain they had left.

The three men left the footpath where it dipped down into the park and followed the rim to the left, passing through a heavy growth of manzanita to a bare hill dotted with scrubby sage, at the other side of which was a small gulch of aspens straggling down into the valley. Back of these a log cabin squatted on the slope. One had to be almost upon it before it could be seen. Its back door looked down upon the entrance to a cañon. This was fenced across to make a corral.

The cattleman and the cowpuncher looked at each other without verbal comment. A message better not put into words flashed from one to the other. This looked like the haunt of rustlers. Here they could pursue their nefarious calling unmolested. Not once a year would anybody except one of themselves enter this valley, and if a stranger did so he would know better than to push his way into the cañon.

Horses were drowsing sleepily in the corral. Dave slid from the saddle and spoke to Crawford in a low voice.

"I'm going down to have a look at those horses," he said, unfastening his rope from the tientos.

The cattleman nodded. He drew from its case beneath his leg a rifle and held it across the pommel. It was not necessary for Sanders to ask, nor for him to promise, protection while the younger man was making his trip of inspection. Both were men who knew the frontier code and each other. At a time of action speech, beyond the curtest of monosyllables, was surplusage.

Dave walked and slid down the rubble of the steep hillside, clambered down a rough face of rock, and dropped into the corral. He wore a revolver, but he did not draw it. He did not want to give anybody in the house an excuse to shoot at him without warning.

His glance swept over the horses, searched the hoofs of each. It found one shod, a rangy roan gelding.

The cowpuncher's rope whined through the air and settled down upon the shoulders of the animal. The gelding went sun-fishing as a formal protest against the lariat, then surrendered tamely. Dave patted it gently, stroked the neck, and spoke softly reassuring words. He picked up one of the front feet and examined the shoe. This was badly worn, and on the left side part of it had broken off.

A man came to the back door of the cabin and stretched in a long and luxuriant yawn. Carelessly and casually his eyes wandered over the aspens and into the corral. For a moment he stood frozen, his arms still flung wide.

From the aspens came down Crawford's voice, cool and ironic. "Much obliged, Shorty. Leave 'em right up and save trouble."

The squat cowpuncher's eyes moved back to the aspens and found there the owner of the D Bar Lazy R. "Wha'dya want?" he growled sullenly.

"You—just now. Step right out from the house, Shorty. Tha's right. Anybody else in the house?"

"No."

"You'll be luckier if you tell the truth."

"I'm tellin' it."

"Hope so. Dave, step forward and get his six-shooter. Keep him between you and the house. If anything happens to you I'm goin' to kill him right now."

Shorty shivered, hardy villain though he was. There had been nobody in the house when he left it, but he had been expecting some one shortly. If his partner arrived and began shooting, he knew that Crawford would drop him in his tracks. His throat went dry as a lime kiln. He wanted to shout out to the man who might be inside not to shoot at any cost. But he was a game and loyal ruffian. He would not spoil his confederate's chance by betraying him. If he said nothing, the man might come, realize the situation, and slip away unobserved.

Sanders took the man's gun and ran his hand over his thick body to make sure he had no concealed weapon.

"I'm going to back away. You come after me, step by step, so close I could touch you with the gun," ordered Dave.

The man followed him as directed, his hands still in the air. His captor kept him in a line between him and the house door. Crawford rode down to join them. The man who claimed not to be foolhardy stayed up in the timber. This was no business of his. He did not want to be the target of any shots from the cabin.

The cattleman swung down from the saddle. "Sure we'll 'light and come in, Shorty. No, you first. I'm right at yore heels with this gun pokin' into yore ribs. Don't make any mistake. You'd never have time to explain it."

The cabin had only one room. The bunks were over at one side, the stove and table at the other. Two six-pane windows flanked the front door.

The room was empty, except for the three men now entering.

"You live here, Shorty?" asked Crawford curtly.

"Yes." The answer was sulky and reluctant.

"Alone?"

"Yes."

"Why?" snapped the cattleman.

Shorty's defiant eyes met his. "My business."

"Mine, too, I'll bet a dollar. If you're nestin' in these hills you cayn't have but one business."

"Prove it! Prove it!" retorted Shorty angrily.

"Some day—not now." Crawford turned to Sanders. "What about the horse you looked at, Dave?"

"Same one we've been trailing. The one with the broken shoe."

"That yore horse, Shorty?"

"Maybeso. Maybe not."

"You've been havin' company here lately," Crawford went on. "Who's yore guest?"

"*You* seem to be right now. You and yore friend the convict," sneered the short cowpuncher.

"Don't use that word again, Shorty," advised the ranchman in a voice gently ominous.

"Why not? True, ain't it? Doesn't deny it none, does he?"

"We'll not discuss that. Where were you yesterday?"

"Here, part o' the day. Where was you?" demanded Shorty impudently. "Seems to me I heard you was right busy."

"What part of the day? Begin at the beginnin' and tell us what you did. You may put yore hands down."

"Why, I got up in the mo'nin' and put on my pants an' my boots," jeered Shorty. "I don't recolleck whether I put on my hat or not. Maybe I did. I cooked breakfast and et it. I chawed tobacco. I cooked dinner and et it. Smoked and chawed some more. Cooked supper and et it. Went to bed."

"That all?"

"Why, no, I fed the critters and fixed up a busted stirrup."

"Who was with you?"

"I was plumb lonesome yesterday. This any business of yours, by the way, Em?"

"Think again, Shorty. Who was with you?"

The heavy-set cowpuncher helped himself to a chew of tobacco. "I told you onct I was alone. Ain't seen anybody but you for a week."

"Then how did you hear yesterday was my busy day?" Crawford thrust at him.

For a moment Shorty was taken aback. Before he could answer Dave spoke.

"Man coming up from the creek."

Crawford took crisp command. "Back in that corner, Shorty. Dave, you stand back, too. Cover him soon as he shows up."

Dave nodded.

124

CHAPTER XXV

MILLER TALKS

A man stood in the doorway, big, fat, swaggering. In his younger days his deep chest and broad shoulders had accompanied great strength. But fat had accumulated in layers. He was a mountain of sagging flesh. His breath came in wheezy puffs.

"Next time you get your own——"

The voice faltered, died away. The protuberant eyes, still cold and fishy, passed fearfully from one to another of those in the room. It was plain that the bottom had dropped out of his heart. One moment he had straddled the world a Colossus, the next he was collapsing like a punctured balloon.

"Goddlemighty!" he gasped. "Don't shoot! I—I give up."

He was carrying a bucket of water. It dropped from his nerveless fingers and spilt over the floor.

Like a bullet out of a gun Crawford shot a question at him. "Where have you hidden the money you got from the stage?"

The loose mouth of the convict opened. "Why, we—I—we—"

"Keep yore trap shut, you durn fool," ordered Shorty.

Crawford jabbed his rifle into the ribs of the rustler. "Yours, too, Shorty."

But the damage had been done. Miller's flabby will had been braced by a stronger one. He had been given time to recover from his dismay. He moistened his lips with his tongue and framed his lie.

"I was gonna say you must be mistaken, Mr. Crawford," he whined.

Shorty laughed hardily, spat tobacco juice at a knot in the floor, and spoke again. "Third degree stuff, eh? It won't buy you a thing, Crawford. Miller wasn't in that hold-up any more'n I—"

"Let Miller do his own talkin', Shorty. He don't need any lead from you."

Shorty looked hard at the cattleman with unflinching eyes. "Don't get on the peck, Em. You got no business coverin' me with that gun. I know you got reasons a-plenty for tryin' to bluff us into sayin' we held up the stage. But we don't bluff worth a cent. See?"

Crawford saw. He had failed to surprise a confession out of Miller by the narrowest of margins. If he had had time to get Shorty out of the room before the convict's appearance, the fellow would have come through. As it was, he had missed his opportunity.

A head followed by a round barrel body came in cautiously from the lean-to at the rear.

"Everything all right, Mr. Crawford? Thought I'd drap on down to see if you didn't need any help."

"None, thanks, Mr. Thomas," the cattleman answered dryly.

"Well, you never can tell." The prospector nodded genially to Shorty, then spoke again to the man with the rifle. "Found any clue to the hold-up yet?"

"We've found the men who did it," replied Crawford.

"Knew 'em all the time, I reckon," scoffed Shorty with a harsh laugh.

Dave drew his chief aside, still keeping a vigilant eye on the prisoners. "We've got to play our hand different. Shorty is game. He can't be bluffed. But Miller can. I found out years ago he squeals at physical pain. We'll start for home. After a while we'll give Shorty a chance to make a getaway. Then we'll turn the screws on Miller."

"All right, Dave. You run it. I'll back yore play," his friend said.

They disarmed Miller, made him saddle two of the horses in the corral, and took the back trail across the valley to the divide. It was here they gave Shorty his chance of escape. Miller was leading the way up the trail, with Crawford, Thomas, Shorty, and Dave in the order named. Dave rode forward to confer with the owner of the D Bar Lazy R. For three seconds his back was turned to the squat cowpuncher.

Shorty whirled his horse and flung it wildly down the precipitous slope. Sanders galloped after him, fired his revolver three times, and after a short chase gave up the pursuit. He rode back to the party on the summit.

Crawford glanced around at the heavy chaparral. "How about off here a bit, Dave?"

The younger man agreed. He turned to Miller. "We're going to hang you," he said quietly.

The pasty color of the fat man ebbed till his face seemed entirely bloodless. "My God! You wouldn't do that!" he moaned.

He clung feebly to the horn of his saddle as Sanders led the horse into the brush. He whimpered, snuffling an appeal for mercy repeated over and over. The party had not left the road a hundred yards behind when a man jogged past on his way into the valley. He did not see them, nor did they see him.

Underneath a rather scrubby cedar Dave drew up. He glanced it over critically. "Think it'll do?" he asked Crawford in a voice the prisoner could just hear.

"Yep. That big limb'll hold him," the old cattleman answered in the same low voice. "Better let him stay right on the horse, then we'll lead it out from under him."

Miller pleaded for his life abjectly. His blood had turned to water. "Honest, I didn't shoot Harrigan. Why, I'm that tender-hearted I wouldn't hurt a kitten. I—I—Oh, don't do that, for God's sake."

Thomas was almost as white as the outlaw. "You don't aim to—you wouldn't—"

Crawford's face was as cold and as hard as steel. "Why not? He's a murderer. He tried to gun Dave here when the boy didn't have a six-shooter. We'll jes' get rid of him now." He threw a rope over the convict's head and adjusted it to the folds of his fat throat.

The man under condemnation could hardly speak. His throat was dry as the desert dust below. "I—I done Mr. Sanders a meanness. I'm sorry. I was drunk."

"You lied about him and sent him to the penitentiary."

"I'll fix that. Lemme go an' I'll make that right."

"How will you make it right?" asked Crawford grimly, and the weight of his arm drew the rope so tight that Miller winced. "Can you give him back the years he's lost?"

"No, sir, no," the man whispered eagerly. "But I can tell how it was—that we fired first at him. Doble did that, an' then—accidental—I killed Doble whilst I was shootin' at Mr. Sanders."

Dave strode forward, his eyes like great live coals. "What? Say that again!" he cried.

"Yessir. I did it—accidental—when Doble run forward in front of me. Tha's right. I'm plumb sorry I didn't tell the cou't so when you was on trial, Mr. Sanders. I reckon I was scairt to."

"Will you tell this of yore own free will to the sheriff down at Malapi?" asked Crawford.

"I sure will. Yessir, Mr. Crawford." The man's terror had swept away all thought of anything but the present peril. His color was a seasick green. His great body trembled like a jelly shaken from a mould.

"It's too late now," cut in Dave savagely. "We came up about this stage robbery. Unless he'll clear that up, I vote to finish the job."

"Maybe we'd better," agreed the cattleman. "I'll tie the rope to the trunk of the tree and you lead the horse from under him, Dave."

Miller broke down. He groveled. "I'll tell. I'll tell all I know. Dug Doble and Shorty held up the stage. I don' know who killed the driver. They didn't say when they come back."

"You let the water into the ditch," suggested Crawford.

"Yessir. I did that. They was shelterin' me and of course I had to do like they said."

"When did you escape?"

"On the way back to the penitentiary. A fellow give the deputy sheriff a drink on the train. It was doped. We had that fixed. The keys to the handcuffs was in the deputy's pocket. When he went to sleep we unlocked the cuffs and I got off at the next depot. Horses was waitin' there for us."

"Who do you mean by us? Who was with you?"

"I don' know who he was. Fellow said Brad Steelman sent him to fix things up for me."

Thomas borrowed the field-glasses of Crawford. Presently he lowered them. "Two fellows comin' hell-for-leather across the valley," he said in a voice that expressed his fears.

The cattleman took the glasses and looked. "Shorty's found a friend. Dug Doble likely. They're carryin' rifles. We'll have trouble. They'll see we stopped at the haid of the pass," he said quietly.

Much shaken already, the oil prospector collapsed at the prospect before him. He was a man of peace and always had been, in spite of the valiant promise of his tongue.

"None of my funeral," he said, his lips white. "I'm hittin' the trail for Malapi right now."

He wheeled his horse and jumped it to a gallop. The roan plunged through the chaparral and soon was out of sight.

"We'll fix Mr. Miller so he won't make us any trouble during the rookus," Crawford told Dave.

He threw the coiled rope over the heaviest branch of the cedar, drew it tight, and fastened it to the trunk of the tree.

"Now you'll stay hitched," he went on, speaking to their prisoner. "And you'd better hold that horse mighty steady, because if he jumps from under you it'll be good-bye for one scalawag."

"If you'd let me down I'd do like you told me, Mr. Crawford," pleaded Miller. "It's right oncomfortable here."

"Keep still. Don't say a word. Yore friends are gettin' close. Let a chirp outa you, and you'll never have time to be sorry," warned the cattleman.

The two men tied their horses behind some heavy mesquite and chose their own cover. Here they crouched down and waited.

They could hear the horses of the outlaws climbing the hill out of the valley to the pass. Then, down in the cañon, they caught a glimpse of Thomas in wild flight. The bandits stopped at the divide.

"They'll be headin' this way in a minute," Crawford whispered.

His companion nodded agreement.

They were wrong. There came the sound of a whoop, a sudden clatter of hoofs, the diminishing beat of horses' feet.

"They've seen Thomas, and they're after him on the jump," suggested Dave.

His friend's eyes crinkled to a smile. "Sure enough. They figure he's the tail end of our party. Well, I'll bet Thomas gives 'em a good run for their money. He's right careless sometimes, but he's no foolhardy idiot and he don't aim to argue with birds like these even though he's a rip-snorter when he gets goin' good and won't stand any devilin'."

"He'll talk them to death if they catch him," Dave answered.

"Back to business. What's our next move, son?"

"Some more conversation with Miller. Probably he can tell us where the gold is hidden."

"Whoopee! I'll bet he can. You do the talkin'. I've a notion he's more scared of you."

The fat convict tried to make a stand against them. He pleaded ignorance. "I don' know where they hid the stuff. They didn't tell me."

"Sounds reasonable, and you in with them on the deal," said Sanders. "Well, you're in hard luck. We don't give two hoots for you, anyhow, but we decided to take you in to town with us if you came through clean. If not——" He shrugged his shoulders and glanced up at the branch above.

Miller swallowed a lump in his throat. "You wouldn't treat me thataway, Mr. Sanders. I'm gittin' to be an old man now. I done wrong, but I'm sure right sorry," he whimpered.

The eyes of the man who had spent years in prison at Cañon City were hard as jade. The fat man read a day of judgment in his stern and somber face.

"I'll tell!" The crook broke down, clammy beads of perspiration all over his pallid face. "I'll tell you right where it's at. In the lean-to of the shack. Southwest corner. Buried in a gunnysack."

They rode back across the valley to the cabin. Miller pointed out the spot where the stolen treasure was cached. With an old axe as a spade Dave dug away the dirt till he came to a bit of sacking. Crawford scooped out the loose earth with his gauntlet and dragged out a gunnysack. Inside it were a number of canvas bags showing the broken wax seals of the express company. These contained gold pieces apparently fresh from the mint.

A hurried sum in arithmetic showed that approximately all the gold taken from the stage must be here. Dave packed it on the back of his saddle while Crawford penciled a note to leave in the cache in place of the money.

The note said:

This is no safe place to leave seventeen thousand dollars, Dug. I'm taking it to town to put in the bank. If you want to make inquiries about it, come in and we'll talk it over, you and me *and Applegate.*

EMERSON CRAWFORD

Five minutes later the three men were once more riding rapidly across the valley toward the summit of the divide. The loop of Crawford's lariat still encircled the gross neck of the convict.

CHAPTER XXVI

DAVE ACCEPTS AN INVITATION

Crawford and Dave, with their prisoner, lay out in the chaparral for an hour, then made their way back to Malapi by a wide circuit. They did not want to meet Shorty and Doble, for that would result in a pitched battle. They preferred rather to make a report to the sheriff and let him attempt the arrest of the bandits.

Reluctantly, under the pressure of much prodding, Miller repeated his story to Sheriff Applegate. Under the circumstances he was not sorry that he was to be returned to the penitentiary, for he recognized that his life at large would not be safe so long as Shorty and Doble were ranging the hills. Both of them were "bad men," in the usual Western acceptance of the term, and an accomplice who betrayed them would meet short shrift at their hands.

The sheriff gave Crawford a receipt for the gold after they had counted it and found none missing.

The old cattleman rose from the table and reached for his hat.

"Come on, son," he said to Dave. "I'll say we've done a good day's work. Both of us were under a cloud. Now we're clear. We're goin' up to the house to have some supper. Applegate, you'll get both of the confessions of Miller fixed up, won't you? I'll want the one about George Doble's death to take with me to the Governor of Colorado. I'm takin' the train to-morrow."

"I'll have the district attorney fix up the papers," the sheriff promised.

Emerson Crawford hooked an arm under the elbow of Sanders and left the office.

"I'm wonderin' about one thing, boy," he said. "Did Miller kill George Doble accidentally or on purpose?"

"I'm wondering about that myself. You remember that Denver bartender said they had been quarreling a good deal. They were having a row at the very time when I met them at the gate of the corral. It's a ten-to-one shot that Miller took the chance to plug Doble and make me pay for it."

"Looks likely, but we'll never know. Son, you've had a rotten deal handed you."

The younger man's eyes were hard as steel. He clamped his jaw tight, but he made no comment.

"Nobody can give you back the years of yore life you've lost," the cattleman went on. "But we'll get yore record straightened out, anyhow, so that won't stand against you. I know one li'l' girl will be tickled to hear the news. Joy always has stuck out that you were treated shameful."

"I reckon I'll not go up to your house to-night," Dave said in a carefully modulated voice. "I'm dirty and unshaven, and anyhow I'd rather not go to-night."

Crawford refused to accept this excuse. "No, sir. You're comin' with me, by gum! I got soap and water and a razor up at the house, if that's what's troublin' you. We've had a big day and I'm goin' to celebrate by talkin' it all over again. Dad gum my hide, think of it, you solemn-faced old owl! This time last night I was 'most a pauper and you sure were. Both of us were under the charge of havin' killed a man each. To-night we're rich as that fellow Crocus; anyhow I am, an' you're haided that way. And both of us have cleared our names to boot. Ain't you got any red blood in that big body of yore's?"

"I'll drop in to the Delmonico and get a bite, then ride out to the Jackpot."

"You will not!" protested the cattleman. "Looky here, Dave. It's a showdown. Have you got anything against me?"

Dave met him eye to eye. "Not a thing, Mr. Crawford. No man ever had a better friend."

"Anything against Joyce?"

"No, sir."

"Don't hate my boy Keith, do you?"

"How could I?"

"Then what in hell ails you? You're not parlor-shy, are you? Say the word, and we'll eat in the kitchen," grinned Crawford.

"I'm not a society man," said Sanders lamely.

He could not explain that the shadow of the prison walls

132

was a barrier he could not cross; that they rose to bar him from all the joy and happiness of young life.

"Who in Mexico's talkin' about society? I said come up and eat supper with me and Joy and Keith. If you don't come, I'm goin' to be good and sore. I'll not stand for it, you darned old killjoy."

"I'll go," answered the invited man.

He went, not because he wanted to go, but because he could not escape without being an ungracious boor.

Joyce flew to meet her father, eyes eager, hands swift to caress his rough face and wrinkled coat. She bubbled with joy at his return, and when he told her that his news was of the best the long lashes of the brown eyes misted with tears. The young man in the background was struck anew by the matronly tenderness of her relation to her father. She hovered about him as a mother does about her son returned from the wars.

"I've brought company for supper, honey," Emerson told her.

She gave Dave her hand, flushed and smiling. "I've been so worried," she explained. "It's fine to know the news is good. I'll want to hear it all."

"We've got the stolen money back, Joy," exploded her father. "We know who took it—Dug Doble and that cowboy Shorty and Miller."

"But I thought Miller—"

"He escaped. We caught him and brought him back to town with us." Crawford seized the girl by the shoulders. He was as keen as a boy to share his pleasure. "And Joy—better news yet. Miller confessed he killed George Doble. Dave didn't do it at all."

Joyce came to the young man impulsively, hand outstretched. She was glowing with delight, eyes kind and warm and glad. "That's the best yet. Oh, Mr. Sanders, isn't it good?"

His impassive face gave no betrayal of any happiness he might feel in his vindication. Indeed, something almost sardonic in its expression chilled her enthusiasm. More than the passing of years separated them from the days when he had shyly but gayly wiped dishes for her in the kitchen, when he had worshiped her with a boy's uncritical adoration.

Sanders knew it better than she, and cursed the habit of repression that had become a part of him in his prison days. He wanted to give her happy smile for smile. But he could not do it. All that was young and ardent and eager in him was dead.

He could not let himself go. Even when emotions flooded his heart, no evidence of it reached his chill eyes and set face.

After he had come back from shaving, he watched her flit about the room while she set the table. She was the competent young mistress of the house. With grave young authority she moved, slenderly graceful. He knew her mind was with the cook in the kitchen, but she found time to order Keith crisply to wash his face and hands, time to gather flowers for the center of the table from the front yard and to keep up a running fire of talk with him and her father. More of the woman than in the days when he had known her, perhaps less of the carefree maiden, she was essentially unchanged, was what he might confidently have expected her to be. Emerson Crawford was the same bluff, hearty Westerner, a friend to tie to in sunshine and in storm. Even little Keith, just escaping from his baby ways, had the same tricks and mannerisms. Nothing was different except himself. He had become arid and hard and bitter, he told himself regretfully.

Keith was his slave, a faithful admirer whose eyes fed upon his hero steadily. He had heard the story of this young man's deeds discussed until Dave had come to take on almost mythical proportions.

He asked a question in an awed voice. "How did you get this Miller to confess?"

The guest exchanged a glance with the host. "We had a talk with him."

"Did you—?"

"Oh, no! We just asked him if he didn't want to tell us all about it, and it seems he did."

"Maybe you touched his better feelin's," suggested Keith, with memories of an hour in Sunday School when his teacher had made a vain appeal to his.

His father laughed. "Maybe we did. I noticed he was near blubberin'. I expect it's 'Adios, Señor Miller.' He's got two years more to serve, and after that he'll have another nice long term to serve for robbin' the stage. All I wish is we'd done the job more thorough and sent some friends of his along with him. Well, that's up to Applegate."

"I'm glad it is," said Joyce emphatically.

"Any news to-day from Jackpot Number Three?" asked the president of that company.

"Bob Hart sent in to get some supplies and had a note left for me at the post-office," Miss Joyce mentioned, a trifle annoyed at herself because a blush insisted on flowing into her cheeks. "He says it's the biggest thing he ever saw, but it's going to be awf'ly hard to control. Where *is* that note? I must have put it somewhere."

Emerson's eyes flickered mischief. "Oh, well, never mind about the note. That's private property, I reckon."

"I'm sure if I can find it—"

"I'll bet my boots you cayn't, though," he teased.

"Dad! What will Mr. Sanders think? You know that's nonsense. Bob wrote because I asked him to let me know."

"Sure. Why wouldn't the secretary and field superintendent of the Jackpot Company keep the daughter of the president informed? I'll have it read into the minutes of our next board meetin' that it's in his duties to keep you posted."

"Oh, well, if you want to talk foolishness," she pouted.

"There's somethin' else I'm goin' to have put into the minutes of the next meetin', Dave," Crawford went on. "And that's yore election as treasurer of the company. I want officers around me that I can trust, son."

"I don't know anything about finance or about bookkeeping," Dave said.

"You'll learn. We'll have a bookkeeper, of course. I want some one for treasurer that's level-haided and knows how to make a quick turn when he has to, some one that uses the gray stuff in his cocoanut. We'll fix a salary when we get goin'. You and Bob are goin' to have the active management of this concern. Cattle's my line, an' I aim to stick to it. Him and you can talk it over and fix yore duties so's they won't conflict. Burns, of course, will run the actual drillin'. He's an A1 man. Don't let him go."

Dave was profoundly touched. No man could be kinder to his own son, could show more confidence in him, than Emerson Crawford was to one who had no claims upon him.

He murmured a dry "Thank you"; then, feeling this to be inadequate, added, "I'll try to see you don't regret this."

The cattleman was a shrewd judge of men. His action now was not based solely upon humanitarian motives. Here was a keen man, quick-witted, steady, and wholly to be trusted, one certain to push himself to the front. It was good business to make it worth his while to stick to Crawford's enterprises. He said as much to Dave bluntly.

"And you ain't in for any easy time either," he added. "We've got oil. We're flooded with it, so I hear. Severe-al thousand dollars' worth a day is runnin' off and seepin' into the desert. Bob Hart and Jed Burns have got the job of puttin' the lid on the pot, but when they do that you've got a bigger job. Looks bigger to me, anyhow. You've got to get rid of that oil—find a market for it, sell it, ship it away to make room for more. Get busy, son." Crawford waved his hand after the manner of one who has shifted a responsibility and does not expect to worry about it. "Moreover an' likewise, we're shy of money to keep operatin' until we can sell the stuff. You'll have to raise scads of mazuma, son. In this oil game dollars sure have got wings. No matter how tight yore pockets are buttoned, they fly right out."

"I doubt whether you've chosen the right man," the ex-cowpuncher said, smiling faintly. "The most I ever borrowed in my life was twenty-five dollars."

"You borrow twenty-five thousand the same way, only it's easier if the luck's breakin' right," the cattleman assured him cheerfully. "The easiest thing in the world to get hold of is money—when you've already got lots of it."

"The trouble is we haven't."

"Well, you'll have to learn to look like you knew where it grew on bushes," Emerson told him, grinning.

"I can see you've chosen me for a nice lazy job."

"Anything but that, son. You don't want to make any mistake about this thing. Brad Steelman's goin' to fight like a son-of-a-gun. He'll strike at our credit and at our market and at our means of transportation. He'll fight twenty-four hours of the day, and he's the slickest, crookedest gray wolf that ever skulked over the range."

The foreman of the D Bar Lazy R came in after supper for a conference with his boss. He and Crawford got their heads together in the sitting-room and the young people gravitated out to the porch. Joyce pressed Dave into service to help her water the roses, and Keith hung around in order to be near Dave. Occasionally he asked questions irrelevant to the conversation. These were embarrassing or not as it happened.

Joyce delivered a little lecture on the culture of roses, not because she considered herself an authority, but because her guest's conversation was mostly of the monosyllabic order. He was not awkward or self-conscious; rather a man given to silence.

"Say, Mr. Sanders, how does it feel to be wounded?" Keith blurted out.

"You mustn't ask personal questions, Keith," his sister told him.

"Oh! Well, I already ast this one?" the boy suggested ingenuously.

"Don't know, Keith," answered the young man. "I never was really wounded. If you mean this scratch in the shoulder, I hardly felt it at all till afterward."

"Golly! I'll bet I wouldn't tackle a feller shootin' at me the way that Miller was at you," the youngster commented in naïve admiration.

"Bedtime for li'l' boys, Keith," his sister reminded him.

"Oh, lemme stay up a while longer," he begged.

Joyce was firm. She had schooled her impulses to resist the little fellow's blandishments, but Dave noticed that she was affectionate even in her refusal.

"I'll come up and say good-night after a while, Keithie," she promised as she kissed him.

To the gaunt-faced man watching them she was the symbol of all most to be desired in woman. She embodied youth, health, charm. She was life's springtime, its promise of fulfillment; yet already an immaculate Madonna in the beauty of her generous soul. He was young enough in his knowledge of her sex to be unaware that nature often gives soft trout-pool eyes of tenderness to coquettes and wonderful hair with the lights and shadows of an autumn-painted valley to giggling fools. Joyce was neither coquette nor fool. She was essential woman in the making, with all the faults and fine brave impulses of her years. Unconsciously, perhaps, she was showing her best side to her guest, as maidens have done to men since Eve first smiled on Adam.

Dave had closed his heart to love. It was to have no room in his life. To his morbid sensibilities the shadow of the prison walls still stretched between him and Joyce. It did not matter that he was innocent, that all his small world would soon know of his vindication. The fact stood. For years he had been shut away from men, a leprous thing labeled "Unclean!" He had dwelt in a place of furtive whisperings, of sinister sounds. His nostrils had inhaled the odor of musty clothes and steamed food. His fingers had touched moisture sweating through the walls, and in his small dark cell he had hunted graybacks. The hopeless squalor of it at times had driven him almost mad. As he saw it now, his guilt was of minor importance. If he had not fired the shot that killed George Doble, that was merely a chance detail. What counted against him was that his soul was marked with the taint of the criminal

137

through association and habit of thought. He could reason with this feeling and temporarily destroy it. He could drag it into the light and laugh it away. But subconsciously it persisted as a horror from which he could not escape. A man cannot touch pitch, even against his own will, and not be defiled.

"You're Keith's hero, you know," the girl told Dave, her face bubbling to unexpected mirth. "He tries to walk and talk like you. He asks the queerest questions. To-day I caught him diving at a pillow on the bed. He was making-believe to be you when you were shot."

Her nearness in the soft, shadowy night shook his self-control. The music of her voice with its drawling intonations played on his heartstrings.

"Think I'll go now," he said abruptly.

"You must come again," she told him. "Keith wants you to teach him how to rope. You won't mind, will you?"

The long lashes lifted innocently from the soft deep eyes, which rested in his for a moment and set clamoring a disturbance in his blood.

"I'll be right busy," he said awkwardly, bluntly.

She drew back within herself. "I'd forgotten how busy you are, Mr. Sanders. Of course we mustn't impose on you," she said, cold and stiff as only offended youth can be.

Striding into the night, Dave cursed the fate that had made him what he was. He had hurt her boorishly by his curt refusal of her friendship. Yet the heart inside him was a wild river of love.

CHAPTER XXVII

AT THE JACKPOT

The day lasted twenty-four hours in Malapi. As Sanders walked along Junipero Street, on his way to the downtown corral from Crawford's house, saloons and gambling-houses advertised their attractions candidly and noisily. They seemed bursting with raw and vehement life. The strains of fiddles and the sound of shuffling feet were pierced occasionally by the whoop of a drunken reveler. Once there rang out the high notes of a woman's hysterical laughter. Cowponies and packed burros drooped listlessly at the hitching-rack. Even loaded wagons were waiting to take the road as soon as the drivers could tear themselves away from the attractions of keno and a last drink.

Junipero Street was not the usual crooked lane that serves as the main thoroughfare for business in a mining town. For Malapi had been a cowtown before the discovery of oil. It lay on the wide prairie and not in a gulch. The street was broad and dusty, flanked by false-front stores, flat-roofed adobes, and corrugated iron buildings imported hastily since the first boom.

At the Stag Horn corral Dave hired a horse and saddled for a night ride. On his way to the Jackpot he passed a dozen outfits of food, tools, timbers, and machinery to the oil camp. Out of the night a mule skinner shouted a profane and drunken greeting to him. A Mexican with a burro train gave him a low-voiced "Buenos noches, señor."

A fine mist of oil began to spray him when he was still a mile away from the well. It grew denser as he came nearer. He found Bob Hart, in oilskins and rubber boots, bossing a gang of scrapers, giving directions to a second one building a dam across a draw, and supervising a third group engaged in siphoning crude oil from one sump to another. From head to foot Hart and his assistants were wet to the skin with the black crude oil.

" 'Lo, Dave! One sure-enough little spouter!" Bob shouted cheerfully. "Number Three's sure a-hittin' her up. She's no cougher—stays right steady on the job. Bet I've wallowed in a million barrels of the stuff since mo'nin'." He waded through a viscid pool to Dave and asked a question in a low voice. "What's the good word?"

"We had a little luck," admitted Sanders, then plumped out his budget of news. "Got the express money back, captured one of the robbers, forced a confession out of him, and left him with the sheriff."

Bob did an Indian war dance in hip boots. "You're the darndest go-getter ever I did see. Tell it to me, you ornery ol' scalawag."

His friend told the story of the day so far as it related to the robbery.

"I could 'a' told you Miller would weaken when you had the rope round his soft neck. Shorty would 'a' gone through and told you-all where to get off at."

"Yes. Miller's yellow. He didn't quit with the robbery, Bob. Must have been scared bad, I reckon. He admitted that he killed George Doble—by accident, he claimed. Says Doble ran in front of him while he was shooting at me."

"Have you got that down on paper?" demanded Hart.

"Yes."

Bob caught his friend's hand. "I reckon the long lane has turned for you, old socks. I can't tell you how damn glad I am. Doble needed killin', but I'd rather you hadn't done it."

The other man made no comment on this phase of the situation. "This brings Dug Doble out into the open at last. He'll come pretty near going to the pen for this."

"I can't see Applegate arrestin' him. He'll fight, Dug will. My notion is he'll take to the hills and throw off all pretense. If he does he'll be the worst killer ever was known in this part of the country. You an' Crawford want to look out for him, Dave."

"Crawford says he wants me to be treasurer of the company, Bob. You and I are to manage it, he says, with Burns doing the drilling."

"Tha's great. He told me he was gonna ask you. Betcha we make the ol' Jackpot hum."

"D' you ever hear of a man land poor, Bob?"

"Sure have."

"Well, right now we're oil poor. According to what the old man says there's no cash in the treasury and we've got bills that have to be paid. You know that ten thousand he paid in to the bank to satisfy the note. He borrowed it from a friend who took it out of a trust fund to loan it to him. He didn't tell me who the man is, but he said his friend would get into trouble a-plenty if it's found out before he replaces the money. Then we've got to keep our labor bills paid right up. Some of the other accounts can wait."

"Can't we borrow money on this gusher?"

"We'll have to do that. Trouble is that oil isn't a marketable asset until it reaches a refinery. We can sell stock, of course, but we don't want to do much of that unless we're forced to it. Our play is to keep control and not let any other interest in to oust us. It's going to take some scratching."

140

"Looks like," agreed Bob. "Any use tryin' the bank here?"

"I'll try it, but we'll not accept any call loan. They say Steelman owns the bank. He won't let us have money unless there's some nigger in the woodpile. I'll probably have to try Denver."

"That'll take time."

"Yes. And time's one thing we haven't got any too much of. Whoever underwrites this for us will send an expert back with me and will wait for his report before making a loan. We'll have to talk it over with Crawford and find out how much treasury stock we'll have to sell locally to keep the business going till I make a raise."

"You and the old man decide that, Dave. I can't get away from here till we get Number Three roped and muzzled. I'll vote for whatever you two say."

An hour later Dave rode back to town.

CHAPTER XXVIII

DAVE MEETS A FINANCIER

On more careful consideration Crawford and Sanders decided against trying to float the Jackpot with local money except by the sale of enough stock to keep going until the company's affairs could be put on a substantial basis. To apply to the Malapi bank for a loan would be to expose their financial condition to Steelman, and it was certain that he would permit no accommodation except upon terms that would make it possible to wreck the company.

"I'm takin' the train for Denver to-morrow, Dave," the older man said. "You stay here for two-three days and sell enough stock to keep us off the rocks, then you hot-foot it for Denver too. By the time you get there I'll have it all fixed up with the Governor about a pardon."

Dave found no difficulty in disposing of a limited amount of stock in Malapi at a good price. This done, he took the stage for the junction and followed Crawford to Denver. An unobtrusive little man with large white teeth showing stood in line behind him at the ticket window. His destination also, it appeared, was the Colorado capital.

If Dave had been a believer in fairy tales he might have thought himself the hero of one. A few days earlier he had come to Malapi on this same train, in a day coach, poorly dressed, with no job and no prospects in life. He had been poor, discredited, a convict on parole. Now he wore good clothes, traveled in a Pullman, ate in the diner, was a man of consequence, and, at least on paper, was on the road to wealth. He would put up at the Albany instead of a cheap rooming-house, and he would meet on legitimate business some of the big financial men of the West. The thing was hardly thinkable, yet a turn of the wheel of fortune had done it for him in an hour.

The position in which Sanders found himself was possible only because Crawford was himself a financial babe in the woods. He had borrowed large sums of money often, but always from men who trusted him and held his word as better security than collateral. The cattleman was of the outdoors type to whom the letter of the law means little. A debt was a debt, and a piece of paper with his name on it did not make payment any more obligatory. If he had known more about capital and its methods of finding an outlet, he would never have sent so unsophisticated a man as Dave Sanders on such a mission.

For Dave, too, was a child in the business world. He knew nothing of the inside deals by which industrial enterprises are underwritten and corporations managed. It was, he supposed, sufficient for his purpose that the company for which he wanted backing was sure to pay large dividends when properly put on its feet.

But Dave had assets of value even for such a task. He had a single-track mind. He was determined even to obstinacy. He thought straight, and so directly that he could walk through subtleties without knowing they existed.

When he reached Denver he discovered that Crawford had followed the Governor to the western part of the State, where that official had gone to open a sectional fair. Sanders had no credentials except a letter of introduction to the manager of the stockyards.

142

"What can I do for you?" asked that gentleman. He was quite willing to exert himself moderately as a favor to Emerson Crawford, vice-president of the American Live Stock Association.

"I want to meet Horace Graham."

"I can give you a note of introduction to him. You'll probably have to get an appointment with him through his secretary. He's a tremendously busy man."

Dave's talk with the great man's secretary over the telephone was not satisfactory. Mr. Graham, he learned, had every moment full for the next two days, after which he would leave for a business trip to the East.

There were other wealthy men in Denver who might be induced to finance the Jackpot, but Dave intended to see Graham first. The big railroad builder was a fighter. He was hammering through, in spite of heavy opposition from transcontinental lines, a short cut across the Rocky Mountains from Denver. He was a pioneer, one who would take a chance on a good thing in the plunging, Western way. In his rugged, clean-cut character was much that appealed to the managers of the Jackpot.

Sanders called at the financier's office and sent in his card by the youthful Cerberus who kept watch at the gate. The card got no farther than the great man's private secretary.

After a wait of more than an hour Dave made overtures to the boy. A dollar passed from him to the youth and established a friendly relation.

"What's the best way to reach Mr. Graham, son? I've got important business that won't wait."

"Dunno. He's awful busy. You ain't got no appointment."

"Can you get a note to him? I've got a five-dollar bill for you if you can."

"I'll take a whirl at it. Jus' 'fore he goes to lunch."

Dave penciled a line on a card.

> If you are not too busy to make $100,000 to-day you had better see me.

He signed his name.

Ten minutes later the office boy caught Graham as he rose to leave for lunch. The big man read the note.

"What kind of looking fellow is he?" he asked the boy.

"Kinda solemn-lookin' guy, sir." The boy remembered the dollar received on account and the five dollars on the horizon.

"Big, straight-standin', honest fellow. From Arizona or Texas, mebbe. Looked good to me."

The financier frowned down at the note in doubt, twisting it in his fingers. A dozen times a week his privacy was assailed by some crazy inventor or crook promoter. He remembered that he had had a letter from some one about this man. Something of strength in the chirography of the note in his hand and something of simple directness in the wording decided him to give an interview.

"Show him in," he said abruptly, and while he waited in the office rated himself for his folly in wasting time.

Underneath bushy brows steel-gray eyes took Dave in shrewdly.

"Well, what is it?" snapped the millionaire.

"The new gusher in the Malapi pool," answered Sanders at once, and his gaze was as steady as that of the big state-builder.

"You represent the parties that own it?"

"Yes."

"And you want?"

"Financial backing to put it on its feet until we can market the product."

"Why don't you work through your local bank?"

"Another oil man, an enemy of our company, controls the Malapi bank."

Graham fired question after question at him, crisply, abruptly, and Sanders gave him back straight, short answers.

"Sit down," ordered the railroad builder, resuming his own seat. "Tell me the whole story of the company."

Dave told it, and in the telling he found it necessary to sketch the Crawford-Steelman feud. He brought himself into the narrative as little as possible, but the grizzled millionaire drew enough from him to set Graham's eye to sparkling.

"Come back to-morrow at noon," decided the great man. "I'll let you know my decision then."

The young man knew he was dismissed, but he left the office elated. Graham had been favorably impressed. He liked the proposition, believed in its legitimacy and its possibilities. Dave felt sure he would send an expert to Malapi with him to report on it as an investment. If so, he would almost certainly agree to put money in it.

A man with prominent white front teeth had followed Dave to the office of Horace Graham, had seen him enter, and later had seen him come out with a look on his face that

144

told of victory. The man tried to get admittance to the financier and failed. He went back to his hotel and wrote a short letter which he signed with a fictitious name. This he sent by special delivery to Graham. The letter was brief and to the point. It said:

> Don't do business with David Sanders without investigating his record. He is a horsethief and a convicted murderer. Some months ago he was paroled from the penitentiary at Cañon City and since then has been in several shooting scrapes. He was accused of robbing a stage and murdering the driver less than a week ago.

Graham read the letter and called in his private secretary. "McMurray, get Cañon City on the 'phone and find out if a man called David Sanders was released from the penitentiary there lately. If so, what was he in for? Describe the man to the warden: under twenty-five, tall, straight as an Indian, strongly built, looks at you level and steady, brown hair, steel-blue eyes. Do it now."

Before he left the office that afternoon Graham had before him a typewritten memorandum from his secretary covering the case of David Sanders.

CHAPTER XXIX

THREE IN CONSULTATION

The grizzled railroad builder fixed Sanders with an eye that had read into the soul of many a shirker and many a dishonest schemer.

"How long have you been with the Jackpot Company?"

"Not long. Only a few days."

"How much stock do you own?"

"Ten thousand shares."

"How did you get it?"

"It was voted me by the directors for saving Jackpot Number Three from an attack of Steelman's men."

Graham's gaze bored into the eyes of his caller. He waited just a moment to give his question full emphasis. "Mr. Sanders, what were you doing six months ago?"

"I was serving time in the penitentiary," came the immediate quiet retort.

"What for?"

"For manslaughter."

"You didn't tell me this yesterday."

"No. It has no bearing on the value of the proposition I submitted to you, and I thought it might prejudice you against it."

"Have you been in any trouble since you left prison?"

Dave hesitated. The blazer of railroad trails rapped out a sharp, explanatory question. "Any shooting scrapes?"

"A man shot at me in Malapi. I was unarmed."

"That all?"

"Another man fired at me out at the Jackpot. I was unarmed then."

"Were you accused of holding up a stage, robbing it, and killing the driver?"

"No. I was twenty miles away at the time of the holdup and had evidence to prove it."

"Then you were mentioned in connection with the robbery?"

"If so, only by my enemies. One of the robbers was captured and made a full confession. He showed where the stolen gold was cached and it was recovered."

The great man looked with chilly eyes at the young fellow standing in front of him. He had a sense of having been tricked and imposed upon.

"I have decided not to accept your proposition to co-operate with you in financing the Jackpot Company, Mr. Sanders." Horace Graham pressed an electric button and a clerk appeared. "Show this gentleman out, Hervey."

But Sanders stood his ground. Nobody could have guessed from his stolid imperturbability how much he was depressed at this unexpected failure.

"Do I understand that you are declining this loan because I am connected with it, Mr. Graham?"

146

"I do not give a reason, sir. The loan does not appeal to me," the railroad builder said with chill finality.

"It appealed to you yesterday," persisted Dave.

"But not to-day. Hervey, I will see Mr. Gates at once. Tell McMurray so."

Reluctantly Dave followed the clerk out of the room. He had been checkmated, but he did not know how. In some way Steelman had got to the financier with this story that had damned the project. The new treasurer of the Jackpot Company was much distressed. If his connection with the company was going to have this effect, he must resign at once.

He walked back to the hotel, and in the corridor of the Albany met a big bluff cattleman the memory of whose kindness leaped across the years to warm his heart.

"You don't remember me, Mr. West?"

The owner of the Fifty-Four Quarter Circle looked at the young man and gave a little whoop. "Damn my skin, if it ain't the boy who bluffed a whole railroad system into lettin' him reload stock for me!" He hooked an arm under Dave's and led him straight to the bar. "Where you been? What you doin'? Whyn't you come to me soon as you . . . got out of a job? What'll you have, boy?"

Dave named ginger ale. They lifted glasses.

"How?"

"How?"

"Now you tell me all about it," said West presently, leading the way to a lounge seat in the mezzanine gallery.

Sanders answered at first in monosyllables, but presently he found himself telling the story of his failure to enlist Horace Graham in the Jackpot property as a backer.

The cattleman began to rumple his hair, just as he had done years ago in moments of excitement.

"Wish I'd known, boy. I've been acquainted with Horace Graham ever since he ran a hardware store on Larimer Street, and that's 'most thirty years ago. I'd 'a' gone with you to see him. Maybe I can see him now."

"You can't change the facts, Mr. West. When he knew I was a convict he threw the whole thing overboard."

The voice of a page in the lobby rose in sing-song. "Mister Sa-a-anders. Mis-ter Sa-a-a-anders."

Dave stepped to the railing and called down. "I'm Mr. Sanders. Who wants me?"

A man near the desk waved a paper and shouted: "Hello,

Dave! News for you, son. I'll come up." The speaker was Crawford.

He shook hands with Dave and with West while he ejaculated his news in jets. "I got it, son. Got it right here. Came back with the Governor this mo'nin'. Called together Pardon Board. Here 'tis. Clean bill of health, son. Resolutions of regret for miscarriage of justice. Big story front page afternoon's papers."

Dave smiled sardonically. "You're just a few hours late, Mr. Crawford. Graham turned us down cold this morning because I'm a penitentiary bird."

"He did?" Crawford began to boil inside. "Well, he can go right plumb to Yuma. Anybody so small as that—"

"Hold yore hawsses, Em," said West, smiling. "Graham didn't know the facts. If you was a capitalist an' thinkin' of loanin' big money to a man you found out had been in prison for manslaughter and that he had since been accused of robbin' a stage an' killing the driver—"

"He was in a hurry," explained Dave. "Going East tomorrow. Some one must have got at him after I saw him. He'd made up his mind when I went back to-day."

"Well, Horace Graham ain't one of those who won't change his views for heaven, hell, and high water. All we've got to do is to get to him and make him see the light," said West.

"When are we going to do all that?" asked Sanders. "He's busy every minute of the time till he starts. He won't give us an appointment."

"He'll see me. We're old friends," predicted West confidently.

Crestfallen, he met the two officers of the Jackpot Company three hours later. "Couldn't get to him. Sent word out he was sorry, an' how was Mrs. West an' the children, but he was in conference an' couldn't break away."

Dave nodded. He had expected this and prepared for it. "I've found out he's going on the eight o'clock flyer. You going to be busy to-morrow, Mr. West?"

"No. I got business at the stockyards, but I can put it off."

"Then I'll get tickets for Omaha on the flyer. Graham will take his private car. We'll break in and put this up to him. He was friendly to our proposition before he got the wrong slant on it. If he's open-minded, as Mr. West says he is—"

Crawford slapped an open hand on his thigh. "Say, you get the *best* ideas, son. We'll do just that."

148

"I'll check up and make sure Graham's going on the flyer," said the young man. "If we fall down we'll lose only a day. Come back when we meet the night train. I reckon we won't have to get tickets clear through to Omaha."

"Fine and dandy," agreed West. "We'll sure see Graham if we have to bust the door of his car."

CHAPTER XXX

ON THE FLYER

West, his friends not in evidence, artfully waylaid Graham on his way to the private car.

"Hello, Henry B. Sorry I couldn't see you yesterday," the railroad builder told West as they shook hands. "You taking this train?"

"Yes, sir. Got business takes me East."

"Drop in to see me some time this morning. Say about noon. You'll have lunch with me."

"Suits me. About noon, then," agreed West.

The conspirators modified their plans to meet a new strategic situation. West was still of opinion that he had better use his card of entry to get his friends into the railroad builder's car, but he yielded to Dave's view that it would be wiser for the cattleman to pave the way at luncheon.

Graham's secretary ate lunch with the two old-timers and the conversation threatened to get away from West and hover about financial conditions in New York. The cattleman brought it by awkward main force to the subject he had in mind.

"Say, Horace, I wanta talk with you about a proposition that's on my chest," he broke out.

Graham helped himself to a lamb chop. "Sail in. Henry B. You've got me at your mercy."

149

At the first mention of the Jackpot gusher the financier raised a prohibitive hand. "I've disposed of that matter. No use reopening it."

But West stuck to his guns. "I ain't aimin' to try to change yore mind on a matter of business, Horace. If you'll tell me that you turned down the proposition because it didn't look to you like there was money in it, I'll curl right up and not say another word."

"It doesn't matter why I turned it down. I had my reasons."

"It matters if you're doin' an injustice to one of the finest young fellows I know," insisted the New Mexican stanchly.

"Meaning the convict?"

"Call him that if you've a mind to. The Governor pardoned him yesterday because another man confessed he did the killin' for which Dave was convicted. The boy was railroaded through on false evidence."

The railroad builder was a fair-minded man. He did not want to be unjust to any one. At the same time he was not one to jump easily from one view to another.

"I noticed something in the papers about a pardon, but I didn't know it was our young oil promoter. There are other rumors about him too. A stage robbery, for instance, and a murder with it."

"He and Em Crawford ran down the robbers and got the money back. One of the robbers confessed. Dave hadn't a thing to do with the hold-up. There's a bad gang down in that country. Crawford and Sanders have been fightin' 'em, so naturally they tell lies about 'em."

"Did you say this Sanders ran down one of the robbers?"

"Yes."

"He didn't tell me that," said Graham thoughtfully. "I liked the young fellow when I first saw him. He looks quiet and strong; a self-reliant fellow would be my guess."

"You bet he is." West laughed reminiscently. "Lemme tell you how I first met him." He told the story of how Dave had handled the stock shipment for him years before.

Horace Graham nodded shrewdly. "Exactly the way I had him sized up till I began investigating him. Well, let's hear the rest. What more do you know about him?"

The Albuquerque man told the other of Dave's conviction, of how he had educated himself in the penitentiary, of his return home and subsequent adventures there.

150

"There's a man back there in the Pullman knows him like he was his own son, a straight man, none better in this Western country," West concluded.

"Who is he?"

"Emerson Crawford of the D Bar Lazy R ranch."

"I've heard of him. He's in this Jackpot company too, isn't he?"

"He's president of it. If he says the company's right, then it's right."

"Bring him in to me."

West reported to his friends, a large smile on his wrinkled face. "I got him goin' south, boys. Come along, Em, it's up to you now."

The big financier took one comprehensive look at Emerson Crawford and did not need any letter of recommendation. A vigorous honesty spoke in the strong hand-grip, the genial smile, the level, steady eyes.

"Tell me about this young desperado you gentlemen are trying to saw off on me," Graham directed, meeting the smile with another and offering cigars to his guests.

Crawford told him. He began with the story of the time Sanders and Hart had saved him from the house of his enemy into which he had been betrayed. He related how the boy had pursued the men who stole his pinto and the reasoning which had led him to take it without process of law. He told the true story of the killing, of the young fellow's conviction, of his attempt to hold a job in Denver without concealing his past, and of his busy week since returning to Malapi.

"All I've got to say is that I hope my boy will grow up to be as good a man as Dave Sanders," the cattleman finished, and he turned over to Graham a copy of the findings of the Pardon Board, of the pardon, and of the newspapers containing an account of the affair with a review of the causes that had led to the miscarriage of justice.

"Now about your Jackpot Company. What do you figure as the daily output of the gusher?" asked Graham.

"Don't know. It's a whale of a well. Seems to have tapped a great lake of oil half a mile underground. My driller Burns figures it at from twenty to thirty thousand barrels a day. I cayn't even guess, because I know so blamed little about oil."

Graham looked out of the window at the rushing landscape and tapped on the table with his finger-tips absent-mindedly. Presently he announced a decision crisply.

151

"If you'll leave your papers here I'll look them over and let you know what I'll do. When I'm ready I'll send McMurray forward to you."

An hour later the secretary announced to the three men in the Pullman the decision of his chief.

"Mr. Graham has instructed me to tell you gentlemen he'll look into your proposition. I am wiring an oil expert in Denver to return with you to Malapi. If his report is favorable, Mr. Graham will co-operate with you in developing the field."

CHAPTER XXXI

TWO ON THE HILLTOPS

It was the morning after his return. Emerson Crawford helped himself to another fried egg from the platter and shook his knife at the bright-eyed girl opposite.

"I tell you, honey, the boy's a wonder," he insisted. "Knows what he wants and goes right after it. Don't waste any words. Don't beat around the bush. Don't let any one bluff him out. Graham says if I don't want him he'll give him a responsible job pronto."

The girl's trim head tilted at her father in a smile of sweet derision. She was pleased, but she did not intend to say so.

"I believe you're in love with Dave Sanders, Dad. It's about time for me to be jealous."

Crawford defended himself. "He's had a hard row to hoe, and he's comin' out fine. I aim to give him every chance in the world to make good. It's up to us to stand by him."

"If he'll let us." Joyce jumped up and ran round the table to him. They were alone, Keith having departed with a top to join his playmates. She sat on the arm of his chair, a straight, slim creature very much alive, and pressed her face of flushed loveliness against his head. "It won't be your fault, old duck,

152

if things don't go well with him. You're good—the best ever —a jim-dandy friend. But he's so—so—Oh, I don't know— stiff as a poker. Acts as if he doesn't want to be friends, as if we're all ready to turn against him. He makes me good and tired, Dad. Why can't he be—human?"

"Now, Joy, you got to remember—"

"—that he was in prison and had an awful time of it. Oh, yes, I remember all that. He won't let us forget it. It's just like he held us off all the time and insisted on us not forgetting it. I'd just like to shake the foolishness out of him." A rueful little laugh welled from her throat at the thought.

"He cayn't be gay as Bob Hart all at onct. Give him time."

"You're so partial to him you don't see when he's doing wrong. But I see it. Yesterday he hardly spoke when I met him. Ridiculous. It's all right for him to hold back and be kinda reserved with outsiders. But with his friends—you and Bob and old Buck Byington and me—he ought not to shut himself up in an ice cave. And I'm going to tell him so."

The cattleman's arm slid round her warm young body and drew her close. She was to him the dearest thing in the world, a never-failing, exquisite wonder and mystery. Sometimes even now he was amazed that this rare spirit had found the breath of life through him.

"You wanta remember you're a li'l' lady," he reproved. "You wouldn't want to do anything you'd be sorry for, honeybug."

"I'm not so sure about that," she flushed, amusement rippling her face. "Someone's got to blow up that young man like a Dutch uncle, and I think I'm elected. I'll try not to think about being a lady; then I can do my full duty, Dad. It'll be fun to see how he takes it."

"Now—now," he remonstrated.

"It's all right to be proud," she went on. "I wouldn't want to see him hold his head any lower. But there's no sense in being so offish that even his friends have to give him up. And that's what it'll come to if he acts the way he does. Folks will stand just so much. Then they give up trying."

"I reckon you're right about that, Joy."

"Of course I'm right. You have to meet your friends halfway."

"Well, if you talk to him don't hurt his feelin's."

There was a glint of mirth in her eyes, almost of friendly malice. "I'm going to worry him about *my* feelings, Dad. He'll not have time to think of his own."

153

Joyce found her chance next day. She met David Sanders in front of a drug-store. He would have passed with a bow if she had let him.

"What does the oil expert Mr. Graham sent think about our property?" she asked presently, greetings having been exchanged.

"He hasn't given out any official opinion yet, but he's impressed. The report will be favorable, I think."

"Isn't that good?"

"Couldn't be better," he admitted.

It was a warm day. Joyce glanced in at the soda fountain and said demurely, "My, but it's hot! Won't you come in and have an ice-cream soda on me?"

Dave flushed. "If you'll go as my guest," he said stiffly.

"How good of you to invite me!" she accepted, laughing, but with a tint of warmer color in her cheeks. Rhythmically she moved beside him to a little table in the corner of the drug-store. "I own stock in the Jackpot. You've got to give an accounting to me. Have you found a market yet?"

"The whole Southwest will be our market as soon as we can reach it."

"And when will that be?" she asked.

"I'm having some hauled to relieve the glut. The railroad will be operating inside of six weeks. We'll keep Number Three capped till then and go on drilling in other locations. Burns is spudding in a new well to-day."

The clerk took their order and departed. They were quite alone, not within hearing of anybody. Joyce took her fear by the throat and plunged in.

"You mad at me, Mr. Sanders?" she asked jauntily.

"You know I'm not."

"How do I know it?" she asked innocently. "You say as little to me as you can, and get away from me as quick as you can. Yesterday, for instance, you'd hardly say 'Good-morning.'"

"I didn't mean to be rude. I was busy." Dave felt acutely uncomfortable. "I'm sorry if I didn't seem sociable."

"So was Mr. Hart busy, but he had time to stop and say a pleasant word." The brown eyes challenged their vis-à-vis steadily.

The young man found nothing to say. He could not explain that he had not lingered because he was giving Bob a chance to see her alone, nor could he tell her that he felt it better for his peace of mind to keep away from her as much as possible.

154

"I'm not in the habit of inviting young men to invite me to take a soda, Mr. Sanders," she went on. "This is my first offense. I never did it before, and I never expect to again. . . . I do hope the new well will come in a good one." The last sentence was for the benefit of the clerk returning with the ice-cream.

"Looks good," said Dave, playing up. "Smut's showing, and you know that's a first-class sign."

"Bob said it was expected in to-day or to-morrow. . . . I asked you because I've something to say to you, something I think one of your friends ought to say, and—and I'm going to do it," she concluded in a voice modulated just to reach him.

The clerk had left the glasses and the check. He was back at the fountain polishing the counter.

Sanders waited in silence. He had learned to let the burden of conversation rest on his opponent, and he knew that Joyce just now was in that class.

She hesitated, uncertain of her opening. Then, "You're disappointing your friends, Mr. Sanders," she said lightly.

He did not know what an effort it took to keep her voice from quavering, her hand from trembling as it rested on the onyx top of the table.

"I'm sorry," he said a second time.

"Perhaps it's our fault. Perhaps we haven't been . . . friendly enough." The lifted eyes went straight into his.

He found an answer unexpectedly difficult. "No man ever had more generous friends," he said at last brusquely, his face set hard.

The girl guessed at the tense feeling back of his words.

"Let's walk," she replied, and he noticed that the eyes and mouth had softened to a tender smile. "I can't talk here, Dave."

They made a pretense of finishing their sodas, then walked out of the town into the golden autumn sunlight of the foothills. Neither of them spoke. She carried herself buoyantly, chin up, her face a flushed cameo of loveliness. As she took the uphill trail a small breath of wind wrapped the white skirt about her slender limbs. He found in her a new note, one of unaccustomed shyness.

The silence grew at last too significant. She was driven to break it.

"I suppose I'm foolish," she began haltingly. "But I had been expecting—all of us had—that when you came home from—from Denver—the first time, I mean—you would be the old Dave Sanders we all knew and liked. We wanted our friendship to—to help make up to you for what you must have suffered. We didn't think you'd hold us off like this."

His eyes narrowed. He looked away at the cedars on the hills painted in lustrous blues and greens and purples, and at the slopes below burnt to exquisite color lights by the fires of fall. But what he saw was a gray prison wall with armed men in the towers.

"If I could tell you!" He said it in a whisper, to himself, but she just caught the words.

"Won't you try?" she said, ever so gently.

He could not sully her innocence by telling of the furtive whisperings that had fouled the prison life, made of it an experience degrading and corrosive. He told her, instead, of the externals of that existence, of how he had risen, dressed, eaten, worked, exercised, and slept under orders. He described to her the cells, four by seven by seven, barred, built in tiers, faced by narrow iron balconies, each containing a stool, a chair, a shelf, a bank. In his effort to show her the chasm that separated him from her he did not spare himself at all. Dryly and in clean-cut strokes he showed her the sordidness of which he had been the victim and left her to judge for herself of its evil effect on his character.

When he had finished he knew that he had failed. She wept for pity and murmured, "You poor boy. . . . You poor boy!"

He tried again, and this time he drew the moral. "Don't you see, I'm a marked man—marked for life." He hesitated, then pushed on. "You're fine and clean and generous—what a good father and mother, and all this have made you." He swept his hand round in a wide gesture to include the sun and the hills and all the brave life of the open. "If I come too near you, don't you see I taint you? I'm a man who was shut up because—"

"Fiddlesticks! You're a man who has been done a wrong. You mustn't grow morbid over it. After all, you've been found innocent."

"That isn't what counts. I've been in the penitentiary. Nothing can wipe that out. The stain of it's on me and can't be washed away."

She turned on him with a little burst of feminine ferocity. "How dare you talk that way, Dave Sanders! I want to be proud of you. We all do. But how can we be if you give up like a quitter? Don't we all have to keep beginning our lives over and over again? Aren't we all forever getting into

156

trouble and getting out of it? A man is as good as he makes himself. It doesn't matter what outside thing has happened to him. Do you dare tell me that my dad wouldn't be worth loving if he'd been in prison forty times?"

The color crept into his face. "I'm not quitting. I'm going through. The point is whether I'm to ask my friends to carry my load for me."

"What are your friends for?" she demanded, and her eyes were like stars in a field of snow. "Don't you see it's an insult to assume they don't want to stand with you in your trouble? You've been warped. You're eaten up with vain pride." Joyce bit her lip to choke back a swelling in her throat. "The Dave we used to know wasn't like that. He was friendly and sweet. When folks were kind to him he was kind to them. He wasn't like—like an old poker." She fell back helplessly on the simile she had used with her father.

"I don't blame you for feeling that way," he said gently. "When I first came out I did think I'd play a lone hand. I was hard and bitter and defiant. But when I met you-all again—and found you were just like home folks—all of you so kind and good, far beyond any claims I had on you—why, Miss Joyce, my heart went out to my old friends with a rush. It sure did. Maybe I had to be stiff to keep from being mushy."

"Oh, if that's it!" Her eager face, flushed and tender, nodded approval.

"But you've got to look at this my way too," he urged. "I can't repay your father's kindness—yes, and yours too—by letting folks couple your name, even in friendship, with a man who—"

She turned on him, glowing with color. "Now that's absurd, Dave Sanders. I'm not a—a nice little china doll. I'm a flesh-and-blood girl. And I'm not a statue on a pedestal. I've got to live just like other people. The trouble with you is that you want to be generous, but you don't want to give other folks a chance to be. Let's stop this foolishness and be sure-enough friends—Dave."

He took her outstretched hand in his brown palm, smiling down at her. "All right. I know when I'm beaten."

She beamed. "That's the first honest-to-goodness smile I've seen on your face since you came back."

"I've got millions of 'em in my system," he promised. "I've been hoarding them up for years."

"Don't hoard them any more. Spend them," she urged.

"I'll take that prescription, Doctor Joyce." And he spent one as evidence of good faith.

The soft and shining oval of her face rippled with gladness as a mountain lake sparkles with sunshine in a light summer breeze. "I've found again that Dave boy I lost," she told him.

"You won't lose him again," he answered, pushing into the hinterland of his mind the reflection that a man cannot change the color of his thinking in an hour.

"We thought he'd gone away for good. I'm so glad he hasn't."

"No. He's been here all the time, but he's been obeying the orders of a man who told him he had no business to be alive."

He looked at her with deep, inscrutable eyes. As a boy he had been shy but impulsive. The fires of discipline had given him remarkable self-restraint. She could not tell he was finding in her face the quality to inspire in a painter a great picture, the expression of that brave young faith which made her a touchstone to find the gold in his soul.

Yet in his gravity was something that disturbed her blood. Was she fanning to flame banked fires better dormant?

She felt a compunction for what she had done. Maybe she had been unwomanly. It is a penalty impulsive people have to pay that later they must consider whether they have been bold and presumptuous. Her spirits began to droop when she should logically have been celebrating her success.

But Dave walked on mountain-tops tipped with mellow gold. He threw off the weight that had oppressed his spirits for years and was for the hour a boy again. She had exorcised the gloom in which he walked. He looked down on a magnificent flaming desert, and it was good. To-day was his. To-morrow was his. All the to-morrows of the world were in his hand. He refused to analyze the causes of his joy. It was enough that beside him moved with charming diffidence the woman of his dreams, that with her soft hands she had torn down the barrier between them.

"And now I don't know whether I've done right," she said ruefully. "Dad warned me I'd better be careful. But of course I always know best. I 'rush in.' "

"You've done me a million dollars' worth of good. I needed some good friend to tell me just what you have. Please don't regret it."

"Well, I won't." She added, in a hesitant murmur, "You won't—misunderstand?"

His look turned aside the long-lashed eyes and brought a faint flush of pink to her cheeks.

"No, I'll not do that," he said.

CHAPTER XXXII

DAVE BECOMES AN OFFICE MAN

From Graham came a wire a week after the return of the oil expert to Denver. It read:

> Report satisfactory. Can you come at once and arrange with me plan of organization?

Sanders was on the next train. He was still much needed at Malapi to look after getting supplies and machinery and to arrange for a wagon train of oil teams, but he dropped or delegated this work for the more important call that had just come.

His contact with Graham uncovered a new side of the state builder, one that was to impress him in all the big business men he met. They might be pleasant socially and bear him a friendly good-will, but when they met to arrange details of a financial plan they always wanted their pound of flesh. Graham drove a hard bargain with him. He tied the company fast by legal control of its affairs until his debt was satisfied. He exacted a bonus in the form of stock that fairly took the breath of the young man with whom he was negotiating. Dave fought him round by round and found the great man smooth and impervious as polished agate.

Yet Dave liked him. When they met at lunch, as they did more than once, the grizzled Westerner who had driven a line of steel across almost impassable mountain passes was simple and frank in talk. He had taken a fancy to this young fellow, and he let him know it. Perhaps he found something of his own engaging, dogged youth in the strong-jawed range-rider.

"Does a financier always hogtie a proposition before he backs it?" Dave asked him once with a sardonic gleam in his eye.

"Always."

"No matter how much he trusts the people he's doing business with?"

"He binds them hard and fast just the same. It's the only way to do. Give away as much money as you want to, but when you loan money look after your security like a hawk."

"Even when you're dealing with friends?"

"Especially when you're dealing with friends," corrected the older man. "Otherwise you're likely not to have your friends long."

"Don't believe I want to be a financier," decided Sanders.

"It takes the hot blood out of you," admitted Graham. "I'm not sure, if I had my life to live over again, knowing what I know now, that I wouldn't choose the outdoors like West and Crawford."

Sanders was very sure which choice he would like to make. He was at present embarked on the business of making money through oil, but some day he meant to go back to the serenity of a ranch. There were times when he left the conferences with Graham or his lieutenants sick at heart because of the uphill battle he must fight to protect his associates.

From Denver he went East to negotiate for some oil tanks and material with which to construct reservoirs. His trip was a flying one. He entrained for Malapi once more to look after the loose ends that had been accumulating locally in his absence. A road had to be built across the desert. Contracts must be let for hauling away the crude oil. A hundred details waited his attention.

He worked day and night. Often he slept only a few hours. He grew lean in body and curt of speech. Lines came into his face that had not been there before. But at his work apparently he was tireless as steel springs.

Meanwhile Brad Steelman moled to undermine the company. Dave's men finished building a bridge across a gulch late one day. It was blown up into kindling wood by dynamite that night. Wagons broke down unexpectedly. Shipments of supplies failed to arrive. Engines were mysteriously smashed.

The sabotage was skillful. Steelman's agents left no evidence that could be used against them. More than one of them, Hart and Sanders agreed, were spies who had found employment with the Jackpot. One or two men were discharged on suspicion, even though complete evidence against them was lacking.

The responsibility that had been thrust on Dave brought out in him unsuspected business capacity. During his prison days there had developed in him a quality of leadership. He had been more than once in charge of a road-building gang of convicts and had found that men naturally turned to him for guidance. But not until Crawford shifted to his shoulders the burdens of the Jackpot did he know that he had it in him to grapple with organization on a fairly large scale.

He worked without nerves, day in, day out, concentrating in a way that brought results. He never let himself get impatient with details. Thoroughness had long since become the habit of his life. To this he added a sane common sense.

Jackpot Number Four came in a good well, though not a phenomenal one like its predecessor. Number Five was already halfway down to the sands. Meanwhile the railroad crept nearer. Malapi was already talking of its big celebration when the first engine should come to town. Its council had voted to change the name of the place to Bonanza.

The tide was turning against Steelman. He was still a very rich man, but he seemed no longer to be a lucky one. He brought in a dry well. On another location the cable had pulled out of the socket and a forty-foot auger stem and bit lay at the bottom of a hole fifteen hundred feet deep. His best producer was beginning to cough a weak and intermittent flow even under steady pumping. And, to add to his troubles, a quiet little man had dropped into town to investigate one of his companies. He was a Government agent, and the rumor was that he was gathering evidence.

Sanders met Thomas on the street. He had not seen him since the prospector had made his wild ride for safety with the two outlaws hard on his heels.

"Glad you made it, Mr. Thomas," said Dave. "Good bit of strategy. When they reached the notch, Shorty and Doble never once looked to see if we were around. They lit out after you on the jump. Did they come close to getting you?"

"It looked like bullets would be flyin'. I won't say who would 'a' got who if they had," he said modestly. "But I wasn't lookin' for no trouble. I don't aim to be one of these here fire-eaters, but I'll fight like a wildcat when I got to."

The prospector looked defiantly at Sanders, bristling like a bantam which has been challenged.

"We certainly owe you something for the way you drew the outlaws off our trail," Dave said gravely.

"Say, have you heard how the Government is gettin' after Steelman? He's a wily bird, old Brad is, but he slipped up when he sent out his advertisin' for the Great Mogul. A photographer faked a gusher for him and they sent it out on the circulars."

Sanders nodded, without comment.

"Steelman can make 'em flow, on paper anyhow," Thomas chortled. "But he's sure in a kettle of hot water this time."

"Mr. Steelman is enterprising," Dave admitted dryly.

"Say, Mr. Sanders, have you heard what's become of Shorty and Doble?" the prospector asked, lapsing to ill-concealed anxiety. "I see the sheriff has got a handbill out offerin' a reward for their arrest and conviction. You don't reckon those fellows would bear me any grudge, do you?"

"No. But I wouldn't travel in the hills alone if I were you. If you happened to meet them they might make things unpleasant."

"They're both killers. I'm a peaceable citizen, as the fellow says. O' course if they crowd me to the wall—"

"They won't," Dave assured him.

He knew that the outlaws, if the chance ever came for them, would strike at higher game than Thomas. They would try to get either Crawford or Sanders himself. The treasurer of the Jackpot did not fool himself with any false promises of safety. The two men in the hills were desperate characters, game as any in the country, gun-fighters, and they owed both him and Crawford a debt they would spare no pains to settle in full. Some day there would come an hour of accounting.

CHAPTER XXXIII

ON THE DODGE

Up in the hills back of Bear Cañon two men were camping. They breakfasted on slow elk, coffee, and flour-and-water biscuits. When they had finished, they washed their tin dishes with sand in the running brook.

"Might's well be hittin' the trail," one growled.

The other nodded without speaking, rose lazily, and began to pack the camp outfit. Presently, when he had arranged the load to his satisfaction, he threw the diamond hitch and stood back to take a chew of tobacco while he surveyed his work. He was a squat, heavy-set man with a Chihuahua hat. Also he was a two-gun man. After a moment he circled an arrow-weed thicket and moved into the chaparral where his horse was hobbled.

The man who had spoken rose with one lithe twist of his big body. His eyes, hard and narrow, watched the shorter man disappear in the brush. Then he turned swiftly and strode toward the shoulder of the ridge.

In the heavy undergrowth of dry weeds and grass he stopped and tested the wind with a bandanna handkerchief. The breeze was steady and fairly strong. It blew down the cañon toward the foothills beyond.

The man stripped from a scrub oak a handful of leaves. They were very brittle and crumbled in his hand. A match flared out. His palm cupped it for a moment to steady the blaze before he touched it to the crisp foliage. Into a nest of twigs he thrust the small flame. The twigs, dry as powder from a four-months' drought, crackled like miniature fireworks. The grass caught, and a small line of fire ran quickly out.

The man rose. On his brown face was an evil smile, in his hard eyes something malevolent and sinister. The wind would do the rest.

He walked back toward the camp. At the shoulder crest he turned to look back. From out of the chaparral a thin column of pale gray smoke was rising.

His companion stamped out the remains of the breakfast fire and threw dirt on the ashes to make sure no live ember could escape in the wind. Then he swung to the saddle.

"Ready, Dug?" he asked.

The big man growled an assent and followed him over the summit into the valley beyond.

"Country needs a rain bad," the man in the Chihuahua hat commented. "Don't know as I recollect a dryer season."

The big hawk-nosed man by his side cackled in his throat with short, splenetic mirth. "It'll be some dryer before the rains," he prophesied.

They climbed out of the valley to the rim. The short man was bringing up the rear along the narrow trail-ribbon. He turned in the saddle to look back, a hand on his horse's rump. Perhaps he did this because of the power of suggestion. Several times Doble had already swung his head to scan with a searching gaze the other side of the valley.

Mackerel clouds were floating near the horizon in a sky of blue. Was that or was it not smoke just over the brow of the hill?

"Cayn't be our camp-fire," the squat man said aloud. "I smothered that proper."

"Them's clouds," pronounced Doble quickly. "Clouds an' some mist risin' from the gulch."

"I reckon," agreed the other, with no sure conviction. Doble must be right, of course. No fire had been in evidence when they left the camping-ground, and he was sure he had stamped out the one that cooked the biscuits. Yet that stringy gray film certainly looked like smoke. He hung in the wind, half of a mind to go back and make sure. Fire in the chaparral now might do untold damage.

Shorty looked at Doble. "If tha's fire, Dug—"

"It ain't. No chance," snapped the ex-foreman. "We'll travel if you don't feel called on to go back an' stomp out the mist, Shorty," he added with sarcasm.

The cowpuncher took the trail again. Like many men, he was not proof against a sneer. Dug was probably right, Shorty

164

decided, and he did not want to make a fool of himself. Doble would ride him with heavy jeers all day.

An our later they rested their horses on the divide. To the west lay Malapi and the plains. Eastward were the heaven-pricking peaks. A long, bright line zigzagged across the desert and reflected the sun rays. It was the bed of the new road already spiked with shining rails.

"I'm goin' to town," announced Doble.

Shorty looked at him in surprise. "Wanta see yore picture, I reckon. It's on a heap of telegraph poles, I been told," he said, grinning.

"To-day," went on the ex-foreman stubbornly.

"Big, raw-boned guy, hook nose, leather face, never took no prize as a lady's man, a wildcat in a roughhouse, an' sudden death on the draw," extemporized the rustler, presumably from his conception of the reward poster.

"I'll lie in the chaparral till night an' ride in after dark."

With the impulsiveness of his kind, Shorty fell in with the idea. He was hungry for the fleshpots of Malapi. If they dropped in late at night, stayed a few hours, and kept under cover, they could probably slip out of town undetected. The recklessness of his nature found an appeal in the danger.

"Damfidon't trail along, Dug."

"Yore say-so about that."

"Like to see my own picture on the poles. Sawed-off li'l' runt. Straight black hair. Some bowlegged. Wears two guns real low. Doncha monkey with him onless you're hell-a-mile with a six-shooter. One thousand dollars reward for arrest and conviction. Same for the big guy."

"Fellow that gets one o' them rewards will earn it," said Doble grimly.

"Goes double," agreed Shorty. "He'll earn it even if he don't live to spend it. Which he's liable not to."

They headed their horses to the west. As they drew down from the mountains they left the trail and took to the brush. They wound in and out among the mesquite and the cactus, bearing gradually to the north and into the foothills above the town. When they reached Frio Cañon they swung off into a timbered pocket debouching from it. Here they unsaddled and lay down to wait for night.

CHAPTER XXXIV

A PLEASANT EVENING

Brad Steelman sat hunched before a fire of piñon knots, head drooped low between his high, narrow shoulders. The restless black eyes in the dark hatchet face were sunk deeper now than in the old days. In them was beginning to come the hunted look of the gray wolf he resembled. His nerves were not what they had been, and even in his youth they were not of the best. He had a way of looking back furtively over his shoulder, as though some sinister shadow were creeping toward him out of the darkness.

Three taps on the window brought his head up with a jerk. His lax fingers crept to the butt of a Colt's revolver. He waited, listening.

The taps were repeated.

Steelman sidled to the door and opened it cautiously. A man pushed in and closed the door. He looked at the sheepman and he laughed shortly in an ugly, jeering way.

"Scared, Brad?"

The host moistened his lips. "What of, Dug?"

"Don't ask me," said the big man scornfully. "You always had about as much sand in yore craw as a rabbit."

"Did you come here to make trouble, Dug?"

"No, I came to collect a bill."

"So? Didn't know I owed you any money right now. How much is it?"

Steelman, as the leader of his gang, was used to levies upon his purse when his followers had gone broke. He judged that he would have to let Doble have about twenty-five dollars now.

"A thousand dollars."

166

Brad shot a quick, sidelong look at him. "Wha's wrong now, Dug?"

The ex-foreman of the D Bar Lazy R took his time to answer. He enjoyed the suspense under which his ally was held. "Why, I reckon nothin' a-tall. Only that this mo'nin' I put a match to about a coupla hundred thousand dollars belongin' to Crawford, Sanders, and Hart."

Eagerly Steelman clutched his arm. "You did it, then?"

"Didn't I say I'd do it?" snapped Doble irritably. "D'ya ever know me rue back on a bargain?"

"Never."

"Wha's more, you never will. I fired the chaparral above Bear Cañon. The wind was right. Inside of twenty-four hours the Jackpot locations will go up in smoke. Derricks, pumps, shacks, an' oil; the whole caboodle's doomed sure as I'm a foot high."

The face of the older man looked more wolfish than ever. He rubbed his hands together, washing one over the other so that each in turn was massaged. "Hell's bells! I'm sure glad to hear it. Fire got a good start, you say?"

"I tell you the whole country'll go up like powder."

If Steelman had not just reached Malapi from a visit to one of his sheep camps he would have known, what everybody else in town knew by this time, that the range for fifty miles was in danger and that hundreds of volunteers were out fighting the menace.

His eyes glistened. "I'll not wear mournin' none if it does just that."

"I'm tellin' you what it'll do," Doble insisted dogmatically.

"Shorty with you?"

"He was, an' he wasn't. I did it while he wasn't lookin'. He was saddlin' his horse in the brush. Don't make any breaks to him. Shorty's got a soft spot in him. Game enough, but with queer notions. Some time I'm liable to have to—" Doble left his sentence suspended in air, but Steelman, looking into his bleak eyes, knew what the man meant.

"What's wrong with him now, Dug?"

"Well, he's been wrong ever since I had to bump off Tim Harrigan. Talks about a fair break. As if I had a chance to let the old man get to a gun. No, I'm not so awful sure of Shorty."

"Better watch him. If you see him make any false moves—"

Doble watched him with a taunting, scornful eye. "What'll I do?"

The other man's gaze fell. "Why, you got to protect yoreself, Dug, ain't you?"

"How?"

The narrow shoulders lifted. For a moment the small black eyes met those of the big man.

"Whatever way seems best to you, Dug," murmured Steelman evasively.

Doble slapped his dusty hat against his thigh. He laughed, without mirth or geniality. "If you don't beat Old Nick, Brad. I wonder was you ever out an' out straightforward in yore life. Just once?"

"I don't reckon you sure enough feel that way, Dug," whined the older man ingratiatingly. "Far as that goes, I'm not making any claims that I love my enemies. But you can't say I throw off on my friends. You always know where I'm at."

"Sure I know," retorted Doble bluntly. "You're on the inside of a heap of rotten deals. So am I. But I admit it and you won't."

"Well, I don't look at it that way, but there's no use arguin'. What about that fire? Sure it got a good start?"

"I looked back from across the valley. It was travelin' good."

"If the wind don't change, it will sure do a lot of damage to the Jackpot. Liable to spoil some of Crawford's range too."

"I'll take that thousand in cash, Brad," the big man said, letting himself down into the easiest chair he could find and rolling a cigarette.

"Soon as I know it did the work, Dug."

"I'm here tellin' you it will make a clean-up."

"We'll know by mornin'. I haven't got the money with me anyhow. It's in the bank."

"Get it soon as you can. I expect to light out again pronto. This town's onhealthy for me."

"Where will you stay?" asked Brad.

"With my friend Steelman," jeered Doble. "His invitation is so hearty I just can't refuse him."

"You'd be safer somewhere else," said the owner of the house after a pause.

"We'll risk that, me 'n' you both, for if I'm taken it's liable to be bad luck for you too. . . . Gimme something to eat and drink."

Steelman found a bottle of whiskey and a glass, then foraged for food in the kitchen. He returned with the shank of a ham and a loaf of bread. His fear was ill-disguised. The presence of the outlaw, if discovered, would bring him trouble; and Doble was so unruly he might out of sheer ennui or bravado let it be known he was there.

"I'll get you the money first thing in the mornin'," promised Steelman.

Doble poured himself a large drink and took it at a swallow. "I would, Brad."

"No use you puttin' yoreself in unnecessary danger."

"Or you. Don't hand me my hat, Brad. I'll go when I'm ready."

Doble drank steadily throughout the night. He was the kind of drinker that can take an incredible amount of liquor without becoming helpless. He remained steady on his feet, growing uglier and more reckless every hour.

Tied to Doble because he dared not break away from him, Steelman's busy brain began to plot a way to take advantage of this man's weakness for liquor. He sat across the table from him and adroitly stirred up his hatred of Crawford and Sanders. He raked up every grudge his guest had against the two men, calling to his mind how they had beaten him at every turn.

"O' course I know, Dug, you're a better man than Sanders or Crawford either, but Malapi don't know it—yet. Down at the Gusher I hear they laugh about that trick he played on you blowin' up the dam. Luck, I call it, but—"

"Laugh, do they?" growled the big man savagely. "I'd like to hear some o' that laughin'."

"Say this Sanders is a wonder; that nobody's got a chance against him. That's the talk goin' round. I said any day in the week you had him beat a mile, and they gave me the laugh."

"I'll show 'em!" cried the enraged bully with a furious oath.

"I'll bet you do. No man livin' can make a fool outa Dug Doble, rustle the evidence to send him to the pen, snap his fingers at him, and on top o' that steal his girl. That's what I told—"

Doble leaned across the table and caught in his great fist the wrist of Steelman. His bloodshot eyes glared into those of the man opposite. "What girl?" he demanded hoarsely.

Steelman looked blandly innocent. "Didn't you know, Dug? Maybe I oughtn't to 'a' mentioned it."

169

Fingers like ropes of steel tightened on the wrist. Brad screamed.

"Don't do that, Dug! You're killin' me! Ouch! Em Crawford's girl."

"What about her and Sanders?"

"Why, he's courtin' her—treatin' her to ice-cream, goin' walkin' with her. Didn't you know?"

"When did he begin?" Doble slammed a hamlike fist on the table. "Spit it out, or I'll tear yore arm off."

Steelman told all he knew and a good deal more. He invented details calculated to infuriate his confederate, to inflame his jealousy. The big man sat with jaw clamped, the muscles knotted like ropes on his leathery face. He was a volcano of outraged vanity and furious hate, seething with fires ready to erupt.

"Some folks say it's Hart she's engaged to," purred the hatchet-faced tempter. "Maybeso. Looks to me like she's throwin' down Hart for this convict. Expect she sees he's gonna be a big man some day."

"Big man! Who says so?" exploded Doble.

"That's the word, Dug. I reckon you've heard how the Governor of Colorado pardoned him. This town's crazy about Sanders. Claims he was framed for the penitentiary. Right now he could be elected to any office he went after." Steelman's restless black eyes watched furtively the effect of his taunting on this man, a victim of wild and uncurbed passions. He was egging him on to a rage that would throw away all caution and all scruples.

"He'll never live to run for office!" the cattleman cried hoarsely.

"They talk him for sheriff. Say Applegate's no good—too easy-going. Say Sanders'll round up you an' Shorty pronto when he's given authority."

Doble ripped out a wild and explosive oath. He knew this man was playing on his vanity, jealousy, and hatred for some purpose not yet apparent, but he found it impossible to close his mind to the whisperings of the plotter. He welcomed the spur of Steelman's two-edged tongue because he wanted to have his purpose of vengeance fed.

"Sanders never saw the day he could take me, dead or alive. I'll meet him any time, any way, an' when I turn my back on him he'll be ready for the coroner."

"I believe you, Dug. No need to tell me you're not afraid of him, for—"

"Afraid of him!" bellowed Doble, eyes like live coals. "Say that again an' I'll twist yore head off."

Steelman did not say it again. He pushed the bottle toward his guest and said other things.

CHAPTER XXXV

FIRE IN THE CHAPARRAL

A carpenter working on the roof of a derrick for Jackpot Number Six called down to his mates:

"Fire in the hills, looks like. I see smoke."

The contractor was an old-timer. He knew the danger of fire in the chaparral at this season of the year.

"Run over to Number Four and tell Crawford," he said to his small son.

Crawford and Hart had just driven out from town.

"I'll shag up the tower and have a look," the younger man said.

He had with him no field-glasses, but his eyes were trained to long-distance work. Years in the saddle on the range had made him an expert at reading such news as the landscape had written on it.

"Fire in Bear Cañon!" he shouted down. "Quite a bit of smoke risin'."

"I'll ride right up and look it over," the cattleman called back. "Better get a gang together to fight it, Bob. Hike up soon as you're ready."

Crawford borrowed without permission of the owner the nearest saddle horse and put it to a lope. Five minutes might make all the difference between a winning and a losing fight.

From the tower Hart descended swiftly. He gathered together all the carpenters, drillers, enginemen, and tool dressers in the vicinity and equipped them with shovels, picks, brush-hooks, saws, and axes. To each one he gave also a gunnysack.

The foot party followed Crawford into the chaparral, making for the hills that led to Bear Cañon. A wind was stirring, and as they topped a rise it struck hot on their cheeks. A flake of ash fell on Bob's hand.

Crawford met them at the mouth of the cañon.

"She's rip-r'arin', Bob! Got too big a start to beat out. We'll clear a fire-break where the gulch narrows just above here and do our fightin' there."

The sparks of a thousand rockets, flung high by the wind, were swept down the gulch toward them. Behind these came a curtain of black smoke.

The cattleman set his crew to work clearing a wide trail across the gorge from wall to wall. The undergrowth was heavy, and the men attacked with brush-hooks, shovels, and axes. One man, with a wet gunnysack, was detailed to see that no flying sparks started a new blaze below the safety zone. The shovelers and grubbers cleared the grass and roots off to the dirt for a belt of twenty feet. They banked the loose dirt at the lower edge to catch flying firebrands. Meanwhile the breath of the furnace grew to a steady heat on their faces. Flame spurts had leaped forward to a grove of small alders and almost in a minute the branches were crackling like fireworks.

"I'll scout round over the hill and have a look above," Bob said. "We've got to keep it from spreading out of the gulch."

"Take the horse," Crawford called to him.

One good thing was that the fire was coming down the cañon. A downhill blaze moves less rapidly than one running up.

Runners of flame, crawling like snakes among the brush, struck out at the fighters venomously and tried to leap the trench. The defenders flailed at these with the wet gunnysacks.

The wind was stiffer now and the fury of the fire closer. The flames roared down the cañon like a blast furnace. Driven back by the intense heat, the men retreated across the break and clung to their line. Already their lungs were sore from inhaling smoke and their throats were inflamed. A pine, its pitchy trunk ablaze, crashed down across the fire-trail and caught in the fork of a tree beyond. Instantly the foliage leaped to red flame.

Crawford, axe in hand, began to chop the trunk and a big Swede swung an axe powerfully on the opposite side. The rest of the crew continued to beat down the fires that started below the break. The chips flew at each rhythmic stroke of the keen blades. Presently the tree crashed down into the trail that had been hewn. It served as a conductor, and along it tongues of fire leaped into the brush beyond. Glowing branches, flung by the wind and hurled from falling timber, buried themselves in the dry undergrowth. Before one blaze was crushed half a dozen others started in its place. Flails and gunnysacks beat these down and smothered them.

Bob galloped into the cañon and flung himself from the horse as he pulled it up in its stride.

"She's jumpin' outa the gulch above. Too late to head her off. We better get scrapers up and run a trail along the top o' the ridge, don't you reckon?" he said.

"Yes, son," agreed Crawford. "We can just about hold her here. It'll be hours before I can spare a man for the ridge. We got to get help in a hurry. You ride to town and rustle men. Bring out plenty of dynamite and gunnysacks. Lucky we got the tools out here we brought to build the sump holes."

"Betcha! We'll need a lot o' grub, too."

The cattleman nodded agreement. "And coffee. Cayn't have too much coffee. It's food and drink and helps keep the men awake."

"I'll remember."

"And for the love o' Heaven, don't forget canteens! Get every canteen in town. Cayn't have my men runnin' around with their tongues hangin' out. Better bring out a bunch of broncs to pack supplies around. It's goin' to be one man-sized contract runnin' the commissary."

The cañon above them was by this time a sea of fire, the most terrifying sight Bob had ever looked upon. Monster flames leaped at the walls of the gulch, swept in an eyebeat over draws, attacked with a savage roar the dry vegetation. The noise was like the crash of mountains meeting. Thunder could scarce have made itself heard.

Rocks, loosened by the heat, tore down the steep incline of the walls, sometimes singly, sometimes in slides. These hit the bed of the ravine with the force of a cannon-ball. The workers had to keep a sharp lookout for these.

A man near Bob was standing with his weight on the shovel he had been using. Hart gave a shout of warning. At the same

173

moment a large rock struck the handle and snapped it off as though it had been kindling wood. The man wrung his hands and almost wept with the pain.

A cottontail ran squealing past them, driven from its home by this new and deadly enemy. Not far away a rattlesnake slid across the hot rocks. Their common fear of man was lost in a greater and more immediate one.

Hart did not like to leave the battle-field. "Lemme stay here. You can handle that end of the job better'n me, Mr. Crawford."

The old cattleman, his face streaked with black, looked at him from bloodshot eyes. "Where do you get that notion I'll quit a job I've started, son? You hit the trail. The sooner the quicker."

The young man wasted no more words. He swung to the saddle and rode for town faster than he had ever traveled in all his hard-riding days.

CHAPTER XXXVI

FIGHTING FIRE

Sanders was in the office of the Jackpot Company looking over some blue-prints when Joyce Crawford came in and inquired where her father was.

"He went out with Bob Hart to the oil field this morning. Some trouble with the casing."

"Thought Dad wasn't giving any of his time to oil these days," she said. "He told me you and Bob were running the company."

"Every once in a while he takes an interest. I prod him up to go out and look things over occasionally. He's president of the company, and I tell him he ought to know what's going on. So to-day he's out there."

"Oh!" Miss Joyce, having learned what she had come in to find out, might reasonably have departed. She declined a chair, said she must be going, yet did not go. Her eyes appeared to study without seeing a field map on the desk. "Dad told me something last night, Mr. Sanders. He said I might pass it on to you and Bob, though it isn't to go farther. It's about that ten thousand dollars he paid the bank when it called his loan. He got the money from Buck Byington."

"Buck!" exclaimed the young man. He was thinking that the Buck he used to know never had ten dollars saved, let alone ten thousand.

"I know," she explained. "That's it. The money wasn't his. He's executor or something for the children of his dead brother. This money had come in from the sale of a farm back in Iowa and he was waiting for an order of the court for permission to invest it in a mortgage. When he heard Dad was so desperately hard up for cash he let him have the money. He knew Dad would pay it back, but it seems what he did was against the law, even though Dad gave him his note and a chattel mortgage on some cattle which Buck wasn't to record. Now it has been straightened out. That's why Dad couldn't tell where he got the money. Buck would have been in trouble."

"I see."

"But now it's all right." Joyce changed the subject. There were teasing pinpoints of mischief in her eyes. "My school physiology used to say that sleep was restful. It builds up worn-out tissue and all. One of these nights, when you can find time, give it a trial and see whether that's true."

Dave laughed. The mother in this young woman would persistently out. "I get plenty of sleep, Miss Joyce. Most people sleep too much."

"How much do you sleep?"

"Sometimes more, sometimes less. I average six or seven hours, maybe."

"Maybe," she scoffed.

"Hard work doesn't hurt men. Not when they're young and strong."

"I hear you're trying to work yourself to death, sir," the girl charged, smiling.

"Not so bad as that." He answered her smile with another, for no reason except that the world was a sunshiny one when he looked at this trim and dainty young woman. "The work gets fascinating. A fellow likes to get things done. There's a

175

satisfaction in turning out a full day and in feeling you get results."

She nodded sagely, in a brisk, businesslike way. "I know. Felt it myself often, but we have to remember that there are other days and other people to lend a hand. None of us can do it all. Dad thinks you overdo. So he told me to ask you to supper for to-morrow night. Bob will be there too."

"I say thanks, Miss Joyce, to your father and his daughter."

"Which means you'll be with us to-morrow."

"I'll be with you."

But he was not. Even as he made the promise a shadow darkened the doorsill and Bob Hart stepped into the office.

His first words were ominous, but before he spoke both of those looking at him knew he was the bearer of bad news. There was in his boyish face an unwonted gravity.

"Fire in the chaparral, Dave, and going strong."

Sanders spoke one word. "Where?"

"Started in Bear Cañon, but it's jumped out into the hills."

"The wind must be driving it down toward the Jackpot!"

"Yep. Like a scared rabbit. Crawford's trying to hold the mouth of the cañon. He's got a man's job down there. Can't spare a soul to keep it from scootin' over the hills."

Dave rose. "I'll gather a bunch of men and ride right out. On what side of the cañon is the fire running?"

"East side. Stop at the wells and get tools. I got to rustle dynamite and men. Be out soon as I can."

They spoke quietly, quickly, decisively, as men of action do in a crisis.

Joyce guessed the situation was a desperate one. "Is Dad in danger?" she asked.

Hart answered. "No—not now, anyhow."

"What can I do to help?"

"We'll have hundreds of men in the field probably, if this fire has a real start," Dave told her. "We'll need food and coffee—lots of it. Organize the women. Make meat sandwiches—hundreds of them. And send out to the Jackpot dozens of coffee-pots. Your job is to keep the workers well fed. Better send out bandages and salve, in case some get burnt."

Her eyes were shining. "I'll see to all that. Don't worry, boys. You fight this fire, and we women will 'tend to feeding you."

Dave nodded and strode out of the room. During the fierce and dreadful days that followed one memory more than once came to him in the fury of the battle. It was of a slim,

176

straight girl looking at him, the call to service stamped on her brave, uplifted face.

Sanders was on the road inside of twenty minutes, a group of horsemen galloping at his heels. At the Jackpot locations the fire-fighters equipped themselves with shovels, sacks, axes, and brush-hooks. The party, still on horseback, rode up to the mouth of Bear Cañon. Through the smoke the sun was blood-red. The air was heavy and heated.

From the fire line Crawford came to meet these new allies. "We're holdin' her here. It's been nip an' tuck. Once I thought sure she'd break through, but we beat out the blaze. I hadn't time to go look, but I expect she's just a-r'arin' over the hills. I've had some teams and scrapers taken up there, Dave. It's yore job. Go to it."

The old cattleman showed that he had been through a fight. His eyes were red and inflamed, his face streaked with black, one arm of his shirt half torn from the shoulder. But he wore the grim look of a man who has just begun to set himself for a struggle.

The horsemen swung to the east and rode up to the mesa which lies between Bear and Cattle Cañons. It was impossible to get near Bear, since the imprisoned fury had burst from its walls and was sweeping the chaparral. The line of fire was running along the level in an irregular, ragged front, red tongues leaping ahead with short, furious rushes.

Even before he could spend time to determine the extent of the fire, Dave selected his line of defense, a ridge of rocky, higher ground cutting across from one gulch to the other. Here he set teams to work scraping a fire-break, while men assisted with shovels and brush-hooks to clear a wide path.

Dave swung still farther east and rode along the edge of Cattle Cañon. Narrow and rock-lined, the gorge was like a boiler flue to suck the flames down it. From where he sat he saw it raging with inconceivable fury. The earth rift seemed to be roofed with flame. Great billows of black smoke poured out laden with sparks and live coals carried by the wind. It was plain at the first glance that the fire was bound to leap from the cañon to the brush-covered hills beyond. His business now was to hold the ridge he had chosen and fight back the flames to keep them from pouring down upon the Jackpot property. Later the battle would have to be fought to hold the line at San Jacinto Cañon and the hills running down from it to the plains.

The surface fire on the hills licked up the brush, mesquite,

177

and young cedars with amazing rapidity. If his trail-break was built in time, Dave meant to back-fire above it. Steve Russell was one of his party. Sanders appointed him lieutenant and went over the ground with him to decide exactly where the clearing should run, after which he galloped back to the mouth of Bear.

"She's running wild on the hills and in Cattle Cañon," Dave told Crawford. "She'll sure jump Cattle and reach San Jacinto. We've got to hold the mouth of Cattle, build a trail between Bear and Cattle, another between Cattle and San Jacinto, cork her up in San Jacinto, and keep her from jumping to the hills beyond."

"Can we back-fire, do you reckon?"

"Not with the wind there is above, unless we have check-trails built first. We need several hundred more men, and we need them right away. I never saw such a fire before."

"Well, get yore trail built. Bob oughtta be out soon. I'll put him over between Cattle and San Jacinto. Three-four men can hold her here now. I'll move my outfit over to the mouth of Cattle."

The cattleman spoke crisply and decisively. He had been fighting fire for six hours without a moment's rest, swallowing smoke-filled air, enduring the blistering heat that poured steadily at them down the gorge. At least two of his men were lying down completely exhausted, but he contemplated another such desperate battle without turning a hair. All his days he had been a good fighter, and it never occurred to him to quit now.

Sanders rode up as close to the west edge of Bear Cañon as he could endure. In two or three places the flames had jumped the wall and were trying to make headway in the scant underbrush of the rocky slope that led to a hogback surmounted by a bare rimrock running to the summit. This natural barrier would block the fire on the west, just as the burnt-over area would protect the north. For the present at least the fire-fighters could confine their efforts to the south and east, where the spread of the blaze would involve the Jackpot. A shift in the wind would change the situation, and if it came in time would probably save the oil property.

Dave put his horse to a lope and rode back to the trench and trail his men were building. He found a shovel and joined them.

From out of Cattle Cañon billows of smoke rolled across the hill and settled into a black blanket above the men. This was acrid from the resinous pitch of the pines. The wind caught the dark pall, drove it low, and held it there till the workers could hardly breathe. The sun was under entire eclipse behind the smoke screen.

The heat of the flames tortured Dave's face and hands, just as the smoke-filled air inflamed his nostrils and throat. Coals of fire pelted him from the river of flame, carried by the strong breeze blowing down. From the cañons on either side of the workers came a steady roar of a world afire. Occasionally, at some slight shift of the wind, the smoke lifted and they could see the moving wall of fire bearing down upon them, wedges of it far ahead of the main line.

The movements of the workers became automatic. The teams had to be removed because the horses had become unmanageable under the torture of the heat. When any one spoke it was in a hoarse whisper because of a swollen larynx. Mechanically they dug, shoveled, grubbed, handkerchiefs over their faces to protect from the furnace glow.

A deer with two fawns emerged from the smoke and flew past on the way to safety. Mice, snakes, rabbits, birds, and other desert denizens appeared in mad flight. They paid no attention whatever to their natural foe, man. The terror of the red monster at their heels wholly obsessed them.

The fire-break was from fifteen to twenty feet wide. The men retreated back of it, driven by the heat, and fought with wet sacks to hold the enemy. A flash of lightning was hurled against Dave. It was a red-hot limb of a pine, tossed out of the gorge by the stiff wind. He flung it from him and tore the burning shirt from his chest. An agony of pain shot through his shoulder, seared for half a foot by the blazing branch.

He had no time to attend to the burn then. The fire had leaped the check-trail at a dozen points. With his men he tried to smother the flames in the grass by using saddle blankets and gunnysacks, as well as by shoveling sand upon it. Sometimes they cut down the smouldering brush and flung it back across the break into the inferno on the other side. Blinded and strangling from the smoke, the fire-fighters would make short rushes into the clearer air, swallow a breath or two of it, and plunge once more into the line to do battle with the foe.

For hours the desperate battle went on. Dave lost count of time. One after another of his men retreated to rest. After a time they drifted back to help make the defense good against the plunging fire devil. Sanders alone refused to retire. His parched eyebrows were half gone. His clothes hung about him in shredded rags. He was so exhausted that he could hardly wield a flail. His legs dragged and his arms hung heavy. But he would not give up even for an hour. Through the confused, shifting darkness of the night he led his band, silhouetted on the ridge like gnomes of the nether world, to attack after attack on the tireless, creeping, plunging flames that leaped the trench in a hundred desperate assaults, that howled and hissed and roared like ravenous beasts of prey.

Before the light of day broke he knew that he had won. His men had made good the check-trail that held back the fire in the terrain between Bear and Cattle Cañons. The fire, worn out and beaten, fell back for lack of fuel upon which to feed.

Reinforcements came from town. Dave left the trail in charge of a deputy and staggered down with his men to the camp that had been improvised below. He sat down with them and swallowed coffee and ate sandwiches. Steve Russell dressed his burn with salve and bandages sent out by Joyce.

"Me for the hay, Dave," the cowpuncher said when he had finished. He stretched himself in a long, tired, luxurious yawn. "I've rid out a blizzard and I've gathered cattle after a stampede till I 'most thought I'd drop outa the saddle. But I give it to this here li'l' fire. It's sure enough a stemwinder. I'm beat. So long, pardner."

Russell went off to roll himself up in his blanket.

Dave envied him, but he could not do the same. His responsibilities were not ended yet. He found his horse in the remuda, saddled, and rode over to the entrance to Cattle Cañon.

Emerson Crawford was holding his ground, though barely holding it. He too was grimy, fire-blackened, exhausted, but he was still fighting to throw back the fire that swept down the cañon at him.

"How are things up above?" he asked in a hoarse whisper.

"Good. We held the check-line."

"Same here so far. It's been hell. Several of my boys fainted."

"I'll take charge awhile. You go and get some sleep," urged Sanders.

The cattleman shook his head. "No. See it through. Say, son, look who's here!" His thumb hitched toward his right shoulder.

Dave looked down the line of blackened, grimy fire-fighters and his eye fell on Shorty. He was still wearing chaps, but his

Chihuahua hat had succumbed long ago. Manifestly the man had been on the fighting line for some hours.

"Doesn't he know about the reward?"

"Yes. He was hidin' in Malapi when the call came for men. Says he's no quitter, whatever else he is. You bet he ain't. He's worth two of most men at this work. Soon as we get through he'll be on the dodge again, I reckon, unless Applegate gets him first. He's a good sport, anyhow. I'll say that for him."

"I reckon I'm a bad citizen, sir, but I hope he makes his getaway before Applegate shows up."

"Well, he's one tough scalawag, but I don't aim to give him away right now. Shorty is a whole lot better proposition than Dug Doble."

Dave came back to the order of the day. "What do you want me to do now?"

The cattleman looked him over. "You damaged much?"

"No."

"Burnt in the shoulder, I see."

"Won't keep me from swinging a sack and bossing a gang."

"Wore out, I reckon?"

"I feel fine since breakfast—took two cups of strong coffee."

Again Crawford's eyes traveled over his ally. They saw a ragged, red-eyed tramp, face and hands and arms blackened with char and grimed with smoke. Outside, he was such a specimen of humanity as the police would have arrested promptly on suspicion. But the shrewd eyes of the cattleman saw more—a spirit indomitable that would drive the weary, tormented body till it dropped in its tracks, a quality of leadership that was a trumpet call to the men who served with him, a soul master of its infirmities. His heart went out to the young fellow. Wherefore he grinned and gave him another job. Strong men to-day were at a premium with Emerson Crawford.

"Ride over and see how Bob's comin' out. We'll make it here."

Sanders swung to the saddle and moved forward to the next fire front, the one between Cattle and San Jacinto Cañons. Hart himself was not here. There had come a call for help from the man in charge of the gang trying to hold the fire in San Jacinto. He had answered that summons long before daybreak and had not yet returned.

The situation on the Cattle-San Jacinto front was not

encouraging. The distance to be protected was nearly a mile. Part of the way was along a ridge fairly easy to defend, but a good deal of it lay in lower land of timber and heavy brush.

Dave rode along the front, studying the contour of the country and the chance of defending it. His judgment was that it could not be done with the men on hand. He was not sure that the line could be held even with reinforcements. But there was nothing for it but to try. He sent a man to Crawford, urging him to get help to him as soon as possible.

Then he took command of the crew already in the field, re-arranged the men so as to put the larger part of his force in the most dangerous locality, and in default of a sack seized a spreading branch as a flail to beat out fire in the high grass close to San Jacinto.

An hour later half a dozen straggling men reported for duty. Shorty was one of them.

"The ol' man cayn't spare any more," the rustler explained. "He had to hustle Steve and his gang outa their blankets to go help Bob Hart. They say Hart's in a helluva bad way. The fire's jumped the trail-check and is spreadin' over the country. He's runnin' another trail farther back."

It occurred to Dave that if the wind changed suddenly and heightened, it would sweep a back-fire round him and cut off the retreat of his crew. He sent a weary lad back to keep watch on it and report any change of direction in that vicinity.

After which he forgot all about chances of danger from the rear. His hands and mind were more than busy trying to drive back the snarling, ravenous beast in front of him. He might have found time to take other precautions if he had known that the exhausted boy sent to watch against a back-fire had, with the coming of night, fallen asleep in a draw.

CHAPTER XXXVII

SHORTY ASKS A QUESTION

When Shorty separated from Doble in Frio Cañon he rode inconspicuously to a tendejon where he could be snugly hidden from the public gaze and yet meet a few "pals" whom he could trust at least as long as he could keep his eyes on them. His intention was to have a good time in the only way he knew how. Another purpose was coupled with this; he was not going to drink enough to interfere with reasonable caution.

Shorty's dissipated pleasures were interfered with shortly after midnight. A Mexican came in to the drinking-place with news. The world was on fire, at least that part of it which interested the cattlemen of the Malapi district. The blaze had started back of Bear Cañon and had been swept by the wind across to Cattle and San Jacinto. The oil field adjacent had been licked up and every reservoir and sump was in flames. The whole range would probably be wiped out before the fire spent itself for lack of fuel. Crawford had posted a rider to town calling for more man power to build trails and wield flails. This was the sum of the news. It was not strictly accurate, but it served to rouse Shorty at once.

He rose and touched the Mexican on the arm. "Where you say that fire started, Pedro?"

"Bear Cañon, señor."

"And it's crossed San Jacinto?"

"Like wildfire." The slim vaquero made a gesture all-inclusive. "It runs, señor, like a frightened jack-rabbit. Nothing will stop it—nothing. It iss sent by heaven for a punishment."

"Hmp!" Shorty grunted.

The rustler fell into a somber silence. He drank no more.

183

The dark-lashed eyes of the Mexican girls slanted his way in vain. He stared sullenly at the table in front of him. A problem had pushed itself into his consciousness, one he could not brush aside or ignore.

If the fire had started back of Bear Cañon, what agency had set it going? He and Doble had camped last night at that very spot. If there had been a fire there during the night he must have known it. Then when had the fire started? And how? They had seen the faint smoke of it as they rode away, the filmy smoke of a young fire not yet under much headway. Was it reasonable to suppose that some one else had been camping close to them? This was possible, but not likely. For they would probably have seen signs of the other evening camp-fire.

Eliminating this possibility, there remained—Dug Doble. Had Dug fired the brush while his companion was saddling for the start? The more Shorty considered this possibility, the greater force it acquired in his mind. Dug's hatred of Crawford, Hart, and especially Sanders would be satiated in part at least if he could wipe their oil bonanza from the map. The wind had been right. Doble was no fool. He knew that if the fire ran wild in the chaparral only a miracle could save the Jackpot reservoirs and plant from destruction.

Other evidence accumulated. Cryptic remarks of Doble made during the day. His anxiety to see Steelman immediately. A certain manner of ill-repressed triumph whenever he mentioned Sanders or Crawford. These bolstered Shorty's growing opinion that the man had deliberately fired the chaparral from a spirit of revenge.

Shorty was an outlaw and a bad man. He had killed, and might at any time kill again. To save the Jackpot from destruction he would not have made a turn of the hand. But Shorty was a cattleman. He had been brought up in the saddle and had known the whine of the lariat and the dust of the drag drive all his days. Every man has his code. Three things stood out in that of Shorty. He was loyal to the hand that paid him, he stood by his pals, and he believed in and after his own fashion loved cattle and the life of which they were the central fact. To destroy the range feed wantonly was a crime so nefarious that he could not believe Doble guilty of it. And yet—

He could not let the matter lie in doubt. He left the tendejon and rode to Steelman's house. Before entering he exam-

184

ined carefully both of his long-barreled forty-fives. He made sure that the six-shooters were in perfect order and that they rested free in the holsters. That sixth sense acquired by "bad men," by means of which they sniff danger when it is close, was telling him that smoke would rise before he left the house.

He stepped to the porch and knocked. There came a moment's silence, a low-pitched murmur of whispering voices carried through an open window, the shuffling of feet. The door was opened by Brad Steelman. He was alone in the room.

"Where's Dug?" asked Shorty bluntly.

"Why, Dug—why, he's here, Shorty. Didn't know it was you. 'Lowed it might be some one else. So he stepped into another room."

The short cowpuncher walked in and closed the door behind him. He stood with his back to it, facing the other door of the room.

"Did you hire Dug to fire the chaparral?" he asked, his voice ominously quiet.

A flicker of fear shot to the eyes of the oil promoter. He recognized signs of peril and his heart was drenched with an icy chill. Shorty was going to turn on him, had become a menace.

"I—I dunno what you mean," he quavered. "I'll call Dug if you wanta see him." He began to shuffle toward the inner room.

"Hold yore hawsses, Brad. I asked you a question." The cold eyes of the gunman bored into those of the other man. "Howcome you to hire Dug to burn the range?"

"You know I wouldn't do that," the older man whined. "I got sheep, ain't I? Wouldn't be reasonable I'd destroy their feed. No, you got a wrong notion about—"

"Yore sheep ain't on the south slope range." Shorty's mind had moved forward one notch toward certainty. Steelman's manner was that of a man dodging the issue. It carried no conviction of innocence. "How much you payin' him?"

The door of the inner room opened. Dug Doble's big frame filled the entrance. The eyes of the two gunmen searched each other. Those of Doble asked a question. Had it come to a showdown? Steelman sidled over to the desk where he worked and sat down in front of it. His right hand dropped into an open drawer, apparently carelessly and without intent.

Shorty knew at once that Doble had been drinking heavily. The man was morose and sullen. His color was high. Plainly he was primed for a killing if trouble came.

"Lookin' for me, Shorty?" he asked.

"You fired Bear Cañon," charged the cowpuncher.

"So?"

"When I went to saddle."

Doble's eyes narrowed. "You aimin' to run my business, Shorty?"

Neither man lifted his gaze from the other. Each knew that the test had come once more. They were both men who had "gone bad," in the current phrase of the community. Both had killed. Both searched now for an advantage in that steady duel of the eyes. Neither had any fear. The emotions that dominated were cold rage and caution. Every sense and nerve in each focalized to one purpose—to kill without being killed.

"When yore's is mine, Dug."

"Is this yore's?"

"Sure is. I've stood for a heap from you. I've let yore ugly temper ride me. When you killed Tim Harrigan you got me in bad. Not the first time either. But I'm damned if I'll ride with a coyote low-down enough to burn the range."

"No?"

"No."

From the desk came the sharp angry bark of a revolver. Shorty felt his hat lift as a bullet tore through the rim. His eyes swept to Steelman, who had been a negligible factor in his calculations. The man fired again and blew out the light. In the darkness Shorty swept out both guns and fired. His first two shots were directed toward the man behind the desk, the next two at the spot where Doble had been standing. Another gun was booming in the room, perhaps two. Yellow fire flashes ripped the blackness.

Shorty whipped open the door at his back, slid through it, and kicked it shut with his foot as he leaped from the porch. At the same moment he thought he heard a groan.

Swiftly he ran to the cottonwood where he had left his horse tied. He jerked loose the knot, swung to the saddle, and galloped out of town.

The drumming of hoofs came down the wind to a young fellow returning from a late call on his sweetheart. He wondered who was in such a hurry.

CHAPTER XXXVIII

DUG DOBLE RIDES INTO THE HILLS

The booming of the guns died down. The acrid smoke that filled the room lifted to shredded strata. A man's deep breathing was the only sound in the heavy darkness.

Presently came a soft footfall of some one moving cautiously. A match flared. A hand cupped the flame for an instant to steady it before the match moved toward the wick of a kerosene lamp.

Dug Doble's first thought was for his own safety. The house door was closed, the window blinds were down. He had heard the beat of hoofs die away on the road. But he did not intend to be caught by a trick. He stepped forward, locked the door, and made sure the blinds were offering no cracks of light. Satisfied that all was well, he turned to the figure sprawled on the floor with outflung arms.

"Dead as a stuck shote," he said callously after he had turned the body over. "Got him plumb through the forehead —in the dark, too. Some shootin', Shorty."

He stood looking down at the face of the man whose brain had spun so many cobwebs of deceit and treachery. Even in death it had none of that dignity which sometimes is lent to those whose lives have been full of meanness and guile. But though Doble looked at his late ally, he was not thinking about him. He was mapping out his future course of action.

If any one had heard the shots and he were found here now, no jury on earth could be convinced that he had not killed Steelman. His six-shooter still gave forth a faint trickle of smoke. An examination would show that three shots had been fired from it.

He must get away from the place at once.

187

Doble poured himself half a tumbler of whiskey and drank it neat. Yes, he must go, but he might as well take with him any money Steelman had in the safe. The dead man owed him a thousand dollars he would never be able to collect in any other way.

He stooped and examined the pockets of the still figure. A bunch of keys rewarded him. An old-fashioned safe stood in the corner back of the desk. Doble stooped in front of it, then waited for an instant to make sure nobody was coming. He fell to work, trying the keys one after another.

A key fitted. He turned it and swung open the door. The killer drew out bundles of papers and glanced through them hurriedly. Deeds, mortgages, oil stocks, old receipts: he wanted none of these, and tossed them to the floor as soon as he discovered there were no banknotes among them. Compartment after compartment he rifled. Behind a package of abstracts he found a bunch of greenbacks tied together by a rubber band at each end. The first bill showed that the denomination was fifty dollars. Doble investigated no farther. He thrust the bulky package into his inside coat pocket and rose.

Again he listened. No sound broke the stillness of the night. The silence got on his nerves. He took another big drink and decided it was time to go.

He blew out the light and once more listened. The lifeless body of his ally lying within touch of his foot did not disturb the outlaw. He had not killed him, and if he had it would have made no difference. Very softly for a large man, he passed to the inner room and toward the back door. He deflected his course to a cupboard where he knew Steelman kept liquor and from a shelf helped himself to an unbroken quart bottle of bourbon. He knew himself well enough to know that during the next twenty-four hours he would want whiskey badly.

Slowly he unlocked and opened the back door. His eyes searched the yard and the open beyond to make sure that neither his enemy nor a sheriff's posse was lurking in the brush for him. He crept out to the stable, revolver in hand. Here he saddled in the dark, deftly and rapidly, thrusting the bottle of whiskey into one of the pockets of the saddlebags. Leading the horse out into the mesquite, he swung to the saddle and rode away.

He was still in the saddle when the peaks above caught the

morning sun glow in a shaft of golden light. Far up in the gulches the new fallen snow reflected the dawn's pink.

In a pocket of the hills Doble unsaddled. He hobbled his horse and turned it loose to graze while he lay down under a pine with the bottle for a companion.

The man had always had a difficult temper. This had grown on him and been responsible largely for his decline in life. It had been no part of his plan to "go bad." There had been a time when he had been headed for success in the community. He had held men's respect, even though they had not liked him. Then, somehow, he had turned the wrong corner and been unable to retrace his steps.

He could even put a finger on the time he had commenced to slip. It had begun when he had quarreled with Emerson Crawford about his daughter Joyce. Shorty and he had done some brand-burning through a wet blanket. But he had not gone so far that a return to respectability was impossible. A little rustling on the quiet, with no evidence to fasten it on one, was nothing to bar a man from society. He had gone more definitely wrong after Sanders came back to Malapi. The young ex-convict, he chose to think, was responsible for the circumstances that made of him an outlaw. Crawford and Sanders together had exposed him and driven him from the haunts of men to the hills. He hated them both with a bitter, morose virulence his soul could not escape.

Throughout the day he continued to drink. This gave him no refuge from himself. He still brooded in the inferno of his own thought-circle. It is possible that a touch of madness had begun to affect his brain. Certainly his subsequent actions would seem to bear out this theory.

Revenge! The thought of it spurred him every waking hour, roweling his wounded pride cruelly. There was a way within reach of his hand, one suggested by Steelman's whisperings, though never openly advocated by the sheepman. The jealousy of the man urged him to it, and his consuming vanity persuaded him that out of evil might come good. He could make the girl love him. So her punishment would bring her joy in the end. As for Crawford and Sanders, his success would be such bitter medicine to them that time would never wear away the taste of it.

At dusk he rose and resaddled. Under the stars he rode back to Malapi. He knew exactly what he meant to do and how he meant to do it.

CHAPTER XXXIX

THE TUNNEL

Dave knew no rest that night. He patrolled his line from San Jacinto to Cattle and back again, stopping always to lend a hand where the attack was most furious. The men of his crew were weary to exhaustion, but the pressure of the fire was so great that they dared not leave the front. As soon as one blaze was beaten out, another started. A shower of sparks close to Cattle Cañon swept over the ridge and set the thick grass afire. This was smothered with saddle blankets and with sand and dirt thrown from shovels.

Nearer to San Jacinto Cañon the danger was more acute. Dave did not dare back-fire on account of the wind. He dynamited the timber to make a trail-break against the howling, roaring wall of fire plunging forward.

As soon as the flames seized the timber the heat grew more intense. The sound of falling trees as they crashed down marked the progress of the fire. The men retreated, staggering with exhaustion, hands and faces flayed, eyes inflamed and blinded by the black smoke that rolled over them.

A stiff wind was blowing, but it was no longer a steady one. Sometimes it bore from the northeast; again in a cross-current almost directly from the east. The smoke poured in, swirling round them till they scarce knew one direction from another.

The dense cloud lifted for a moment, swept away by an air current. To the fire-fighters that glimpse of the landscape told an appalling fact. The demon had escaped below from San Jacinto Cañon and been swept westward by a slant of wind with the speed of an express train. They were trapped by the back-fire in a labyrinth from which there appeared no escape.

190

Every path of exit was blocked. The flames had leaped from hilltop to hilltop.

The men gathered together to consult. Many of them were on the verge of panic.

Dave spoke quietly. "We've got a chance if we keep our heads. There's an old mining tunnel hereabouts. Follow me, and stay together."

He plunged into the heavy smoke that had fallen about them again, working his way by instinct rather than by sight. Twice he stopped, to make sure that his men were all at heel. Several times he left them, diving into the smoke to determine which way they must go.

The dry, salt crackle of a dead pine close at hand would have told him, even if the oppressive heat had not, that the fire would presently sweep over the ground where they stood. He drew the men steadily toward Cattle Cañon.

In that furious, murk-filled world he could not be sure he was moving in the right direction, though the slope of the ground led him to think so. Falling trees crashed about them. The men staggered on in the uncanny light which tinged even the smoke.

Dave stopped and gave sharp, crisp orders. His voice was even and steady. "Must be close to it now. Lie back of these down trees with your faces close to the ground. I'll be back in a minute. Shorty, you're boss of the crew while I'm away."

"You're gonna leave us to roast," a man accused, in a voice that was half a scream.

Sanders did not stop to answer him, but Shorty took the hysterical man in hand. "Git down by that log pronto or I'll bore a hole in you. Ain't you got sense enough to see he'll save us if there's a chance?"

The man fell trembling to the ground.

"Two men behind each log," ordered Shorty. "If yore clothes git afire, help each other put it out."

They lay down and waited while the fire swept above and round them. Fortunately the woods here were not dense. Men prayed or cursed or wept, according to their natures. The logs in front of some of them caught fire and spread to their clothing. Shorty's voice encouraged them.

"Stick it out, boys. He'll be back if he's alive."

It could have been only minutes, but it seemed hours before the voice of Sanders rang out above the fury of the blast.

"All up! I've found the tunnel! Step lively now!"

They staggered after their leader, Shorty bringing up the

rear to see that none collapsed by the way. The line moved drunkenly forward. Now and again a man went down, overcome by the smoke and heat. With brutal kicks Shorty drove him to his feet again.

The tunnel was a shallow one in a hillside. Dave stood aside and counted the men as they passed in. Two were missing. He ran along the back trail, dense with smoke from the approaching flames, and stumbled into a man. It was Shorty. He was dragging with him the body of a man who had fainted. Sanders seized an arm and together they managed to get the unconscious victim to the tunnel.

Dave was the last man in. He learned from the men in the rear that the tunnel had no drift. The floor was moist and there was a small seepage spring in it near the entrance.

Some of the men protested at staying.

"The fire'll lick in and burn us out like rats," one man urged. "This ain't no protection. We've just walked into a trap. I'll take my chance outside."

Dave reached forward and lifted one of Shorty's guns from its holster. "You'll stay right here, Dillon. We didn't make it one minute too soon. The whole hill out there's roaring."

"I'll take my chance out there. That's my lookout," said the man, moving toward the entrance.

"No. You'll stay here." Dave's hard, chill gaze swept over his crew. Several of them were backing Dillon and others were wavering. "It's your only chance, and I'm here to see you take it. Don't take another step."

Dillon took one, and went crumpling to the granite floor before Dave could move. Shorty had knocked him down with the butt of his nine-inch-barrel revolver.

Already smoke was filling the cave. The fire had raced to its mouth and was licking in with long, red, hungry tongues. The tunnel timbers were smouldering.

"Lie down and breathe the air close to the ground," ordered Dave, just as though a mutiny had not been quelled a moment before. "Stay down there. Don't get up."

He found an old tomato can and used it to throw water from the seep-spring upon the burning wood. Shorty and one or two of the other men helped him. The heat near the mouth was so intense they could not stand it. All but Sanders collapsed and staggered back to sink down to the fresher air below.

Their place of refuge packed with smoke. A tree crashed down at the mouth and presently a second one. These, blaz-

192

ing, sent more heat in to cook the tortured men inside. In that bakehouse of hell men showed again their nature, cursing, praying, storming, or weeping as they lay.

The prospect hole became a madhouse. A big Hungarian, crazed by the torment he was enduring, leaped to his feet and made for the blazing hill outside.

"Back there!" Dave shouted hoarsely.

The big fellow rushed him. His leader flung him back against the rock wall. He rushed again, screaming in crazed anger. Sanders struck him down with the long barrel of the forty-five. The Hungarian lay where he fell for a few minutes, then crawled back from the mouth of the pit.

At intervals others tried to break out and were driven back.

Dave's eyebrows crisped away. He could scarcely draw a breath through his inflamed throat. His eyes were swollen and almost blinded with smoke. His lungs ached. Whenever he took a step he staggered. But he stuck to his job hardily. The tomato can moved more jerkily. It carried less water. But it still continued to drench the blazing timbers at the mouth of the tunnel.

So Dave held the tunnel entrance against the fire and against his own racked and tortured men. Occasionally he lay down to breathe the air close to the floor. There was no circulation, for the tunnel ended in a wall face. But the smoke was not so heavy close to the ground.

Man after man succumbed to the stupor of unconsciousness. Men choked, strangled, and even died while their leader, his hair burnt and his eyes almost sightless, face and body raw with agonizing wounds, crept feebly about his business of saving their lives.

Fire-crisped and exhausted, he dropped down at last into forgetfulness of pain. And the flames, which had fought with such savage fury to blot out the little group of men, fell back sullenly in defeat. They had spent themselves and could do no more.

The line of fire had passed over them. It left charred trees still burning, a hillside black and smoking, desolation and ruin in its path.

Out of the prospect hole a man crawled over Dave's prostrate body. He drew a breath of sweet, delicious air. A cool wind lifted the hair from his forehead. He tried to give a cowpuncher's yell of joy. From out of his throat came only a cracked and raucous rumble. The man was Shorty.

He crept back into the tunnel and whispered hoarsely the

good news. Men came out on all fours over the bodies of those who could not move. Shorty dragged Dave into the open. He was a sorry sight. The shirt had been almost literally burned from his body.

In the fresh air the men revived quickly. They went back into the cavern and dragged out those of their companions not yet able to help themselves. Three out of the twenty-nine would never help themselves again. They had perished in the tunnel.

CHAPTER XL

A MESSAGE

The women of Malapi responded generously to the call Joyce made upon them to back their men in the fight against the fire in the chaparral. They were simple folk of a generation not far removed from the pioneer one which had settled the country. Some of them had come across the plains in white-topped movers' wagons. Others had lain awake in anxiety on account of raiding Indians on the war-path. All had lived lives of frugal usefulness. It is characteristic of the frontier that its inhabitants help each other without stint when the need for service arises. Now they cooked and baked cheerfully to supply the wants of the fire-fighters.

Joyce was in command of the commissary department. She ordered and issued supplies, checked up the cooked food, and arranged for its transportation to the field of battle. The first shipment went out about the middle of the afternoon of the first day of the fire. A second one left town just after midnight. A third was being packed during the forenoon of the second day.

Though Joyce had been up most of the night, she showed no signs of fatigue. In spite of her slenderness, the girl was possessed of a fine animal vigor. There was vitality in her crisp tread. She was a decisive young woman who got results competently.

A bustling old lady with the glow of winter apples in her wrinkled cheeks remonstrated with her.

"You can't do it all, dearie. If I was you I'd go home and rest now. Take a nice long nap and you'll feel real fresh," she said.

"I'm not tired," replied Joyce. "Not a bit. Think of those poor men out there fighting the fire day and night. I'd be ashamed to quit."

The old lady's eyes admired the clean, fragrant girl packing sandwiches. She sighed, regretfully. Not long since—as her memory measured time—she too had boasted a clear white skin that flushed to a becoming pink on her smooth cheeks when occasion called.

"A-well a-well, dearie, you'll never be young but once. Make ye the most of it," she said, a dream in her faded eyes.

Out of the heart of the girl a full-throated laugh welled. "I'll do just that, Auntie. Then I'll grow some day into a nice old lady like you." Joyce recurred to business in a matter-of-fact voice. "How many more of the ham sandwiches are there, Mrs. Kent?"

About sunset Joyce went home to see that Keith was behaving properly and snatched two hours' sleep while she could. Another shipment of food had to be sent out that night and she did not expect to get to bed till well into the small hours.

Keith was on hand when she awakened to beg for permission to go out to the fire.

"I'll carry water, Joy, to the men. Someone's got to carry it, ain't they, 'n' if I don't mebbe a man'll haf to."

The young mother shook her head decisively. "No, Keithie, you're too little. Grow real fast and you'll be a big boy soon."

"You don't ever lemme have any fun," he pouted. "I gotta got to bed an' sleep an' sleep an' sleep."

She had no time to stay and comfort him. He pulled away sulkily from her good-night kiss and refused to be placated. As she moved away into the darkness, it gave Joyce a tug of the heart to see his small figure on the porch. For she knew that as soon as she was out of sight he would break down and wail.

He did. Keith was of that temperament which wants what it wants when it wants it. After a time his sobs subsided.

There wasn't much use crying when nobody was around to pay any attention to him.

He went to bed and to sleep. It was hours later that the voice of some one calling penetrated his dreams. Keith woke up, heard the sound of a knocking on the door, and went to the window. The cook was deaf as a post and would never hear. His sister was away. Perhaps it was a message from his father.

A man stepped out from the house and looked up at him. "Mees Crawford, ees she at home maybeso?" he asked. The man was a Mexican.

"Wait a jiffy. I'll get up," the youngster called back.

He hustled into his clothes, went down, and opened the door.

"The señorita. Ees she at home?" the man asked again.

"She's down to the Boston Emporium cuttin' sandwiches an' packin' 'em," Keith said. "Who wants her?"

"I have a note for her from Señor Sanders."

Master Keith seized his opportunity promptly. "I'll take you down there."

The man brought his horse from the hitching-rack across the road. Side by side they walked downtown, the youngster talking excitedly about the fire, the Mexican either keeping silence or answering with a brief *"Si, muchacho."*

Into the Boston Emporium Keith raced ahead of the messenger. "Joy, Joy, a man wants to see you! From Dave!" he shouted.

Joyce flushed. Perhaps she would have preferred not to have her private business shouted out before a roomful of women. But she put a good face on it.

"A letter, señorita," the man said, presenting her with a note which he took from his pocket.

The note read:

Miss Joyce:
Your father has been hurt in the fire. This man will take you to him.

Dave Sanders

Joyce went white to the lips and caught at the table to steady herself. "Is—is he badly hurt?" she asked.

The man took refuge in ignorance, as Mexicans do when they do not want to talk. He did not understand English, he

196

said, and when the girl spoke in Spanish he replied sulkily that he did not know what was in the letter. He had been told to deliver it and bring the lady back. That was all.

Keith burst into tears. He wanted to go to his father too, he sobbed.

The girl, badly shaken herself in soul, could not refuse him. If his father was hurt he had a right to be with him.

"You may ride along with me," she said, her lip trembling.

The women gathered round the boy and his sister, expressing sympathy after the universal fashion of their sex. They were kinder and more tender than usual, pressing on them offers of supplies and service. Joyce thanked them, a lump in her throat, but it was plain that the only way in which they could help was to expedite her setting out.

Soon they were on the road, Keith riding behind his sister and clinging to her waist. Joyce had slipped a belt round the boy and fastened it to herself so that he would not fall from the saddle in case he slept. The Mexican rode in complete silence.

For an hour they jogged along the dusty road which led to the new oil field, then swung to the right into the low foothills among which the mountains were rooted.

Joyce was a bit surprised. She asked questions, and again received for answers shrugs and voluble Spanish irrelevant to the matter. The young woman knew that the battle was being fought among the cañons leading to the plains. This trail must be a short cut to one of them. She gave up trying to get information from her guide. He was either stupid or sulky; perhaps a little of each.

The hill trail went up and down. It dipped into valleys and meandered round hills. It climbed a mountain spur, slipped through a notch, and plumped sharply into a small mountain park. At the notch the Mexican drew up and pointed a finger. In the dim pre-dawn grayness Joyce could see nothing but a gulf of mist.

"Over there, señorita, he waits."

"Where?"

"In the arroyo. Come."

They descended, letting the horses pick their way cautiously through the loose rubble of the steep pitch. The heart of the girl beat fast with anxiety about her father, with the probability that David Sanders would soon come to meet her out of the silence, with some vague prescience of unknown evil clutching at her bosom. There had been growing in Joyce a feeling that something was wrong, something sinister was at work which she did not understand.

A mountain corral took form in the gloom. The Mexican slipped the bars of the gate to let the horses in.

"Is he here?" asked Joyce breathlessly.

The man pointed to a one-room shack huddled on the hillside.

Keith had fallen sound asleep, his head against the girl's back. "Don't wake him when you lift him down," she told the man. "I'll just let him sleep if he will."

The Mexican carried Keith to a pile of sheepskins under a shed and lowered him to them gently. The boy stirred, turned over, but did not awaken.

Joyce ran toward the shack. There was no light in it, no sign of life about the place. She could not understand this. Surely some one must be looking after her father. Whoever this was must have heard her coming. Why had he not appeared at the door? Dave, of course, might be away fighting fire, but some one . . .

Her heart lost a beat. The shadow of some horrible thing was creeping over her life. Was her father dead? What shock was awaiting her in the cabin?

At the door she raised her voice in a faint, ineffective call. Her knees gave way. She felt her body shaking as with an ague. But she clenched her teeth on the weakness and moved into the room.

It was dark—darker than outdoors. But as her eyes grew accustomed to the absence of light she made out a table, a chair, a stove. From the far side of the room came a gurgle that was half a snore.

"Father," she whispered, and moved forward.

Her outstretched hand groped for the bed and fell on clothing warm with heat transmitted from a human body. At the same time she subconsciously classified a strong odor that permeated the atmosphere. It was whiskey.

The sleeper stirred uneasily beneath her touch. She felt stifled, wanted to shout out her fears in a scream. Far beyond the need of proof she knew now that something was very wrong, though she still could not guess at what the dreadful menace was.

But Joyce had courage. She was what the wind and the sun and a long line of sturdy ancestors had made her. She leaned

198

forward toward the awakening man just as he turned in the bunk.

A hand fell on her wrist and closed, the fingers like bands of iron. Joyce screamed wildly, her nerve swept away in a reaction of terror. She fought like a wildcat, twisting and writhing with all her supple strength to break the grip on her arm.

For she knew now what the evil was that had been tolling a bell of warning in her heart.

CHAPTER XLI

HANK BRINGS BAD NEWS

The change in the wind had cost three lives, but it had saved the Jackpot property and the feed on the range. After the fire in San Jacinto Cañon had broken through Hart's defense by its furious and persistent attack, nothing could have prevented it from spreading over the plains on a wild rampage except a cloudburst or a decided shift of wind. This last had come and had driven the flames back on territory already burnt over.

The fire did not immediately die out, but it soon began to dwindle. Only here and there did it leap forward with its old savage fury. Presently these sporadic plunges wore themselves out for lack of fuel. The devastated area became a smouldering, smoking char showing a few isolated blazes in the barren ruin. There were still possibilities of harm in them if the wind should shift again, but for the present they were subdued to a shadow of their former strength. It remained the business of the fire-fighters to keep a close watch on the red-hot embers to prevent them from being flung far by the breeze.

Fortunately the wind died down soon, reducing the danger to a minimum.

Dave handed back to Shorty the revolver he had borrowed so peremptorily from his holster.

"Much obliged. I won't need this any more."

The cowpuncher spoke grimly. "I'm liable to."

"Mexico is a good country for a cattleman," Sanders said, looking straight at him.

Shortly met him eye to eye. "So I've been told."

"Good range and water-holes. Stock fatten well."

"Yes."

"A man might do worse than go there if he's worn out this country."

"Stage-robbers and rustlers right welcome, are they?" asked Shorty hardily.

"No questions asked about a man's past if his present is O.K."

"Listens good. If I meet anybody lookin' to make a change I'll tell him you recommended Mexico." The eyes of the two men still clashed. In each man's was a deep respect for the other's gameness. They had been tried by fire and come through clean. Shorty voiced this defiantly. "I don't like a hair of yore head. Never did. You're too damned interferin' to suit me. But I'll say this. You'll do to ride the river with, Sanders."

"I'll interfere again this far, Shorty. You're too good a man to go bad."

"Oh, hell!" The outlaw turned away; then thought better of it and came back. "I'll name no names, but I'll say this. Far as I'm concerned Tim Harrigan might be alive to-day."

Dave, with a nod, accepted this as true.

"I guessed as much. You've been running with a mighty bad pardner."

"Have I?" asked the rustler blandly. "Did I say anything about a pardner?"

His eye fell on the three still figures lying on the hillside in a row. Not a twitching muscle in his face showed what he was thinking, that they might have been full of splendid life and vigor if Dug Doble had not put a match to the chaparral back of Bear Cañon. The man had murdered them just as surely as though he had shot them down with a rifle. For weeks Shorty had been getting his affairs in order to leave the country, but before he went he intended to have an accounting with one man.

Dillon came up to Sanders and spoke in an awed voice.

"What do you aim to do with—these, Sanders?" His hand indicated the bodies lying near.

"Send horses up for them," Dave said. "You can take all the men back to camp with you except three to help me watch the fire. Tell Mr. Crawford how things are." The men crept down the hill like veterans a hundred years old. Ragged, smoke-blackened, and grimy, they moved like automatons. So great was their exhaustion that one or two dropped out of line and lay down on the charred ground to sleep. The desire for it was so overmastering that they could not drive their weighted legs forward.

A man on horseback appeared and rode up to Dave and Shorty. The man was Bob Hart. The red eyes in his blackened face were sunken and his coat hung on him in crisped shreds. He looked down at the bodies lying side by side. His face worked, but he made no verbal comment.

"We piled into a cave. Some of the boys couldn't stand it," Dave explained.

Bob's gaze took in his friend. The upper half of his body was almost naked. Both face and torso were raw with angry burns. Eyebrows had disappeared and eyes were so swollen as to be almost closed. He was gaunt, ragged, unshaven, and bleeding. Shorty, too, appeared to have gone through the wars.

"You boys oughtta have the doc see you," Hart said gently. "He's down at camp now. One of Em's men had an arm busted by a limb of a tree fallin' on him. I've got a coupla casualties in my gang. Two or three of 'em runnin' a high fever. Looks like they may have pneumonia, doc says. Lungs all inflamed from swallowin' smoke. . . . You take my hawss and ride down to camp, Dave. I'll stick around here till the old man sends a relief."

"No, you go down and report to him, Bob. If Crawford has any fresh men I'd like mine relieved. They've been on steady for 'most two days and nights. Four or five can hold the fire here. All they need do is watch it."

Hart did not argue. He knew how Dave stuck to a thing like a terrier to a rat. He would not leave the ground till orders came from Emerson Crawford.

"Lemme go an' report," suggested Shorty. "I wanta get my bronc an' light out pronto. Never can tell when Applegate might drap around an' ask questions. Me, I'm due in the hills."

201

"All right," agreed Bob. "See Crawford himself, Shorty."

The outlaw pulled himself to the saddle and cantered off.

"Best man in my gang," Dave said, following him with his eyes. "There to a finish and never a whimper out of him. Dragged a man out of the fire when he might have been hustling for his own skin."

"Shorty's game," admitted Hart. "Pity he went bad."

"Yes. He told me he didn't kill Harrigan."

"Reckon Dug did that. More like him."

Half an hour later the relief came. Hart, Dave, and the three fire-fighters who had stayed to watch rode back to camp.

Crawford had lost his voice. He had already seen Hart since the fire had subsided, so his greeting was to Sanders.

"Good work, son," he managed to whisper, a quaver in his throat. "I'd rather we'd lost the whole works than to have had that happen to the boys, a hundred times rather. I reckon it must 'a' been mighty bad up there when the back-fire caught you. The boys have been tellin' me. You saved all their lives, I judge."

"I happened to know where the cave was."

"Yes." Crawford's whisper was sadly ironic. "Well, I'm sure glad you happened to know that. If you hadn't—" The old cattleman gave a little gesture that completed the sentence. The tragedy that had taken place had shaken his soul. He felt in a way responsible.

"If the doc ain't busy now, I reckon Dave could use him," Bob said. "I reckon he needs a li'l' attention. Then I'm ready for grub an' a sleep twice round the clock. If any one asks me, I'm sure enough dead beat. I don't ever want to look at a shovel again."

"Doc's fixin' up Lanier's burnt laig. He'd oughtta be through soon now. I'll have him 'tend to Dave's burns right away then," said Crawford. He turned to Sanders. "How about it, son? You sure look bunged up pretty bad."

"I'm about all in," admitted Dave. "Reckon we all are. Shorty gone yet?"

"Yes. Lit out after he'd made a report. Said he had an engagement to meet a man. Expect he meant he had an engagement *not* to meet the sheriff. I rec'lect when Shorty was a mighty promisin' young fellow before Brad Steelman got a-holt of him. He punched cows for me twenty years ago. He hadn't took the wrong turn then. You cayn't travel crooked trails an' not reach a closed pocket o' the hills sometime."

For several minutes they had heard the creaking of a wagon working up an improvised road toward the camp. Now it moved into sight. The teamster called to Crawford.

"Here's another load o' grub, boss. Miss Joyce she rustled up them canteens you was askin' for."

Crawford stepped over to the wagon. "Don't reckon we'll need the canteens, Hank, but we can use the grub fine. The fire's about out."

"That's bully. Say, I got news for you, Mr. Crawford. Brad Steelman's dead. They found him in his house, shot plumb through the head. I reckon he won't do you any more meanness."

"Who killed him?"

"They ain't sayin'," returned the teamster cautiously. "Some folks was guessin' that mebbe Dug Doble could tell, but there ain't any evidence far's I know. Whoever it was robbed the safe."

The old cattleman made no comment. From the days of their youth Steelman had been his bitter enemy, but death had closed the account between them. His mind traveled back to those days twenty-five years ago when he and the sheepman had both hitched their horses in front of Helen Radcliff's home. It had been a fair fight between them, and he had won as a man should. But Brad had not taken his defeat as a man should. He had nourished bitterness and played his successful rival many a mean despicable trick. Out of these had grown the feud between them. Crawford did not know how it had come about, but he had no doubt Steelman had somehow fallen a victim in the trap he had been building for others.

A question brought his mind back to the present. The teamster was talking: ". . . so she started pronto. I s'pose you wasn't as bad hurt as Sanders figured."

"What's that?" asked Crawford.

"I was sayin' Miss Joyce she started right away when the note come from Sanders."

"What note?"

"The one tellin' how you was hurt in the fire."

Crawford turned. "Come here, Dave," he called hoarsely. Sanders moved across.

"Hank says you sent a note to Joyce sayin' I'd been hurt. What about it?"

"Why would I do that when you're not hurt?"

"Then you didn't?"

"Of course not," answered Dave, perplexed.

"Some one's been stringin' you, Hank," said Crawford, smiling.

The teamster scratched his head. "No, sir. I was there when she left. About twelve o'clock last night, mebbe later."

"But Sanders says he didn't send a note, and Joyce didn't come here. So you must 'a' missed connections somewhere."

"Probably you saw her start for home," suggested Dave.

Hank stuck to his guns. "No, sir. She was on that sorrel of hers, an' Keith was ridin' behind her. I saddled myself and took the horse to the store. They was waitin' there for me, the two young folks an' Juan."

"Juan?"

"Juan Otero. He brought the note an' rode back with her."

The old cattleman felt a clutch of fear at his heart. Juan Otero was one of Dug Doble's men.

"That all you know, Hank?"

"That's all. Miss Joyce said for me to get this wagonload of grub out soon as I could. So I come right along."

"Doble been seen in town lately?" asked Dave.

"Not as I know of. Shorty has."

"Shorty ain't in this."

"Do you reckon—?"

Sanders cut the teamster short. "Some of Doble's work. But I don't see why he sent for Keith too."

"He didn't. Keith begged to go along an' Miss Joyce took him."

In the haggard, unshaven face of the cattleman Dave read the ghastly fear of his own soul. Doble was capable of terrible evil. His hatred, jealousy, and passion would work together to poison his mind. The corners of his brain had always been full of lust and obscenity. There was this difference between him and Shorty. The squat cowpuncher was a clean scoundrel. A child, a straight girl, an honest woman, would be as safe with him as with simple-hearted old Buck Byington. But Dug Doble—it was impossible to predict what he would do. He had a vein of caution in his make-up, but when in drink he jettisoned this and grew ugly. His vanity—always a large factor in determining his actions—might carry him in the direction of decency or the reverse.

"I'm glad Keith's with her," said Hart, who had joined the group. "With Keith and the Mexican there—" His meaning did not need a completed sentence.

"Question is, where did he take her," said Crawford. "We

might comb the hills a week and not find his hole. I wish to God Shorty was still here. He might know."

"He's our best bet, Bob," agreed Dave.

"Find him. He's gone off somewhere to sleep. Rode away less than half an hour since."

"Which way?"

'Rode toward Bear Cañon," said Crawford.

"That's a lead for you, Bob. Figure it out. He's done—completely worn out. So he won't go far—not more than three-four miles. He'll be in the hills, under cover somewhere, for he won't forget that thousand dollars reward. So he'll be lying in the chaparral. That means he'll be above where the fire started. If I was looking for him, I'd say somewhere back of Bear, Cattle, or San Jacinto would be the likeliest spot."

"Good guess, Dave. Somewheres close to water," said Bob. "You goin' along with me?"

"No. Take as many men as you can get. I'm going back, if I can, to find the place where Otero and Miss Joyce left the road. Mr. Crawford, you'd better get back to town, don't you think? There may be clues there we don't know anything about here. Perhaps Miss Joyce may have got back."

"If not, I'll gather a posse to rake the hills, Dave. If that villain's hurt my li'l' girl or Keith—" Crawford's whisper broke. He turned away to conceal the working of his face.

"He hasn't," said Bob with decision. "Dug ain't crazy even if his actions look like it. I've a notion when Mr. Crawford gets back to town Miss Joyce will be there all right. Like as not Dug brought her back himself. Maybe he sent for her just to brag awhile. You know Dug."

That was the worst of it, so far as any allaying of their fear went. They did know Doble. They knew him for a thorough black-hearted scoundrel who might stop at nothing.

The three men moved toward the remuda. None of them had slept for forty-eight hours. They had been through a grueling experience that had tried soul and body to the limit. But none of them hesitated for an instant. They belonged to the old West which answers the call no matter what the personal cost. There was work to do. Not one of them would quit as long as he could stick to the saddle.

CHAPTER XLII

SHORTY IS AWAKENED

The eyes that looked into those of Joyce in the gloom of the cabin abruptly shook off sleep. They passed from an amazed incredulity to a malicious triumph.

"So you've come to old Dug, have you, my pretty?" a heavy voice jeered.

The girl writhed and twisted regardless of the pain, exerting every muscle of the strong young arm and shoulder. As well she might have tried to beat down an iron door with her bare hands as to hope for escape from his strong grip. He made a motion to draw her closer. Joyce flung herself back and sank down beside the bunk, straining away.

"Let me go!" she cried, terror rampant in her white face. "Don't touch me! Let me go!"

The force of her recoil had drawn him to his side. His cruel, mirthless grin seemed to her to carry inexpressible menace. Very slowly, while his eyes taunted her, he pulled her manacled wrist closer.

There was a swift flash of white teeth. With a startled oath Doble snatched his arm away. Savage as a tigress, Joyce had closed her teeth on his forearm.

She fell back, got to her feet, and fled from the house. Doble was after her on the instant. She dodged round a tree, doubled on her course, then deflected toward the corral. Swift and supple though she was, his long strides brought him closer. Again she screamed.

Doble caught her. She fought in his arms, a prey to wild and unreasoning terror.

"You young hell-cat, I'm not gonna hurt you," he said. "What's the use o' actin' crazy?"

He could have talked to the waves of the sea with as much effect. It is doubtful if she heard him.

There was a patter of rapid feet. A small body hurled itself against Doble's leg and clung there, beating his thigh with a valiant little fist.

"You le' my sister go! You le' my sister go!" the boy shouted, repeating the words over and over.

Doble looked down at Keith. "What the hell?" he demanded, amazed.

The Mexican came forward and spoke in Spanish rapidly. He explained that he could not have prevented the boy from coming without arousing the suspicions of his sister and her friends.

The outlaw was irritated. All this clamor of fear annoyed and disturbed him. This was not the scene he had planned in his drink-inspired reveries. There had been a time when Joyce had admired the virile force of him, when she had let herself be kind to him under the impression she was influencing him for his good. He had misunderstood the reaction of her mind and supposed that if he could get her away from the influence of her father and the rest of his enemies, she would again listen to what he called reason.

"All right. You brought the brat here without orders. Now take him home again," directed Doble harshly.

Otero protested fluently, with gestures eloquent. He had not yet been paid for his services. By this time Malapi might be too hot for him. He did not intend ever to go back. He was leaving the country pronto—muy pronto. The boy could go back when his sister went.

"His sister's not going back. Soon as it gets dark we'll travel south. She's gonna be my wife. You can take the kid back to the road an' leave him there."

Again the Mexican lifted hands and shoulders while he pattered volubly, trying to make himself heard above the cries of the child. Dug had silenced Joyce by the simple expedient of clapping his big hand over her mouth.

Doble's other hand went into his pocket. He drew out a flat package of currency bound together with rubber bands. His sharp teeth drew off one of the rubbers. From the bundle he stripped four fifty-dollar bills and handed them to Otero.

"Peel this kid off'n my leg and hit the trail, Juan. I don' care where you leave him so long as you keep an eye on him till afternoon."

With difficulty the Mexican dragged the boy from his hold

207

on Doble and carried him to a horse. He swung to the saddle, dragged Keith up in front of him, and rode away at a jogtrot. The youngster was screaming at the top of his lungs.

As his horse climbed toward the notch, Otero looked back. Doble had picked up his prisoner and was carrying her into the house.

The Mexican formulated his plans. He must get out of the country before the hue and cry started. He could not count on more than a few hours before the chase began. First, he must get rid of the child. Then he wanted to go to a certain tendejon where he would meet his sweetheart and say goodbye to her.

It was all very well for Doble to speak of taking him to town or to the road. Juan meant to do neither. He would leave him in the hills above the Jackpot and show him the way down there, after which he would ride to meet the girl who was waiting for him. This would give him time enough to get away safely. It was no business of his whether or not Doble was taken. He was an overbearing brute, anyhow.

An hour's riding through the chaparral brought him to the watershed far above the Jackpot. Otero picked his way to the upper end of a gulch.

"Leesten, muchacho. Go down—down—down. First the gulch, then a cañon, then the Jackpot. You go on thees trail."

He dropped the boy to the ground, watched him start, then turned away at a Spanish trot.

The trail was a rough and precipitous one. Stumbling as he walked, Keith went sobbing down the gulch. He had wept himself out, and his sobs had fallen to a dry hiccough. A forlorn little chap, tired and sleepy, he picked his way among the mesquite, following the path along the dry creek bed. The catclaw tore his stockings and scratched him. Stone bruises hurt his tender feet. He kept traveling, because he was afraid to give up.

He reached the junction of the gulch and the cañon. A small stream, which had survived the summer drought, trickled down the bed of the latter. Through tangled underbrush Keith crept to the water. He lay down and drank, after which he sat on a rock and pitied himself. In five minutes he would have been asleep if a sound had not startled him. Some one was snoring on the other side of a mesquite thicket.

Keith jumped up, pushed his way through, and almost stumbled over a sleeping man. He knelt down and began to shake the snorer. The man did not awaken. The foghorn in

208

his throat continued to rumble intermittently, now in crescendo, now in diminuendo.

"Wake up, man!" Keith shouted in his ear in the interval between shakes.

The sleeper was a villainous-looking specimen. His face and throat were streaked with black. There was an angry weal across his cheek. One of the genus tramp would have scorned his charred clothes. Keith cared for none of these details. He wanted to unload his troubles to a "grown-up."

The youngster roused the man at last by throwing water in his face. Shorty sat up, at the same time dragging out a revolver. His gaze fastened on the boy, after one swift glance round.

"Who's with you, kid?" he demanded.

Keith began to sniffle. "Nobody."

"Whadya doin' here?"

"I want my daddy."

"Who is yore daddy? What's yore name?"

"Keith Crawford."

Shortly bit off an oath of surprise. "Howcome you here?"

"A man brought me."

The rustler brushed the cobwebs of sleep from his eyes and brain. He had come up here to sleep undisturbed through the day and far into the night. Before he had had two hours of rest this boy had dragged him back from slumber. He was prepared to be annoyed, but he wanted to make sure of the facts first.

As far as he understood them, the boy told the story of the night's adventures. Shorty's face grew grim. He appreciated the meaning back of them far better than the little fellow. Keith's answers to his questions told him that the men figuring in the episode must be Doble and Otero. Though the child was a little mixed as to the direction from which Otero had brought him, the man was pretty sure of the valley where Doble was lying hid.

He jumped to his feet. "We'll go, kid."

"To daddy?"

"Not right away. We got hurry-up business first."

"I wanta go to my daddy."

"Sure. Soon as we can. But we'll drift over to where yore sister's at first off. We're both wore to a frazzle, mebbe, but we got to trail over an' find out what's bitin' Dug."

The man saddled and took the up-trail, Keith clinging to his waist. At the head of the gulch the boy pointed out the way he and Otero had come. This confirmed Shorty's opinion as to the place where Doble was to be found.

With the certainty of one who knew these hills as a preacher does his Bible, Shorty wound in and out, always moving by the line of least resistance. He was steadily closing the gap of miles that separated him from Dug Doble.

CHAPTER XLIII

JUAN OTERO IS CONSCRIPTED

Crawford and Sanders rode rapidly toward Malapi. They stopped several times to examine places where they thought it possible Otero might have left the road, but they looked without expectation of any success. They did not even know that the Mexican had started in this direction. As soon as he reached the suburbs, he might have cut back across the plain and followed an entirely different line of travel.

Several miles from town Sanders pulled up. "I'm going back for a couple of miles. Bob was telling me of a Mexican tendejon in the hills kept by the father of a girl Otero goes to see. She might know where he is. If I can get hold of him likely I can make him talk."

This struck Crawford as rather a wild-goose chase, but he had nothing better to offer himself in the way of a plan.

"Might as well," he said gloomily. "I don't reckon you'll find him. But you never can tell. Offer the girl a big reward if she'll tell where Doble is. I'll hustle to town and send out posses."

They separated. Dave rode back up the road, swung off at the place Hart had told him of, and turned up a valley which pushed to the roots of the hills. The tendejon was a long, flat-roofed adobe building close to the trail.

Dave walked through the open door into the barroom. Two

or three men were lounging at a table. Behind a counter a brown-eyed Mexican girl was rinsing glasses in a pail of water.

The young man sauntered forward to the counter. He invited the company to drink with him.

"I'm looking for Juan Otero," he said presently. "Mr. Crawford wanted me to see him about riding for him."

There was a moment's silence. All of those present were Mexicans except Dave. The girl flashed a warning look at her countrymen. That look, Sanders guessed at once, would seal the lips of all of them. At once he changed his tactics. What information he got would have to come directly through the girl. He signaled her to join him outside.

Presently she did so. The girl was a dusky young beauty, plump as a partridge, with the soft-eyed charm of her age and race.

"The señor wants to see me?" she asked.

Her glance held a flash of mockery. She had seen many dirty, poverty-stricken mavericks of humanity, but never a more battered specimen than this gaunt, hollow-eyed tramp, black as a coal-heaver, whose flesh showed grimy with livid wounds through the shreds of his clothing. But beneath his steady look the derision died. Tattered his coat and trousers might be. At least he was a prince in adversity. The head on the splendid shoulders was still finely poised. He gave an impression of indomitable strength.

"I want Juan Otero," he said.

"To ride for Señor Crawford." Her white teeth flashed and she lifted her pretty shoulders in a shrug of mock regret. "Too bad he is not here. Some other day—"

"—will not do. I want him now."

"But I have not got him hid."

"Where is he? I don't want to harm him, but I must know. He took Joyce Crawford into the hills last night to Dug Doble —pretended her father had been hurt and he had been sent to lead her to him. I must save her—from Doble, not from Otero. Help me. I will give you money—a hundred dollars, two hundred."

She stared at him. "Did Juan do that?" she murmured.

"Yes. You know Doble. He's a devil. I must find him . . . soon."

"Juan has not been here for two days. I do not know where he is."

The dust of a moving horse was traveling toward them

211

from the hills. A Mexican pulled up and swung from the saddle. The girl called a greeting to him quickly before he could speak. "Buenos dios, Manuel. My father is within, Manuel."

The man looked at her a moment, murmured "Buenos, Bonita," and took a step as though to enter the house.

Dave barred the way. The flash of apprehension in Bonita's face, her unnecessary repetition of the name, the man's questioning look at her, told Sanders that this was the person he wanted.

"Just a minute, Otero. Where did you leave Miss Crawford?"

The Mexican's eyes contracted. To give himself time he fell again into the device of pretending that he did not understand English. Dave spoke in Spanish. The loafers in the barroom came out to listen.

"I do not know what you mean."

"Don't lie to me. Where is she?"

The keeper of the tendejon asked a suave question. He, too, talked in Spanish. "Who are you, señor? A deputy sheriff, perhaps?"

"No. My name is Dave Sanders. I'm Emerson Crawford's friend. If Juan will help me save the girl he'll get off light and perhaps make some money. I'll stand by him. But if he won't, I'll drag him back to Malapi and give him to a mob."

The sound of his name was a potent weapon. His fame had spread like wildfire through the hills since his return from Colorado. He had scored victory after victory against bad men without firing a gun. He had made the redoubtable Dug Doble an object of jeers and had driven him to the hills as an outlaw. Dave was unarmed. They could see that. But his quiet confidence was impressive. If he said he would take Juan to Malapi with him, none of them doubted he would do it. Had he not dragged Miller back to justice—Miller who was a killer of unsavory reputation?

Otero wished he had not come just now to see Bonita, but he stuck doggedly to his statement. He knew nothing about it, nothing at all.

"Crawford is sending out a dozen posses. They will close the passes. Doble will be caught. They will kill him like a wolf. Then they will kill you. If they don't find him, they will kill you anyhow."

Dave spoke evenly, without raising his voice. Somehow he made what he said seem as inevitable as fate.

Bonita caught her lover by the arm and shoulder. She was

212

afraid, and her conscience troubled her vicariously for his wrongdoing.

"Why did you do it, Juan?" she begged of him.

"He said she wanted to come, that she would marry him if she had a chance. He said her father kept her from him," the man pleaded. "I didn't know he was going to harm her."

"Where is he? Take me to him, quick," said Sanders, relapsing into English.

"Si, señor. At once," agreed Otero, thoroughly frightened.

"I want a six-shooter. Some one lend me one."

None of them carried one, but Bonita ran into the house and brought back a small bulldog. Dave looked it over without enthusiasm. It was a pretty poor concern to take against a man who carried two forty-fives and knew how to use them. But he thrust it into his pocket and swung to the saddle. It was quite possible he might be killed by Doble, but he had a conviction that the outlaw had come to the end of the passage. He was going to do justice on the man once for all. He regarded this as a certainty.

CHAPTER XLIV

THE BULLDOG BARKS

Joyce fainted for the first time in her life.

When she recovered consciousness Doble was splashing water in her face. She was lying on the bunk from which she had fled a few minutes earlier. The girl made a motion to rise and he put a heavy hand on her shoulder.

"Keep your hand off me!" she cried.

"Don't be a fool," he told her irritably. "I ain't gonna hurt you none—if you behave reasonable."

"Let me go," she demanded, and struggled to a sitting position on the couch. "You let me go or my father—"

"What'll he do?" demanded the man brutally. "I've stood a heap from that father of yore's. I reckon this would even the score even if I hadn't—" He pulled up, just in time to keep from telling her that he had fired the chaparral. He was quite sober enough to distrust his tongue. It was likely, he knew, to let out some things that had better not be told.

She tried to slip by him and he thrust her back.

"Let me go!" she demanded. "At once!"

"You're not gonna go," he told her flatly. "You'll stay here —with me. For keeps. Un'erstand?"

"Have you gone crazy?" she asked wildly, her heart fluttering like a frightened bird in a cage. "Don't you know my father will search the whole country for me?"

"Too late. We travel south soon as it's dark." He leaned forward and put a hand on her knee, regardless of the fact that she shrank back quivering from his touch. "Listen, girl. You been a high-stepper. Yore heels click mighty loud when they hit the sidewalk. Good enough. Go far as you like. I never did fancy the kind o' women that lick a man's hand. But you made one mistake. I'm no doormat, an' nobody alive can wipe their feet on me. You turned me down cold. You had the ol' man kick me outa my job as foreman of the ranch. I told him an' you both I'd git even. But I don't aim to rub it in. I'm gonna give you a chance to be Mrs. Doble. An' when you marry me you git a man for a husband."

"I'll never marry you! Never! I'd rather be dead in my grave!" she broke out passionately.

He went to the table, poured himself a drink, and gulped it down. His laugh was sinister and mirthless.

"Please yorese'f, sweetheart," he jeered. "Only you won't be dead in yore grave. You'll be keepin' house for Dug Doble. I'm not insistin' on weddin' bells none. But women have their fancies an' I aim to be kind. Take 'em or leave 'em."

She broke down and wept, her face in her hands. In her sheltered life she had known only decent, clean-minded people. She did not know how to cope with a man like this. The fear of him rose in her throat and choked her. This dreadful thing he threatened could not be, she told herself. God would not permit it. He would send her father or Dave Sanders or Bob Hart to rescue her. And yet—when she looked at the man, big, gross, dominant, flushed with drink and his triumph —the faith in her became a weak and fluid stay for her soul. She collapsed like a child and sobbed.

Her wild alarm annoyed him. He was angered at her un-

controllable shudders when he drew near. There was a savage
desire in him to break through the defense of her helplessness
once for all. But his caution urged delay. He must give her
time to get accustomed to the idea of him. She had sense
enough to see that she must make the best of the business.
When the terror lifted from her mind she would be reasonable.

He repeated again that he was not going to hurt her if she
met him halfway, and to show good faith went out and left
her alone.

The man sat down on a chopping-block outside and
churned his hatred of Sanders and Crawford. He spurred
himself with drink, under its influence recalling the injuries
they had done him. His rage and passion simmered, occasionally exploded into raucous curses. Once he strode into the
house, full of furious intent, but the eyes of the girl daunted
him. They looked at him as they might have looked at a tiger
padding toward her.

He flung out of the house again, snarling at his own weakness. There was something in him stronger than passion,
stronger than his reckless will, that would not let him lay a
hand on her in the light of day. His bloodshot eyes looked for
the sun. In a few hours now it would be dark.

While he lounged sullenly on the chopping-block, shoulders
and head sunken, a sound brought him to alert attention. A
horseman was galloping down the slope on the other side of
the valley.

Doble eased his guns to make sure of them. Intently he
watched the approaching figure. He recognized the horse,
Chiquito, and then, with an oath, the rider. His eyes gleamed
with evil joy. At last! At last he and Dave Sanders would settle accounts. One of them would be carried out of the valley
feet first.

Sanders leaped to the ground at the same instant that he
pulled Chiquito up. The horse was between him and his
enemy.

The eyes of the men crossed in a long, level look.

"Where's Joyce Crawford?" asked Dave.

"That yore business?" Doble added to his retort the insult
unmentionable.

"I'm makin' it mine. What have you done with her?" The
speech of the younger man took on again the intonation of
earlier days. "I'm here to find out."

A swish of skirts, a soft patter of feet, and Joyce was beside her friend, clinging to him, weeping in his arms.

Doble moved round in a wide circumference. When shooting began he did not want his foe to have the protection of the horse's body. Not even for the beat of a lid did the eyes of either man lift from the other.

"Go back to the house, Joyce," said Dave evenly. "I want to talk with this man alone."

The girl clung the tighter to him. "No, Dave, no! It's been . . . awful."

The outlaw drew his long-barreled six-shooter, still circling the group. He could not fire without running a risk of hitting Joyce.

"Hidin' behind a woman, are you?" he taunted, and again flung the epithet men will not tolerate.

At any moment he might fire. Dave caught the wrists of the girl, dragged them down from his neck, and flung her roughly from him to the ground. He pulled out his little bulldog.

Doble fired and Dave fell. The outlaw moved cautiously closer, exultant at his marksmanship. His enemy lay still, the pistol in his hand. Apparently Sanders had been killed at the first shot.

"Come to git me with that popgun, did you? Hmp! Fat chance." The bad man fired again, still approaching very carefully.

Round the corner of the house a man had come. He spoke quickly. "Turn yore gun this way, Dug."

It was Shorty. His revolver flashed at the same instant. Doble staggered, steadied himself, and fired.

The forty-fives roared. Yellow flames and smoke spurted. The bulldog barked. Dave's parlor toy had come into action.

Out of the battle Shorty and Sanders came erect and uninjured. Doble was lying on the ground, his revolver smoking a foot or two from the twitching, outstretched hand.

The outlaw was dead before Shorty turned him over. A bullet had passed through the heart. Another had struck him on the temple, a third in the chest.

"We got him good," said Shorty. "It was comin' to him. I reckon you don't know that he fired the chaparral on purpose. Wanted to wipe out the Jackpot, I s'pose. Yes, Dug sure had it comin' to him."

Dave said nothing. He looked down at the man, eyes hard

216

as jade, jaw clamped tight. He knew that but for Shorty's arrival he would probably be lying there himself.

"I was aimin' to shoot it out with him before I heard of this last scullduggery. Soon as the kid woke me I hustled up my intentions." The bad man looked at Dave's weapon with the flicker of a smile on his face. "He called it a popgun. I took notice it was a right busy li'l' plaything. But you got yore nerve all right. I'd say you hadn't a chance in a thousand. You played yore hand fine, keelin' over so's he'd come clost enough for you to get a crack at him. At that, he'd maybe 'a' got you if I hadn't drapped in."

"Yes," said Sanders.

He walked across to the corral fence, where Joyce sat huddled against the lower bars.

She lifted her head and looked at him from wan eyes out of which the life had been stricken. They stared at him in dumb, amazed questioning.

Dave lifted her from the ground.

"I . . . I thought you . . . were dead," she whispered.

"Not even powder-burnt. His six-shooter outranged mine. I was trying to get him closer."

"Is he . . . ?"

"Yes. He'll never trouble any of us again."

She shuddered in his arms.

Dave ached for her in every tortured nerve. He did not know, and it was not his place to ask, what price she had had to pay.

Presently she told him, not in words, without knowing what he was suffering for her. A ghost of a smile touched her eyes.

"I knew you would come. It's all right now."

His heart leaped. "Yes, it's all right, Joyce."

She recurred to her fears for him. "You're not . . . hiding any wounds from me? I saw you fall and lie there while he shot at you."

"He never touched me."

She disengaged herself from his arms and looked at him, wan, haggard, unshaven, eyes sunken, a tattered wretch scarred with burns.

"What have you done to yourself?" she asked, astonished at his appearance.

"Souvenirs of the fire," he told her. "They'll wash and wear off. Don't suppose I look exactly pretty."

He had never looked so handsome in her eyes.

CHAPTER XLV

JOYCE MAKES PIES

Juan Otero carried the news back to Malapi. He had been waiting on the crest of the hill to see the issue of the adventure and had come forward when Dave gave him a signal.

Shorty brought Keith in from where he had left the boy in the brush. The youngster flew into his sister's arms. They wept over each other and she petted him with caresses and little kisses.

Afterward she made some supper from the supplies Doble had laid in for his journey south. The men went down to the creek, where they bathed and washed their wounds. Darkness had not yet fallen when they went to sleep, all of them exhausted by the strain through which they had passed.

Not until the cold crystal dawn did they awaken. Joyce was the first up. She had breakfast well under way before she had Keith call the still sleeping men. With the power of quick recuperation which an outdoor life had given them, both Shorty and Dave were fit for any exertion again, though Sanders was still suffering from his burns.

After they had eaten they saddled. Shorty gave them a casual nod of farewell.

"Tell Applegate to look me up in Mexico if he wants me," he said.

Joyce would not let it go at that. She made him shake hands. He was in the saddle, and her eyes lifted to his and showered gratitude on him.

"We'll never forget you—never," she promised. "And we do so hope you'll be prosperous and happy."

He grinned down at her sheepishly. "Same to you, Miss," he said; and added, with a flash of audacity, "To you and Dave both."

He headed south, the others north.

From the hilltop Dave looked back at the squat figure steadily diminishing with distance. Shorty was moving toward Mexico, unhasting and with a certain sureness of purpose characteristic of him.

Joyce smiled. It was the first signal of unquenchable youth she had flashed since she had been trapped into this terrible adventure. "I believe you admire him, Dave," she mocked. "You're just as grateful to him as I am, but you won't admit it. He's not a bad man at all, really."

"He's a good man gone bad. But I'll say this for Shorty. He's some *man*. He'll do to ride the river with."

"Yes."

"At the fire he was the best fighter in my gang—saved one of the boys at the risk of his own life. Shorty's no quitter."

She shut her teeth on a little wave of emotion. Then, "I am awful sorry for him," she said.

He nodded appreciation of her feeling. "I know, but you don't need to worry any. He'll not worry about himself. He's sufficient, and he'll get along."

They put their horses to the trail again.

Crawford met them some miles nearer town. He had been unable to wait for their arrival. Neither he nor the children could restrain their emotion at sight of each other. Dave felt they might like to be alone and he left the party, to ride across to the tendejon with Bonita's bulldog revolver.

That young woman met him in front of the house. She was eager for news. Sanders told her what had taken place. They spoke in her tongue.

"And Juan—is it all right about him?" she asked.

"Juan has wiped the slate clean. Mr. Crawford wants to know when Bonita is to be married. He has a wedding present for her."

She was all happy smiles when he left her.

Late that afternoon Bob Hart reached town. He and Dave were alone in the Jackpot offices when the latter forced himself to open a subject that had always been closed between them. Sanders came to it reluctantly. No man had ever found a truer friend than he in Bob Hart. The thing he was going to do seemed almost like a stab in the back.

"How about you and Joyce, Bob?" he asked abruptly.

The eyes of the two met and held. "What about us, Dave?"

"It's like this," Sanders said, flushed and embarrassed. "You were here first. You're entitled to first chance. I meant to keep out of it, but things have come up in spite of me. I want to do whatever seems right to you. My idea is to go away till —till you've settled how you stand with her. Is that fair?"

Bob smiled, ruefully. "Fair enough, old-timer. But no need of it. I never had a chance with Joyce, not a dead man's look-in. Found that out before ever you came home. The field's clear far as I'm concerned. Hop to it an' try yore luck."

Dave took his advice, within the hour. He found Joyce at home in the kitchen. She was making pies energetically. The sleeves of her dress were rolled up to the elbows and there was a dab of flour on her temple where she had brushed back a rebellious wisp of hair.

She blushed prettily at sight of her caller. "I didn't know it was you when I called to come in. Thought it was Keith playing a trick on me."

Both of them were embarrassed. She did not know what to do with him in the kitchen and he did not know what to do with himself. The girl was acutely conscious that yesterday she had flung herself into his arms without shame.

"I'll go right on with my pies if you don't mind," she said. "I can talk while I work."

"Yes."

But neither of them talked. She rolled pie-crust while the silence grew significant.

"Are your burns still painful?" she asked at last, to make talk.

"Yes—no. Beg pardon, I—I was thinking of something else."

Joyce flashed one swift look at him. She knew that an emotional crisis was upon her. He was going to brush aside the barriers between them. Her pulses began to beat fast. There was the crash of music in her blood.

"I've got to tell you, Joyce," he said abruptly. "It's been a fight for me ever since I came home. I love you. I think I always have—even when I was in prison."

She waited, the eyes in her lovely, flushed face shining.

"I had no right to think of you then," he went on. "I kept away from you. I crushed down hope. I nursed my bitterness to prove to me there could never be anything between us. Then Miller confessed and—and we took our walk over the hills. After that the sun shone. I came out from the mists where I had been living."

"I'm glad," she said in a low voice. "But Miller's confession made no difference in my thought of you. I didn't need that to know you."

"But I couldn't come to you even then. I knew how Bob Hart felt, and after all he'd done for me it was fair he should have first chance."

She looked at him, smiling shyly. "You're very generous."

"No. I thought you cared for him. It seemed to me any woman must. There aren't many men like Bob."

"Not many," she agreed. "But I couldn't love Bob because" —her steadfast eyes met his bravely—"because of another man. Always have loved him, ever since that night years ago when he saved my father's life. Do you really truly love me, Dave?"

"God knows I do," he said, almost in a whisper.

"I'm glad—oh, awf'ly glad." She gave him her hands, tears in her soft brown eyes. "Because I've been waiting for you so long. I didn't know whether you ever were coming to me."

Crawford found them there ten minutes later. He was looking for Joyce to find him a collar-button that was missing.

"Dawggone my hide!" he fumed, and stopped abruptly, the collar-button forgotten.

Joyce flew out of Dave's arms into her father's.

"Oh, Daddy, Daddy, I'm so happy," she whispered from the depths of his shoulder.

The cattleman looked at Dave, and his rough face worked. "Boy, you're in luck. Be good to her, or I'll skin you alive." He added, by way of softening this useless threat, "I'd rather it was you than anybody on earth, Dave."

The young man looked at her, his Joy-in-life, the woman who had brought him back to youth and happiness, and he answered with a surge of emotion:

"I'll sure try."

It's
ALL IN THE FAMILY